Pop Secrets

Jackie Notter

Climate Publishing
Seattle

First Edition for North America published by Climate Publishing, LLC

All inquiries should be emailed to info@climatepublishing.com

This story is 100% a work of fiction: the names, characters, and incidents are products of the author's imagination or are used fictitiously. Any resemblance to actual events or persons, living or dead, is entirely coincidental. All celebrity encounters and their personalities are fictional and used in a satirical manner.

The character Brixton Webber is fictional. Any resemblance to entertainers, living or dead, is entirely coincidental.

Some product and company names have been used and may be trademarks of their respective manufacturers or sellers.

Conceived and written by Jackie Notter
Editor: Julie Kay Clayton
Cover Design: Ink Slinger Designs for Writers
Cover photograph: Fuse, Getty Images
Back Cover photograph: Alex_L, 123RF

ISBN: 978-0-692-19810-0

Songs mentioned or sung (in order of appearance):

"Royals"
Performed by Lorde
Written by Lorde and Joel Little
Lava / Republic / Universal / Virgin

"Sex and Candy"
Performed by Marcy Playground
Written by John Wozniak
Capitol

"Jennifer"
Performed by the Eurythmics
Written by Annie Lennox and David Stewart
RCA Records

"Call Me Maybe"
Performed by Carly Rae Jepsen
Written by Carly Rae Jepsen, Josh Ramsay and Tavish Crowe
604 / Schoolboy / Interscope

"Road to Nowhere"
Performed by the Talking Heads
Written by David Byrne
Sire

"When Doves Cry"
Witten and performed by Prince
Warner Bros.

"Friends in Low Places"
Performed by Garth Brooks
Written by Dewayne Blackwell and Earl Bud Lee
Capitol Nashville

"Groove is in the Heart"
Performed by Deee-Lite
Written by Dmitry Brill, Chung Dong-Hwa, Kierin Kirby,
Herbie Hancock & Jonathan Davis
Elektra Records

"Orinoco Flow" (Sail Away)
Performed by Enya
Written by Enya and Roma Ryan
Warner Music / Geffen

"Shattered"
Performed by The Rolling Stones
Written by Mick Jagger and Keith Richards
Rolling Stones

"What's My Age Again?"
Performed by Blink-182
Written by Mark Hoppus and Tom DeLonge
MCA

"Magic Carpet Ride"
Performed by The Mighty Dub Katz
Written by Norman Cook
Southern Fried Records

"Without You"
Performed by Harry Nilsson
Written by Pete Ham and Tom Evans of Welsh rock group Badfinger
RCA Victor

Movies mentioned:

Footloose
Directed by Herbert Ross
Written by Dean Pitchford
Paramount Pictures / IndieProd Company Productions

Titanic
Written and Directed by James Cameron
Produced by James Cameron & Jon Landau
Paramount Pictures / 20th Century Fox / Lightstorm Entertainment

For Lucile

To Daniel Higgins, Climate Publishing

A couple of months ago my sister Jackie was murdered. While going through her belongings, I found her journals and it was soon apparent that she was having an affair with pop star Brixton Webber. Since this discovery, I've met with him on several occasions. As you are aware, he insists that I publish Jackie's story. Brixton feels it's time for the world to meet her. I'm still uncomfortable presenting her intimate moments and thoughts for all to read, but if that's what it will take to give him closure, you have my approval.

Enclosed is Jackie's manuscript. Brixton helped fill in a few vague areas—song lyrics and such. I'm proud of my sister's writing. I didn't know she inherited our grandmother's gift of storytelling. I'm not as talented in that department. The chapter I wrote will need work. All I ask is that you handle Jackie's book with care.

Sincerely,

Randy Notter

Peeking Ahead

There wasn't the slightest bend to Brixton Webber's amazingly straight seven-inch cock. It stood proud and taut against his ripped abs. The shaft was perfect in its girth, nice and thick but not so large it would cripple a girl. There were no bulging veins or unsightly redness, just smooth, silky skin. The kissable head was a work of art — soft, bulbous, and pink.

His dark blond pubic hair was meticulously manicured. A light trail of fuzz flowed downward from his bellybutton. On the inside of each hip was a well-defined sex seam that drew the eye inward. He had shaved his balls. I salivated at the thought of rolling them around in my mouth.

The freshness of Brixton's shower did little to mask the scent of his raging pheromones. One whiff and my endorphins shot into overdrive. I grabbed hold of his shaft and was surprised to find he was uncircumcised. I'd never been with anyone who was uncut. The loose skin produced a fluid motion as I stroked his manhood up and down. It came alive in my hand. I gazed up at Brixton thankfully and slid his cock into my mouth.

The Concert

Lidia and I snaked through the crowded hallway of Seattle's Key Arena and down onto the main floor. The excitement in the auditorium grew as we approached the stage. I was more thrilled by how great our seats were than to see Brixton Webber. What little I knew of him came from snippets I'd read in the grocery line tabloids. Brixton's pop music was a bit young for us, but I wasn't about to turn down front row tickets.

We had spent the afternoon downtown. Lidia and I work together, so it's rare for both of us to have a Saturday off. The day began with power shopping and a long lunch with several cocktails at the Pink Door. Next up was Gene Juarez for a mani/pedi and a more current hairstyle. Throughout lunch, Lidia tried to talk me into chopping off my hair. With three strong drinks in me, I gave in and allowed the stylist to cut off six inches. Lidia was right—my new look was long overdue. It was still below my shoulders, but getting used to the drastic change would take some time.

Lidia was sporting thick black frames that went well with her dark hair and new bob. The style complimented her olive skin and sharp Italian nose. I wasn't sure if she was wearing glasses to look hip or if she needed them to see the show. Whatever the case, they worked; she was cool as hell. I liked her new bangs, especially with her cute sixties dress—a geometric black and white number with primary colors filling in random squares.

"Where did you get that dress?" I asked.

"Le Frock on Capitol Hill. It's vintage, baby," she said, twirling her petite frame in a half spin.

"I love it. You look fabulous, as always."

"Thank you, my dear. I love your blue hoodie. It brings out the color of your eyes." The little minx leaned over and unzipped my sweatshirt, exposing my cleavage.

"Stop," I protested.

"I'm sorry," Lidia said. "I just wish you'd get back into the dating scene."

"As soon as I'm ready, you'll be the first to know."

I didn't understand her rush. Maybe she just wanted to see one of us happy.

"Check this guy out," Lidia said. I sighed with exasperation, but she was only pointing to a man walking in front of us, holding a young girl's hand.

"That's sweet, taking his daughter to the show."

"No, look at his headphones," Lidia insisted. "They're noise canceling."

"Well, that's not supportive at all."

"Dude must hate Brixton's music."

"Or he's a big pussy," I said a little too loud. The man didn't seem to notice.

When we reached the stage, an usher showed us to our seats. I let Lidia go in first, putting her closer to center. The tickets were hers after all, a gift from a generous client. Having a retail job in an upscale department store has its perks.

I looked behind us at the packed audience of young girls. They all seemed afflicted with the same nervous energy and crazed look of anticipation. I remember being a part of this phenomenon when I saw 'U Nifi as a teen. Robbie Cumberlake was a god to me.

"I've never been in the front row," I told Lidia.

The crowd went wild as a roadie appeared for a last-minute sound check.

"We're going to have fun tonight," Lidia yelled over the piercing screams of Brixton's fans. She was smiling, showing off the diastema between her top front teeth. I love that gap. It's pop-star-fabulous, like Magdalene's.

"Hell to the yes!" I said with goofy enthusiasm. I was in a fantastic mood. Being around Lidia has that effect on me. The last month was rough. It was nice having a chance to let loose.

"You rock, Jackie Jones!" she said.

"Can you stop calling me by my married name? I left his sorry ass a year ago."

"My apologies, Naughty Notter." That was her joke, as my legs had been tighter than Fort Knox since my divorce.

Lidia and I both married into cool names. With the name Jackie Jones, I should have been the CEO of Bellstrom instead of a salesgirl. Lidia Ledbetter wasn't too shabby a name, either. She could have been a reporter or the host of her own talk show. But no matter how cool my married name was, I had to return to Notter after the divorce.

"Thanks for inviting me," I said. "I needed this."

Lidia hugged me. "There's no one I'd rather be here with than you." Before letting go, she held me at arm's length, putting us face to face. She rarely let me see her motherly side, but it shone through. "What's awesome is you're smiling again. I hope that's here to stay."

"You and me both. So, how are you and Paul doing?"

Lidia let out a sigh that would have been funny under different circumstances. I regretted asking.

"We can't seem to get out of this rut. I don't know if we ever will. I'm trying. Believe me, I am."

"Don't give up. Once you break this cycle, life will be better." That wasn't the case in my marriage, but I'd heard it somewhere. Sounded like the right thing to say.

"I sure hope so. When things are good, they're really good."

"How's Ellie holding up? Is she too young to know what's going on?"

"No, unfortunately, she picks up on everything."

7

The lights went out and Lidia screamed with the schoolgirls surrounding us. I joined her after laughing. Brixton Webber's name flashed across the giant screen in bright neon colors. Lasers shot out in random directions as a spotlight on each side of the stage swayed back and forth. The beams joined together, highlighting Brixton in the rafters, strapped into a zipline harness. A collective high-pitched scream rang through the crowd.

I followed the zipline cable to the stage, where a close-up of Brixton was on the big screen. He was dressed in black, looking a little steampunk with a mix of Goth and all-American boy. Shoulder length blond hair fell loosely over his right eye. He had thick dark eyebrows and a strong, angular European nose. The soft shape of his cheeks and round chin balanced out his masculine features.

My gaze lowered to an unexpected sight. The harness was cinched against his pelvis, pushing his bulge front and center. The outline of his balls and the head were prominently on display. I felt my face grow flush, yet couldn't look away.

Brixton adjusted his hands-free mic and shouted, "Let's get this mutha started!" He reached for the overhead bar with gloved hands and leaped off the platform with a primal scream. The weight of his body caused a noticeable drag on the line as he zipped to the stage. He flew in swiftly but with streamlined precision. At the last second, he grabbed the cable to slow down, landing easily on his feet. He unhooked the line and unfastened the harness, letting it drop to the floor. Pictures do not do him justice. He was more handsome in person than on any tabloid cover.

A thunderous explosion kicked off the first song. I recognized the beat from Brixton's CD Lidia bought for the ride to the show. It was a silly song that was a play on his last name:

What is a spider doing in my web?
What is this spider doing in my bed?
Soon as you leave you're stuck in my head.
Can only think of you stuck on my thread.

Black Widow, you're a heartbreaker.
Black Widow, you're a love taker.
Black Widow, I will make you mine!

Heartbreaker? Love taker? Who is he, *Patrick Benatar?*

Six male dancers emerged from the tunnel in the center of the stage and began working the beat. They were professionals, yet Brixton stood out. He was an incredible dancer — sexy as hell and dripping with sensuality. His moves were smooth and natural, almost effortless, each complementing the last. I imagined how amazing he would be in bed.

Brixton broke away from the dancers in a sideways slide, arms outstretched like a surfer. He strutted toward us, which resulted in a stream of girls trying to occupy our space. Lidia and I held fast, locking our hands. We were pushed against the security barrier less than five feet from Brixton. I've never been in the presence of such beauty. His kissable mouth drew me in; the top lip pushed up with a predominant dip in the middle, the bottom full and pouty. My knees gave way as if he was sucking the oxygen from the room. I was mesmerized.

He rubbed his crotch seductively before belting out, "*I've had my share of girls. What I want is a woman!*" And then he winked at me.

Lidia and I looked at each other and gasped. Was Brixton Webber flirting with me? Before I could respond, he danced away with a devious grin.

The girls who had invaded our area took Brixton's lead and attempted to follow him. Unfortunately for them,

9

they were intercepted by a security guard and escorted back to their seats.

"I'm totally perving out on Brixton," Lidia said. Her look of shame was priceless.

"Jailbait," I shouted as the music swelled.

"I think he's legal," Lidia replied.

The next song had a fun and bouncy rhythm. Everyone in the crowd was singing along, hopping up and down. Lidia and I didn't have a clue about the lyrics.

"He sure grabs his dick a lot," I screamed in Lidia's ear. I made a cock sucking motion with my hand, trying to shock her. I hadn't noticed that Brixton was dancing in front of us. He looked at me with his eyes wide and tripped over his feet but caught himself before he fell, then ran to the other side of the stage, leaving us in a heap of laughter.

Near the end of the song Brixton sang, *You could be my Supergirl – I could be your Superman.* He took off running and jumped into the crowd face first. I thought he was doing a stage dive, but he stuck his arms out at the last moment, flying like Superman. Even as close as we were, the wires were barely visible. He swung out a good hundred yards in an arc, where he made a perfect running landing, disappearing into the tunnel. A roadie walked out with the harness and whisked it away. Lidia and I were awestruck.

Brixton reemerged from the tunnel to uproarious applause. He danced across the stage as a purple bra came hurling through the air, smacking him in the crotch. He leaned over and retrieved something that had landed at his feet.

"What am I going to do with your grocery store club card?" he said, cracking up the audience and himself. Brixton laughed so hard his body buckled, sending him to the ground like a puppet collapsing. The crowd erupted in joined laughter. It took him a while to regain his composure. I pictured myself in his arms, the two of us rolling around on the floor laughing.

"Damn, that was off the chain," he said, jumping back on his feet. "Thanks, I needed that." He tossed the card into the crowd and continued with the show.

A tight mix of dance songs had us shaking our stuff. I was hungry for more but Brixton slowed the mood by taking a seat center stage with an acoustic guitar. At that point, he was down to a tank top, which revealed the definition in his arms. He was no longer the boy we'd seen in pictures—a handsome ruggedness was showing through. I shifted my stance, rubbing the insides of my thighs together, fully aware of the tingling below.

The song he played was full of melancholy, with words of suffering and loss swirling around as if caught in the wind. The lyrics were about slipping away, which made me think of my best friend Jennifer, who I'd lost to cancer five weeks earlier. I looked away and tried to force back the tears. It wasn't working. Lidia hugged me as I cried on her shoulder. She squeezed tighter, holding me through the rest of the song.

We had consumed our fair share of drinks before the show. After two more songs, the pressure on my bladder became unbearable. I excused myself and made a beeline to the bathroom. I had to go so badly I sat down on the toilet without using a seat cover. The stream was full force and loud as hell, but I was particularly embarrassed by how long it lasted. I grabbed a wad of toilet paper. It slid out of my hand with one wipe. I wadded up another handful and wiped again. My crotch felt like a Slip 'N Slide. Brixton had really put me in a lather.

I made it back to our row while he was in the middle of a ballad. I stood to the side so I wouldn't disturb his seated fans. The song ended, and a security guard motioned for me to go. I waited until Brixton walked in the other direction. Lidia fist-bumped me when I reached my seat.

11

A few songs later, Brixton returned from backstage draped in oversized gold chains and his ass hanging out of his pants.

"He's so urban," Lidia said in a mockingly dry tone that made me laugh.

I felt like telling him to pull his damn pants up but at the same time fantasized about them falling to the floor. Brixton's white Prada boxer briefs were exposed in the back, showcasing his tight bubble butt to perfection. I wanted to bite him.

The show ended with an elaborate dance number and a dazzling array of pyrotechnics. A skateboard shot from the stage and Brixton caught it with one hand. He ran to the top of a landing and hopped on his board. Without hesitation, he dropped into the ramp and skated toward the crowd. At the last minute, he turned and exited through the tunnel. A giant fireball shot from the same tunnel, and a collective gasp echoed throughout the arena. Brixton emerged from the smoke and everybody went wild. He stood tall as he soaked up the adoration, then took a bow and disappeared back into the tunnel.

The house lights came on halfway. Do we get an encore? Why did I care so much?

A rumble shook the stadium as thousands of girls pounded their feet and chanted, "Brixton, Brixton!"

Smoke started to pour from a crevasse in the middle of the stage. Brixton reappeared, standing on a platform that spun as he rose. The smoke spiraling around him offered an impressive visual. He was lost in the moment and ripped off his shirt, sending the buttons flying into the audience. The screams were deafening. A button shot toward us, clipping Lidia on the side of her head. I tried to catch it but a girl behind us was more aggressive.

Brixton's physique was thin but muscular. There wasn't a scar or tattoo in sight—he was pristine. By then, I was so wet I checked to make sure I wasn't soaking through my jeans. I touched myself and my fingers lingered. Brixton stopped in front of me and grinned. I pulled my hand from my pants and gave him the rock 'n' roll salute. I'd seen the girls giving him the stupid W sign for Webber and thought he would enjoy my gesture more. He smiled and began gyrating his pelvis to the beat. The ten feet between us seemed to evaporate. I followed his lead and in my mind it was just the two of us—dancing in unison as if we were one. When I moved forward, he stepped back. As I ventured sideways, he was already there.

It had been so long since anyone was there mentally with me. Dennis never was.

Brixton radiated masculinity so powerfully it drew me into his sexual aura. He licked the underside of his upper teeth, igniting my imagination. I stopped dancing and unconsciously rocked my hips back and forth like we were having sex. This caught Brixton off guard. The front of his jeans were bursting with the fullness of his erection. Awash in an adorable look of panic, he ran to the back of the stage to adjust himself.

Lidia and I held onto each other and jumped around, squealing like teenagers.

Brixton closed the concert with his biggest hit and sprinted up the stairs to the upper platform. He towered above us, drenched in sweat, his long hair cascading against his moistened skin in sexy waves. That was the image I would pleasure myself with when I got home.

His mic was no longer working. A stagehand came to his rescue and adjusted something on Brixton's back.

"Are we live?" he asked. "Good." The roadie took the cue and slipped into the darkness. "Every day, I thank God for the strength given to me by you—my fans. Your love and support is the reason I'm here today. I am humbled by each of you, and want you to know that I have as much faith in you as you have in me." Brixton had ditched his street facade and was speaking from the heart.

13

"I am living proof that you can do whatever you want if you want it bad enough. Follow your dreams. Do *not* settle for mediocrity. Thank you for making my dream a reality. I love you, Seattle. Peace."

The arena grew dark and an immense blue ball of light materialized from the ceiling. It descended upon Brixton until his entire body was illuminated and aglow. The light expanded, pulsing in and out, then shot him swiftly to the rafters and through the roof, leaving a trail of smoke in his wake. Electrical sparks whipped across the ceiling in all directions. Brixton was gone.

I have no idea how the effect was achieved, but it blew my mind. The house lights came on, revealing all the wild-eyed girls surrounding us. You'd think they had seen the Beatles the way they were bawling and carrying on. I don't remember that happening at the 'U Nifi concert, but maybe I had been crying too hard to notice.

Lidia grabbed my hand. "Did you see Brixton dancing with me?"

I was about to say, "Oh no, Honey," but picked up on the conversations around us. The girls were all bickering; each one convinced that Brixton danced with them. Lidia heard it too and we both giggled.

We were waiting for the arena to thin out before making our way to the side.

"Pushing through a crowd is so pedestrian," Lidia said, pretending to be a spoiled rich girl.

"Peasants," I said.

It took a while for the masses to dissipate.

"Let's blow this joint," Lidia declared. We reluctantly said goodbye to the front row.

"How do his pants hang so low in the back without them falling off?" I asked. "What's keeping them up?"

"I know. Seriously. Is he a wizard?"

"Maybe his wand is holding them up," I joked. We looked at each other and burst into laughter.

At the end of the aisle, an enormous security guard stopped me and hung a laminated pass around my neck.

"Brixton has requested your presence backstage," he said.

"Me?" I said in shock.

"Oh yeah." The security guard grinned and nodded.

"Well, I guess we know who he was dancing with," Lidia said.

My excitement drove me to the brink of hyperventilation. I grabbed Lidia by the wrist.

"Just you," the guard said sternly.

I held my hands out to Lidia and tried to think of something to say.

"Go," she said, pushing me forward. "I'll meet you back at the bar."

Backstage

The security guard led me to where a handsome blazer-clad gentleman was waiting. I honed right in on his Bally shoes—one of the most expensive pairs we sell. Unfortunately, they didn't compensate for his severe case of raccoon eyes. The man was obviously not an aficionado of high SPF.

"I'll take her from here," he said.

"All yours, boss," the guard said and walked away.

"Dusty Cohen," the man said matter-of-factly.

"Jackie Notter," I said, clueless.

He turned his head curiously and a grin formed. "You have no idea who I am, do you?"

I studied him more intently but couldn't place his face. He looked like a slick New York lawyer. His thin lips accentuated a hairline that only recently began receding. The two-day stubble worked wonders on him. Still, the whiteness left from his sunglasses was so distracting I had to ask if he was a superhero.

"Funny," he said, not laughing. "I couldn't resist the rays yesterday—had to go skiing. Seriously though, I manage Mr. Webber."

"Oh, nice to meet you." We shook hands and he gave me an awkward pat on the back.

"I take it you're not a big fan?" Dusty asked with a quizzical look.

"I wasn't. Well, not until tonight. My friend had an extra ticket. Couldn't pass up front row."

"It's actually refreshing—Brixton's fans can be a bit much," he admitted.

"I can imagine." Christ, look at the effect he had on me in just a few hours.

"Walk with me, Jackie," he said, motioning toward the back.

We strolled past a lot full of tour buses and entered a large room filled with concert equipment. Roadies were packing up for the next show. A guard flung open a set of double doors that led to a dingy yellow corridor. I don't know what I expected, but I thought backstage would be more glamorous. The enormity of the moment wasn't lost on me, though. I absorbed every sight and sound.

The door to the dancer's room was ajar; *B's Crüe* was inscribed on the nameplate. Toned bodies in various stages of undress were milling about. The next room was Brixton's. A stocky man with tattooed sleeves and a shaved head stood guard. He looked pissed about something. The door opened and a woman emerged carrying an oxygen tank and mask. I caught a glimpse of Brixton sitting shirtless on the couch, slumped over with his head low. My heart melted.

"Is he all right?" I asked Dusty.

"A few hits off the tank and he's good as new."

"That can't be healthy," I said.

"Life isn't healthy," he said flatly.

A group of tween girls were lined against the wall, giggling with each other. I recognized them as the dance troupe that Brixton invited on stage from the crowd. The girls danced with him during one of his songs. They knew every move. I wondered if he invites amateur dancers up at each show.

"All right, girls. It's time," a woman my age announced. "Are you ready?"

They all screamed hysterically.

The woman held her hand up. "No screaming. Brixton won't appreciate you screaming in his face. I need you girls to be cool," she said like an exhausted den mother. "Can you do that for me?" They calmed down and shook their heads enthusiastically. "All right then." She walked the girls over to his door. "What are we?"

18

"Cool," they said in unison. With that, she led them to his room. As soon as they saw Brixton the girls started screaming again.

"Let's step into my office," Dusty said. "Time's a wasting."

I followed him to a room with a red Ikea couch and an old desk.

"Love what you've done with the place," I said.

"The talent gets the VIP room. Have a seat. Can I get you anything?"

"Vodka-cran?"

"Brixton doesn't allow liquor backstage," he said.

"Yeah, right," I responded sardonically.

"We have to protect his reputation. Earn the trust of the parents and you're golden." He gave me the same wink that Brixton had given me. "Let's get down to business. Brixton has four active death threats against him. I need to do a background check."

"Of course. Did you say four death threats?"

"Do *not* mention that to him," he said sternly. "He only knows about the one in the news."

"I'm cool," I said, which caused him to do a double-take. "Really, I am."

Dusty sat in the desk chair beside me and removed an iPad from an oversized Louis Vuitton satchel. It took him a while to find the link for the background check. Once he did, he passed it to me.

"I need your social security number."

I typed in my nine digits and hit enter.

He looked briefly at the results and said, "You're good."

"That's what they tell me," I said, smiling. I instantly regretted saying it but he wasn't paying attention to me anyway.

"Driver's license," he demanded.

I retrieved my wallet from my purse and handed over my I.D.

He glanced at it without looking up and remarked, "You're thirty."

"Just turned."

Dusty threw his hands up and pushed away from the desk, causing him to roll back a few feet in his chair.

"No!" he said.

"What do you mean no?" I asked incredulously.

"He's not sleeping with a 30-year-old."

"Whoa, whoa!" I protested. "Who said anything about fucking him? I'm just along for the ride."

"All of his handlers are in their early thirties—all of us. I won't allow you to cross that line. I'm sorry, but you have to leave."

Tears welled up in my eyes. I said nothing for fear of restarting the waterworks that Brixton's ballad had let loose.

He put an arm around my shoulder and led me out of the room past Bricton's closed door. My mind was a centrifuge of conflicting thoughts spiraling out of control. We walked through the corridor toward the exit but were hedged off by a woman with short, spiky, black hair. She was waiflike with soft porcelain skin.

"What are you doing?" the woman snapped at Dusty.

"She's thirty, for fuck's sake."

The woman contemplated this for half a second before shaking it off. "Can you excuse us for a moment?" she said to me.

I walked a few feet ahead and listened intently to their conversation, hoping with all my heart that this woman would change Dusty's mind.

"There are boundaries," Dusty argued. "Brix has his world, and we have ours. We meet in the middle to get the job done. That's where it has to end."

"Christ, Dusty, look beyond the dollar signs. Brixton has been a wreck since Candice. There's something about this chick that caught his eye. He wants to spend time with her. I am not going to deny him that. Maybe he'll quit moping around."

In my head I was screaming and jumping up and down. This might actually happen.

"I can't be a part of this," Dusty said, storming off.

"Don't let him bother you," the woman apologized as she caught up with me. "Dusty has good intentions, but he can be a bit of an ass-pain."

I laughed.

"I'm Stephanie, Brixton's stylist."

"Jackie," I said. She gave me a warm hug that brightened my day. I liked her immediately.

"We have a few minutes. Do you want me to work some of my magic on you?"

"Sure," I said enthusiastically. "I'd be a fool to pass that up."

She took my hand and led me to the hair and makeup room.

"Can I use the restroom?" I asked, spotting the door in the corner. "I have to pee so badly my back teeth are floating."

"Of course, Jackie," she laughed.

I caught my reflection in the bathroom mirror as I was washing up. My eyes were red and swollen.

"Thank you for doing this," I said after returning.

"My pleasure," she said. "Have a seat."

Stephanie removed her sweater, revealing more tattoos. She rummaged around in her hard-sided black makeup case. "Ah, here it is." She produced a small white tube and squeezed a dab of ointment onto her finger. "This should take the puffiness away from those eyes."

"I wasn't crying because of Brixton," I responded, embarrassed. "My best friend died of cancer a few weeks back. One of his songs reminded me of her."

"I'm sorry," she said, looking deep into my eyes. "Believe me, I know what you're going through."

I wanted to say something comforting, but my mind went blank.

"I bet the song was Fallen Leaves. He wrote that about a classmate who committed suicide."

"That's horrible."

"Yeah, it haunts him to this day."

Stephanie started singing, *"Billy's the one who was picked on for fun. He had nowhere to turn in his life."*

I was so caught up in the song's emotions during his show I missed half the lyrics.

"He still feels some of the blame is on him. Like if he had been there instead of L.A. he could have stopped the bullying."

"What? He shouldn't blame himself."

"That's what I tell him, but he's a sensitive guy underneath all that cocksureness."

"There is something about him," I concurred.

"Close your eyes and look down," she said and applied beigey-gold eyeshadow to my upper lids with a small triangular sponge. "He does have a presence. I can feel him walk into a room without even looking. It's spooky. The president is the only other person I know with a presence that strong. You should see those two together. They're like the Glimmer Twins."

I knew who Stephanie was talking about. My mother is a huge Stones fan. "Mick and Keith," I said.

"Yeah, baby!" Stephanie exclaimed. "You're old school but young and fresh."

"Speaking of school, is Brixton even legal?" I asked.

"For almost a year now." She stepped back to study my face. "Oh, I am good," she boasted, admiring her artistry.

Stephanie handed me a mirror. I grinned with delight at my reflection. She gave me a no-makeup look, and the result was spectacular. "I love it!" I said.

"Fabulous!"

"You should fix Dusty's eyes," I suggested.

"Brixton won't let me. He thinks his sunburn is hilarious. It's probably why Dusty has been in a pissy mood today."

I heard the girls screaming outside our door as they were escorted from the hallway.

"Well," Stephanie said as she clapped her palms together. "Showtime!"

She led me into the hall and over to Brixton's room. I couldn't believe this was happening. I was sure I would wake up and discover it was all a dream.

The guard with the shaved head gave me the once-over. "Her?" he said, looking perplexed.

"Jimmy!" Stephanie pounced.

His questioning tone tore through my confidence, allowing my insecurities to push their way up front.

"Phone," Jimmy demanded, holding out his hand. I was confused.

"He wants your cell phone," Stephanie said. "No dressing room pictures."

I reluctantly handed it over.

Jimmy unlocked the door and said, "Welcome to Oz."

I detected an odd annoyance from him, but in retrospect, it was just the natural slope of his eyebrows. The way they curve down in the middle makes him look perpetually angry.

"Hey Jackie, you're beautiful," Stephanie said as I entered the room.

I smiled back at her. "Thank you."

Stephanie lay into Jimmy. "Don't you ever make anyone feel bad around Brixton."

"What did I do?" he asked.

"No negativity. You should know that by now."

The door shut behind me and I stood alone in the room. Brixton was nowhere to be found. An antique lamp produced a soft glow across an oversized couch with plush pillows. Metal-framed photographs of beaches, sunsets, and fast cars hung on the walls. Remnants of pizza and finger food were scattered everywhere. I shut my eyes and imagined the roar of the crowd chanting my name. Instead, I heard a shower.

"Hello? Is someone there?" Brixton called out from behind a closed door.

I was speechless for a few seconds but regained my composure. "Uh, it's Jackie. Blonde hair, blue hoodie?"

"And that amazing smile," he added.

A few simple words and I was his.

"I'll be right out." He turned off the water, and with only a wall separating us I imagined him standing there, naked and dripping wet.

I sat on the couch beside a leather-bound notebook protruding from a cushion. It was his writing journal. Before I could stop myself, I opened it and read the beginning of what appeared to be a new song:

you're not alone
everyone's a freak
you're not alone
everyone is weak
you're not alone

His words touched my heart. I wanted more but the bathroom door began to creak open. I jammed the notebook back under the cushion.

Brixton walked in with a swagger, clad only in dark blue basketball shorts and a white tank top. His long blond hair was wet and slicked back. He was intimidatingly handsome.

"What's up, Goodness?" he purred. His eyes were a tropical blue sea of desire, washing over my body with fevered intensity.

"I… it's nice to meet you," I stammered.

Brixton offered his hand and pulled me from the sofa. The pulse of his eager heart beat rapidly against my palm.

I was somewhat surprised by his stature. He couldn't have been more than 5' 11". Brixton seemed larger than life on stage, but standing next to him we were nearly the same height.

"My, you *are* lovely," he said.

"Lovely?" I laughed.

"Sorry, I picked that up from one of my mates in England."

"No need to apologize, young bloke," I said, with a horrible English accent that made us both grin.

"I mean it. You're stunning." The compliment sent my lust into overdrive.

"Thank you," I said, trying hard not to break his stare. "Do you mind if I take off my shoes?" I pretended my feet were sore but really I needed him to be taller than me.

"*Mi casa es su casa*," he said.

"Who'd you pick that up from, a conquistador in Spain?"

He responded, "Noooo," in a drawn-out Spanish accent that made me laugh.

I steadied myself on his shoulder as I kicked off my shoes. He smelled wonderful—so fresh and clean. I glanced at his shorts and caught a glimpse of the outline of his cock. I looked at him, embarrassed.

"Jesus Christ!" he exclaimed, peering down at himself. "I'll go put on some underwear."

The foreplay of his concert had reduced me to a quivering mess of sexual desire. Being in his presence intensified the effect. I'd never felt a stronger attraction to anyone. The feeling came from deep inside, almost primal. I wasn't about to let this opportunity slip away. Gathering my courage, I took a giant leap out of my comfort zone.

"Don't even think about it," I said, grabbing his arm and reeling him in to me. Our faces were now inches apart. His hot breath warmed my lips, tempting me, luring me in. I desperately wanted to kiss him but waited for Brixton to take the lead.

He looked me in the eyes, "I want you to know you're the first girl I've ever invited backstage."

I smiled, half believing him.

Brixton held me close and kissed me on my neck, leaving a trail of tender kisses as he worked his way to my ear. The adrenalin jolting through my body sent my heart aflutter. He traced my lobe with his soft lips and whispered something unintelligible. I grabbed his ass and pressed him against me. His wet, silky tongue found mine and soon we were making out feverishly.

I cupped Brixton's face and brought him closer. He quivered and dove in harder, clutching my hair in one hand. His probing tongue triggered a thousand sensations in my body. I wanted his mouth everywhere.

I reached for his manhood but he caught my wrist. His grip was unyielding. He backed me up against the vanity, knocking his electronic keyboard to the floor. Not even his security guards could have pulled us apart.

Being young, I was expecting him to go straight for my breasts, but he zoned in on my pants. Before I could react, he had the buttons free and his face buried in my underwear. I gasped as he took a deep breath through his nose, and shoved him away. All of the old fears and insecurities came flooding back. My ex-husband Dennis used every excuse not to go down on me. He never did — not once in ten years. I realize now that he was covering up for his hidden sexuality. Nonetheless, I had acquired quite a complex.

"I want to taste you," he said with pleading eyes.

Reluctantly, I let go of his head. He shimmied my pants off and threw them on the floor. I was glad I wore my sexiest white lace panties, although Brixton couldn't peel them off fast enough. Once he did, something stopped him dead in his tracks. He stared at my vagina with a dazed look on his face and stroked the small patch of pubic hair with his finger. I froze, unsure of what he was thinking.

"Your pussy is fucking gorgeous," he said in wonder.

With sheer gratitude I waved him into home plate. He leaped in with unbridled enthusiasm.

In one long, fluid motion he licked me from taint to clit. Ever so slowly he repeated this move. I quivered each time his tongue passed. He was testing my sensitivity — trying to figure out what aroused me. The thought of a man actually caring about my sexual needs was more erotic than anything he was doing physically.

His mouth landed at last. He held tightly as if capturing my clit, slapping it with his tongue to show my little man who's boss. Next came a barrage of quick jabs that caused me to flinch. Reading my body language, he softened his touch, gently flicking the tip of his tongue along my clit in a finely tuned dance. Pulses of lightning shot through my loins. I had never felt anything so amazing. I closed my eyes and floated out of my body.

He found the perfect rhythm and kept pace with hyper-focus. In my mind, we were running hand in hand toward a cliff. I was drawn to the edge with an intense energy but something kept pulling me back. Thankfully, he was patient.

Waves of pleasure permeated my clitoris until it was engorged and tingling. I was getting close. My body tensed and my mind faded to black.

I grabbed Brixton by the ears and let him know his efforts were about to pay off. "Don't stop," I begged. "Yes. Yes. Right there. Oh my God!"

I felt weightless as I dove off the cliff into a sea of splendor.

The relief I experienced afterward reduced me to tears. There were so many emotions colliding with each other it didn't take long before I was a sobbing mess.

Brixton leaned his head back and looked at me with shock and confusion. "Did I do something wrong?"

I wiped the tears from my eyes and gathered myself the best I could. It took a moment to find my voice.

"Nobody's ever made me feel like that," I said.

"So those are tears of joy?"

"Oh, yeah."

"Good, because we're not finished." He slid between my legs and moved in for a second course.

It was strange looking down and seeing Brixton-fucking-Webber eating my pussy. I was off and running toward the cliff, but it was easier to reach this time. I felt somewhat disconnected from my body, as if my mind was hovering along the ceiling, witnessing what was happening to me below. Pulses of ecstasy coursed through my veins until they reached a crescendo. I exploded in a fevered pitch, moaning, "Brixton."

I unclamped my legs from around his neck and allowed him to surface for some much-needed air. "How you doing up there?" he asked with those big puppy dog eyes, his mouth a glistening grin. Brixton seemed quite pleased with himself. "Ready for another?"

I hesitated for a second before saying, "Yes, please."

"My pleasure," he said and started lapping me up again.

The third orgasm sent me rocketing into orbit with such ferocity that my screams of delight were uncontrollable.

"You'll get me in trouble," he silenced, placing a hand over my mouth. I couldn't help biting it. He winced a little but laughed.

As I was coming down, I combed my fingers through his long, silky hair. The strands parted effortlessly as they flowed tenderly across my skin. How many girls would have killed to be in my shoes right then? That simple act of intimacy would blow their pubescent minds.

"It's my turn," I whispered seductively. I couldn't contain myself any longer. I'd never wanted anything so strongly in my life. I had to have Brixton's cock.

The erection pushing through his basketball shorts begged for attention. I kneeled on the floor and attempted to set it free, but the head was caught in the waistband. I pulled up and out, and his fully erect cock sprang upwards, snapping tight against his abs. It was larger than I'd expected. He hadn't let me touch it earlier, which made me wonder if he had a weird pygmy penis, but nothing could be further from the truth. His cock was sublime.

Brixton's alluring scent intensified my lust. I grabbed hold of his shaft and was surprised to find he was uncircumcised. The feel of the loose skin as I pumped back and forth was incredible. I was instantly a fan of the uncut. I gazed up at him and enthusiastically shoved his cock into my mouth. It had a soft, inviting texture. I wanted to explore every inch, but for the moment was compelled to suck on that glorious phallus as if my life depended on it. Brixton shuddered and moaned. He began fucking my mouth in sync with my rhythm.

A harsh knock at the door stopped us dead in our tracks.

"Yo, Jimmy!" he said angrily.

"It's Mama, Brixton. Open the door!" His body tensed and he removed his cock from my mouth.

"Your mom?" I whispered, shocked.

He closed his eyes and clenched his fists. "This isn't a good time, Mom. You need to come back later."

"I need to talk to you *now*," she demanded, her tone frighteningly authoritative. "It's important."

"Hang on a minute. I'm getting out of the shower." Brixton hurried to the bathroom, his sweet derrière bouncing with each stride. That's when I noticed the spider tattoo on his right cheek. This small act of rebellion in such an inconspicuous place was cute as hell.

He grabbed a fresh pair of underwear from the counter and attempted to put them on, but missed a leg and fell to the floor. I somehow managed to stifle my laughter.

It wasn't until my shoes were on that I noticed my panties sitting on the vanity. I was about to put them in my pocket but thought his backpack would be a better place.

He turned and faced me with a look of utter frustration. "I am so sorry."

"Don't worry about it," I whispered. "I had a great time."

He smiled and gave me a delicious lingering kiss. He led me to the adjoining door to the dancer's room and guided me in. There were several guys from the show lounging about. The door shut softly and Brixton was gone.

"His mom is here," I told no one in particular. The room fell silent.

I heard Brixton's mother storm into his room.

"Where is she?"

"Where is who?"

"Don't act wise with me, Brixton Marcell Webber."

"Mom, I'm eighteen."

"Really? Playing the age card, young man?" she snapped, her voice echoing as she searched the bathroom.

"I'm an adult," he said firmly. "You can't treat me like this."

An attractive young dancer with a short haircut on the sides and a crazy mess on top like the college kids wear grabbed my hand and led me to the couch. He dragged it from the wall and shoved me behind. That pissed me off but I complied, trying to flatten my body as they pushed the sofa close to the wall. Two guys sat down and pretended to be deep in conversation. I felt ridiculous hiding.

The door to Brixton's room burst open. I closed my eyes, wishing I could vanish. "Hey, Mrs. W," one of the dancers above me said. "How's it hanging?" He had brazenly steered her attention to where I was hiding.

There was an uncomfortable silence as she searched the room without responding. She lingered momentarily and then exited with a huff through the main door. Outside in the hallway, she scurried around before giving up and returning to Brixton's room. When I thought we were safe, the main door to the dancer's room opened again. I pressed tighter but the couch slid out away from me. I was relieved to see Dusty but completely mortified about hiding.

"Did she see you?" he whispered.

"No."

"Thank God. Let's get you the hell out of here," he said, grabbing my arm.

I could hear his mom in the other room saying, "Let us pray."

"Enough with the passive-aggressive prayers," Brixton said. "What are you even doing here?"

There was no response from his mother. I pictured her on bent knee, pleading with Jesus for her baby boy's salvation.

Dusty led me from the room, rushed me around the corner and stopped at a door.

I wanted to tell him it wasn't my idea to hide but he was so mad I was afraid to say anything.

"Look," he said tersely, "Brixton has worked his ass off to earn the trust of his fans. He's safe to them and their parents. I will not let you destroy his world."

"I won't tell anyone," I said, nearly in tears. "Nobody."

"*Nobody*," he barked. "You were never here." He yanked the pass from my neck and practically shoved me out the door.

Just like that I was back in the real world. The chill of the early March air sent a shiver to my core. My body trembled, not from the cold but from the hurt and anger. For ten years, I was denied what Brixton had given me. Ten fucking years! I cried so hard my legs gave out, and I slid down the cold steel door to the ground. Between sobs, I realized I left my purse in his room.

Dusty had dumped me near the back of the arena, outside the fence where all the semis and tour buses were parked. I pounded on the door for five minutes but no one came to my rescue. My fear of the dark was getting the best of me, and I hurried to the front entrance. An unsuccessful attempt to get back in through the main gate led me to the mother of two enthusiastic young girls. The woman looked exhausted.

"I'm sorry to bother you," I said. "Do you have a phone I could use? I've lost my purse."

"Sure, no problem," the woman said. She retrieved her cell phone, oblivious to my fragile state of mind.

I dialed my number but it went straight to voicemail. I tried again to no avail. The battery must be dead. I thought about calling Lidia but always relied on my contact list for her number. I returned the phone and thanked the woman for her kindness.

The bar where I was meeting Lidia was across the street. The place would usually be packed after a concert but not tonight since most adults were chaperones. I headed into the bathroom to freshen up and ran into Lidia.

"Oh my God," she laughed. "Your hair is a mess!"

I didn't know what to say.

"Go fix yourself up, woman," she said. "I'll order you a drink."

I made myself presentable and found our table. Lidia stared at me and grinned. "Good for you," she said, patting me on the leg.

"Nothing happened," I professed.

"Sure, nothing happened," she said mockingly.

"Please. Don't tell anyone."

"Tell anyone what?"

"Just please don't tell anyone. All we did was kiss."

"It's *where* he kissed you that matters."

I felt myself blush. An image popped into my mind of Brixton looking up at me, his mouth buried in my crotch. "I promised I wouldn't tell."

"I knew it!" she exclaimed. "I could see it on your face. It's about time."

"I need to borrow your phone," I said, ignoring her. "I left my damn purse in his room."

"You can use it if you describe his cock to me," she said, holding her phone back.

"Please stop," I said. Lidia handed her phone over and I dialed my number, but again it went straight to voicemail. "I have tomorrow's soccer tickets in my purse. Randy's going kill me."

I called my brother to see if there were any messages but he didn't answer.

"Do you mind if we head back so I can take care of this?"

"Not at all. I should get home to the *fam damily* anyway."

I could tell she didn't want to go but I needed to get home. I'd have to make it up to her.

We polished off our drinks and exited the bar.

"Are you OK to drive?" I asked once we were buckled in her car.

"Quite," she affirmed. "But to be safe, no drag racing tonight." I laughed at the thought of Lidia racing in her hot rod Prius.

With the sweet sounds of Brixton Webber playing on the stereo, we headed into the night.

After crossing over the West Seattle Bridge, we exited onto Harbor Avenue. Trees lined the first mile, but once we reached Salty's Restaurant the Seattle skyline shimmered in its nighttime glory from across the bay. I never get tired of seeing that magnificent view.

We cruised along Alki's deserted moonlit drive and rolled into the curbside spot in front of my house. I was relieved that my ex-husband's light was off in the basement apartment.

The day I filed for divorce, my brother Randy swapped places with Dennis, moving upstairs with me. When we have enough equity in the house, we're getting a second mortgage to buy Dennis out. Until then, I'm stuck living above the prick.

Lidia put the car in park and left the engine running.

"You'll never guess what Brixton called me," I said.

"What?"

"Goodness."

"No way!" Lidia exclaimed. "That's what you used to call Jennifer. Did you say anything?"

"No, I was freaked out enough just meeting him."

She paused for a moment. "Well, I'm glad you had fun tonight," she said.

"You have no idea."

"I think I do—but I want to hear more!"

I shook my head and laughed. "You will."

I gave her an extra-long hug. "Thanks for everything."

I had barely jumped out of the car before Lidia took off. I was surprised she didn't wait to see me safely in the house. Now I really was worried she had too much to drink.

A wave of panic washed over me as I imagined a deranged man lurking in the dark. I made a mad dash to my car to retrieve my .22 from the glove box but stopped short when I realized I didn't have my keys. Randy better be home.

I ran around the side of the house and up the stairs, where I bumped into my brother smoking a cigarette.

"Whoa, Sis, it's me," Randy said, blowing smoke over his shoulder. He was wearing an old T-shirt that had paint all over it. His blond hair was trimmed short on the sides with a half inch on top, same as he's worn it for most of his adult life. It nicely complements his baby-faced athletic look. He's four years older than me, but you can't tell.

It was good that I couldn't retrieve my pistol—he would have confiscated it.

"Did you have fun tonight?"

I wanted to say more than you'll ever know, but couldn't get it out through my tears.

"Oh my God, Jacks, what's wrong?"

"I had the best night of my life," I sobbed.

"Then why are you crying?"

"Why did I waste all those years with Dennis?"

"What are you talking about?" he asked. "I thought you just had the best night of your life?"

"I did. It was. I know."

Why the hell was I bringing negativity into the evening? Brixton had taken a giant sledgehammer to my self-doubt. What I liked best is he thought my pussy was beautiful. He made that abundantly clear. How I had allowed Dennis to put such a shitty thing in my head I will never know.

"Let's get you a drink," Randy said.

"I could use one," I said, wiping away the tears and following him inside.

My brother is the original chill factor. He's my one saving grace. Randy isn't overly burdened with ambition, but for me, he's been remodeling our half of the house to get rid of the stench of the was-band.

35

"You finished the bookshelf!" I exclaimed.

"Do you like it?"

"It's wonderful."

"Hey, someone from Key Arena called. They have your purse."

"Oh, thank God."

I didn't recognize the area code on the caller ID but quickly dialed.

"Hey, Jackie," Dusty said. I was disappointed to hear his voice, hoping for Brixton on the other end.

"Hi, Dusty."

"You're probably looking for your purse," he said.

"Uh, yeah."

"Sorry about that. I'll have someone bring it by in the morning."

"Thank you. My tickets are in there for tomorrow's Spinnakers game."

"I saw that. Do you need a ride? I'm sending a car with the purse. You might as well use it."

"That would be great. Thanks."

I didn't understand why he was so nice, especially after how he treated me.

"Is the address on your license correct?"

"That's the one."

"You get some sleep, girl," he said, trying to imitate Brixton's stage persona. He wasn't even close.

"I will," I said and hung up.

My brother was staring at me with a knowing look.

"What?" I said.

"You got laid tonight, didn't you?"

My face flushed.

"I knew it!" he exclaimed. "It's about damn time."

"Weren't you making drinks?"

The Game

The following morning there was a loud, obnoxious knock at the door. I peered through the peephole and saw Dennis standing on my doorstep. His black hair was combed to the side the way he used to wear it when he was pretending to be straight. He was trying to grow a beard on his altar boy face but still couldn't get his mustache to connect with the rest. It actually looked cute, making me hate him even more. He was wearing the Spinnakers jacket I bought him for Christmas a few years back. I was happy he dialed his flamboyance down for the game. Dennis was going through that in-your-face stage of coming out. It could be a bit much.

I opened the door and was startled to see Brixton's bodyguard, Jimmy, standing behind Dennis. What the hell was he doing here? Perhaps he was being punished for treating me poorly. Or was Brixton waiting in the car? A surge of adrenalin raced through my body.

"Hello," I said nervously.

"Good morning," Jimmy responded with a smile. He was quite dapper in his black suit. His angry eyebrows punctuated every aspect of his cool and polished demeanor.

I snapped my finger and pointed at the tan Prada sitting at his feet. "My purse."

"Here you go," he said, bending down and handing it over.

I grabbed my hobo bag and dug into my wallet, triumphantly producing three tickets.

"You guys ready?" Dennis asked impatiently.

"I think so." I turned to yell for Randy but he was right behind me. His blue knitted cap and impeccable posture screamed handsome Navy boy, although he's never spent a day in the military. The recruiter is probably still waiting for him to show up for that appointment he made fifteen years ago.

He walked over to Jimmy and shook his hand. "I'm Randy."

"Jimmy," he said, shaking it firmly.

"Hello, sailor," Dennis said to Randy. My brother laughed and threw his hat on the love seat. That was the end of that. He was going to freeze at the game but I let it go, not wanting to start anything with Dennis.

I felt the need to explain the men in my house to Jimmy. "This is my brother," I said, motioning to Randy. "And I believe you've already met my was-band."

"Ah!" he responded. "Well, let's go, kids. Move 'em out." He spun his finger in the air a few times then pointed toward the road.

I looked around the corner. A shiny black Range Rover with dark tinted windows and murdered wheels was in our driveway. I gathered my coat and Spinnakers scarf and bounced down the stairs after Jimmy.

My excitement grew as I approached the car. Jimmy opened the rear door to let me in. A pair of manly legs protruded from the back seat. My heart skipped a beat until I realized they belonged to Dusty. I waved hello. He leaned forward and nodded but continued talking on his phone.

Jimmy caught my arm, holding me back. His touch was surprisingly gentle.

"Jackie," he said hesitantly, "I want to apologize for last night."

"No need for that," I said.

"Yes, I need to explain. Brixton usually prefers brunettes. That's why I was confused and said, 'Her?' I wasn't aware of how bad it sounded. I'm sorry that I hurt you."

Usually prefers brunettes? I doubt he understood how awful his apology was, but I let it go. "It's OK,

Jimmy." I had a feeling Brixton was behind this adequate plea of remorse.

I climbed into the back of the Range Rover with Randy and Dennis. Jimmy walked around the front and slid into the driver's seat. The layout in back was similar to a limo. I moved in next to Dusty. Randy and Dennis sat across from us, both looking confused. The plan had been to call for an Uber.

Dusty was wearing a gaudy pair of designer sunglasses. It was obvious he was trying to hide his still-visible raccoon eyes. A thunderclap rumbled in the distance. I turned away, biting my cheek to suppress my amusement.

"Look, you have to reschedule," Dusty insisted, his phone conversation becoming heated. "Have them all meet us at BC Place. Spider can do a Q&A session instead. It will be fine." He ended the conversation without a goodbye.

Dennis is all about appearances and how he is perceived in public life. He says that part of being important is looking important, but get him in a fancy Range Rover and he's bouncing around like a two-year-old, opening drawers and checking things out. He was starting to piss me off. I think Dusty picked up on this.

"Stop!" Dusty scolded him.

Dennis' eyes grew wide. "You're Dusty Cohen!" He looked over at me while pointing at Dusty. "He's Brixton Webber's manager! What the fuck?"

I turned to Dusty, totally embarrassed and not knowing what to say. Dusty took my hand and held it. "There's nothing to see here," he said to Dennis, like a cop trying to disperse a crowd from a crime scene.

My brother laughed to himself.

In the year since I'd left him, Dennis was already on his third boyfriend. It was nice to have someone to flaunt in front of him even if it was pretend.

"It's cool," Dennis said, somewhat defeated. I was shocked he gave up so easily. He's such a master manipulator he can usually get himself out of most situations. "Will Brixton be joining us?" He had a big stupid grin on his bearded face.

"In your dreams," Dusty said.

"You've got that right," Dennis retorted.

Jimmy parked in front of a bar a few blocks from the arena.

"I'll take that gum you put in your pocket," Dusty said to Dennis as he was getting out.

I looked at my ex and grimaced.

"What?" Dennis said. He handed over a used piece of gum balled up in a wrapper.

"This isn't Brixton's if that's what you were thinking," Dusty said. "It's mine."

"You chew grape bubble gum?" Dennis asked sarcastically.

"You have a problem with that?"

"Whatever," Dennis said.

I pushed him out with my foot. Dusty grabbed hold of my coat as I was trying to exit.

"You're not dating any of those guys, are you?"

"No, the jackass with the gum is my ex and the other one is my brother."

"I thought the two of you might be related," he said. "You have the same smile. Well, enjoy the game."

I wanted to ask about Brixton's whereabouts but Dusty's abruptness made me uncomfortable. "Thanks for the ride."

I was going for a hug when he offered his hand, squeezing mine firmly.

The car drove off and I sprinted ahead to catch up with Randy. He was standing with his hands in his coat pockets. I slipped an arm through his and we walked along together. We decided to skip the bar and head straight to the stadium. Dennis lagged behind, smoking one of his disgusting clove cigarettes.

Randy stopped and shook his head. "You never cease to amaze me, sis."

Our seats are near the entrance where the Spinnakers come out on the field. The walkway for our level is directly in front of us, and the tunnel to the concession stands to the right, providing ample opportunity for people watching. The space feels like a private box with three seats to the row, eliminating the need to get up a bunch of times to let people in and out. Unfortunately, both Dennis and I still want to see the Spinnakers play. We resolved the problem by alternating games. Opening Day is the only one we share.

We arrived at our area and Dennis brazenly sat in my seat. He knew from last year that I needed to sit there. I can't have him in my line of sight. I wouldn't last ten minutes if I had to look past him the whole game.

"Come on, Dennis," Randy said, picking up on my irritation. "Give Jacks her seat." Dennis didn't move but Randy held strong. "Let's have a good day, all right?"

"She's the one riding my ass," Dennis snapped. "Fine, I'll move,"

How does he make me out to be the jerk when it's him acting like an idiot? I slid in and Randy took a seat between us.

"Thank you, Dennis," I forced myself to say.

"It's cool," he said. "So, did you get to meet Brixton last night?"

"No, he was gone by the time I was backstage," I said, lying poorly.

"I tried to get tickets but they were sold out," Dennis said. "I think he's fucking hot." He adjusted himself awkwardly.

"Creepy," I said.

"Are we a pedophile, Dennis?" Randy joked.

"What? No. He turns nineteen this Wednesday."

"Stop," I said. Nineteen—really? I liked that. Somehow it made a difference.

41

I was on my second Mike's Hard Lemonade by game time. The crowd had worked itself into a frenzy. It took a few years but Seattle was becoming a genuine soccer town.

At the far end of the stadium, a group of Boy Scouts walked onto the field carrying an enormous folded-up American flag. They unfurled and shook it vigorously as if waving in the breeze. The excitement of opening day permeated the air.

"Ladies and gentlemen," the announcer said in a deep voice. "Today we have a special guest to sing the national anthem. This talented artist has taken time away from his world tour to be here today."

No fucking way.

"Please give a warm welcome to Brixton Webber."

On the jumbotron appeared Brixton in all his glory. My boy was there! Was it for me? He was wearing a green and blue Spinnakers uniform, not the kind you buy in the team store but an actual uniform. His blond hair was disheveled and fell across his face in long, straight strands, partially covering his eyes. He combed it back with his fingers, revealing those drop-dead baby blues. The crowd went wild. I looked over at Dennis and realized the loudest screams were coming from him. I shook my head but had to laugh.

I searched the field for Brixton. He was on our side but so far away I could barely make him out. I turned back to the monitor.

Brixton raised his mic and began singing "The Star-Spangled Banner." His rendition was so moving that tears welled up in his eyes. He brought the song home at the end, digging deep from the bottom of his soul. His beautiful voice resonated through my body. The crowd erupted with enthusiastic approval.

"Go Spinnakers," he cheered and walked off the field. "Webber" was embroidered on the back of his uniform.

Jimmy guided him over to our side of the stadium flanked by a dozen police officers and an impressive entourage. Brixton smiled in my direction before disappearing into the Spinnakers' tunnel.

"Mr. Webber will be playing a sold-out show tonight at BC Place in Vancouver, Canada." The announcer's voice echoed over the loudspeaker. "He hopes to see you there. Some lucky folks at this game will get to go to the show. Brixton is giving away two sets of four tickets at halftime. You can purchase raffle tickets for the drawing at the auction table by the team store. All proceeds go to the Boys & Girls Club of Seattle." The unmistakable screams of young pubescent girls rang throughout the stadium, and with a flash, Dennis was gone.

"Now, ladies and gentlemen, please direct your attention to center field for the coin toss."

My head would have been in the game, but I spent the first fifteen minutes scanning the suites for Brixton, hoping he was still there. I was so engrossed in my search I didn't see Dusty standing on the walkway below us. He tapped my ankle to get my attention.

"Well, hello there," I said.

"Hey, baby," Dusty responded, still pretending to be my lover. "Want to get a drink?"

"Sure," I said and told Randy I'd be right back.

"Take your time," he said.

Dennis wasn't as happy. I pushed my way past him. "Can I come?" he pleaded. I ignored him.

"I'll be good," he called out as I followed Dusty.

"You have great seats," Dusty said.

I looked at him, a bit perplexed. "What is all this?" I asked, gesturing to where Brixton had sung.

"That's just Brixton," he said, shrugging his shoulders.

A girl screamed "Dusty" from the section above us.

43

"Oh, crap," he said, grabbing my hand and leading me briskly to the club level.

By the time security let us pass, six girls were chasing after us. They were stuck on the other side of the glass door, pleading with the guard to let them through.

I removed my Spinnakers cap and handed it to Dusty to use as a disguise.

"I'll be fine," he said, placing it back on my head. "But I do need to ask you something."

"What's on your mind?" I said.

He asked point-blank, "Is your ex-husband gay?"

"Is it that obvious?"

"Kind of. Is he?"

"Yeah."

"Well, it's just."

"Oh, don't worry," I said, understanding the direction he was heading. "I've been tested. Trust me, I'm so clean you could eat off it." My eyes grew large. "I can't believe I just said that!" My filter tends to disappear at the most inopportune times.

Dusty laughed even though he tried not to. "I need you to understand something. Brixton seems mature because he spends a lot of time with people our age. You may want to tone it down around him."

The way he was talking down to me struck a nerve. I wanted to tell him that Brixton was old enough to handle himself. Instead, I offered a pathetic, "I'll be good."

"I still think this is a mistake but follow me," he said, leading us to the escalator.

Oh my God, he was taking me to see my man!

"Brixton told me he's been thinking about you since you rushed out."

Rushed out? Dusty practically dragged me from the arena. What the fuck? I was about to object but my common sense kicked in. "That's sweet," I said.

Dusty handed me a keycard and whispered, "Yours is the suite past the one where Jimmy is standing. Have fun."

The girls hanging out in the hallway recognized Dusty and rushed toward him. I entered the other door, braced for a party, but the room was dark. As I turned the corner, Brixton moved his arm back from the counter with a sheepish look. He was amazingly hot in his Spinnakers uniform.

"Oh, hello," I said nervously.

"Hi, Jackie!"

"Were you sneaking liquor?" I asked.

"No," Brixton said, sounding like a boy. He retrieved his drink from behind a jug of cranberry juice. I could tell by the pale color he added way too much vodka. Brixton took a swig and winced, then shuddered. He was so remarkably handsome even his look of disgust was appealing.

"Let me help you with that," I said, opening the bottle of cranberry juice.

"I'm not really a fan of cranberry," he admitted.

"I'm with you. It's horrible stuff, but vodka does something magical to it. Knocks out the bitter."

"All right," he said hesitantly and presented his glass. I topped his drink off and stirred with a spoon. He took a sip. "Tasty."

"If you don't enjoy your liquor there's no use drinking it. So, do we have the whole place to ourselves?"

"We do. They snuck me in over the bulkhead from the suite next door." He motioned toward the windows. Two burly security guards were lounging in our area, watching the game.

Brixton put an arm around my shoulder and held me close. "What's up, Goodness?"

"Oh no, honey, you have that all wrong. I'm Badness."

"Well, OK then. Hey, sorry about last night."

"We all have mothers."

"I have one that won't be hanging around as much anymore. I'm just glad Dad wasn't with her. Where are my manners? Can I make you a drink?"

"It would probably be safer if I made it."

He laughed. "Probably true. Vodka-cran?"

"Yes, how did you know?"

"A little birdy told me that's what you ordered last night."

I was flattered that he had taken note of my preference in alcohol. I filled a glass with ice and poured myself a double from the half-gallon bottle of Grey Goose.

He rested his arms on my waist. "I can't shake you from my head. You're adorable."

I don't know why I couldn't take the compliment. "Come on. I bet you hang out with supermodels."

He looked me straight in the eyes. "Supermodels have nothing on you. There's beautiful, and then there's adorable, which is on a much higher plane. You're adorable."

Was he really this fabulous?

Brixton leaned forward and kissed me softly on the lips. He brushed the tip of his tongue across my front teeth and then ventured further. Soon we were engaged in a tongue-wrestling match that left us both breathless. The chemistry I'd felt the night before was real.

He removed my baseball cap and placed it on his head.

"I believe I owe you something from last night," I said, glancing at his bulge. I bit against my lower lip, hoping to juxtapose my intentions with an air of innocence. "Are we cool in here?" I asked, concerned about being exposed.

"Absolutely, I had the glass tinted."

I reached down and grabbed him through his soccer pants. He was already hard.

"Hold up," he said. "Let's get high first."

"What?" I said, shocked, releasing his cock. "Look at you, big stoner. So, the video on the news really was you?"

"Nah," he said, "Well yeah, but this weed's not mine. A fan gave it to me in a pen when I signed her autograph." He popped the cap off and a thin joint fell into my hand.

"A pinner in a pen. That's the cutest thing I've ever seen." I took a whiff. "This is some quality shit."

"My fans are the best." He took my hand and led me to the bathroom. It had been a while since I'd smoked pot. Randy is a marine mechanic for the Seattle PD, so I've been good about keeping drugs out of the house.

We entered the bathroom and I shut the door behind us.

"You first," Brixton said. I leaned against the counter and held the joint to my lips. He sparked it up with a chartreuse-colored lighter.

"Love your nails," he said. "The blue trumps the purple."

"Thanks," I said, coughing out smoke. I was flattered that he noticed I had painted my nails that morning. I can't remember the last time anybody paid that much attention.

I passed the joint over. Brixton tried not to cough but couldn't help himself. "Smooth!" he said, which made me laugh. He reached around my waist and turned on the fan.

"You know it's legal here," I said.

"In the suite?"

"No, you dope, in Washington State. Don't you keep up with the news?"

"The news? Please." He handed the joint back. "Can I ask something weird?"

"The weirder the better," I said.

"We were driving around this morning taking in the city, and I noticed a sign that said Catholic Seamen's Club. What is that? A gay bar?"

I laughed, and then laughed harder when I realized he was serious. "It's seamen, as in sailor."

"Oh," he said. "Oh!" His eyes lit up when it registered. The weed sent us into uncontrollable stoned laughter — one of those long gutturals that's good for the soul. We rolled around on the floor until we were both in tears.

"I've never heard sailors called seamen before," Brixton said. He was embarrassed but at the same time looked extraordinarily cute. "Thanks for setting me straight. No one outside my crew corrects me anymore. They all just kiss my ass. I'm man enough to admit I don't know everything."

"Well then, you have most 18-year-olds beat," I said.

He winked at me.

I was roasting. "Do you mind if I ditch my long underwear?" I stood up not waiting for an answer, kicked off my shoes, shimmied my jeans past my pink long johns then hesitated. "I'm not wearing any panties."

"Allow me." Brixton dropped to his knees and rested his arms on my thighs. He took a long drag off the joint then snubbed it out on the metal edge of the sink. Before I knew what was happening, my silk lace thermals were being peeled off like a snake shedding its skin. He buried his face deep into my crotch.

"Hold on," I said. "I've been waiting long enough."

"It's all yours," he said, waving his hand toward his manhood.

I brought him to his feet and slipped my hand inside his underwear, caressing his smooth balls. He grew instantly hard.

"Let's get out of the bathroom," Brixton said. He took my hand and led us to the kitchen, where we both went straight for our drinks. I had serious cottonmouth and took three healthy swallows.

"I'm really high," I said. There was no response, which made me wonder if my words had left my mouth.

He walked to the couch and stretched out with his hands tucked behind his head. I lowered myself onto the floor next to him and pushed his soccer pants down around his ankles. He was wearing regulation issued soccer shorts. Christ, could he be any sexier? I pulled off his shorts, revealing skintight boxer briefs. The head of his cock was peeking from the elastic like a curious turtle.

I ripped off his underwear, wrapped a hand around his rigid cock and slammed it into my mouth. I furiously sucked on it, worshiping every inch of that star-studded phallus. I pounded him deep into my throat and to my surprise, my gag reflex was nonexistent.

"What did I do to deserve this?" he said.

His gratitude fueled my fire. I slid my tongue down the shaft, popping one of his silky balls into my mouth. I rolled it around with my tongue while simultaneously stroking his cock in a spiral motion. Brixton whimpered. I went for the other ball, licking at first then sucking gently until I had them both captured. There's something amazing about having a mouthful of balls; it's one of my favorite things.

I took a drink of my vodka-cran, then guided him back into my mouth, swirling the juice around his cock as I sucked up and down. I swallowed when the liquid turned warm. My hand and mouth were in perfect harmony when I felt his body begin to tense. I didn't slow down. The one thing trying to save my marriage taught me was to enjoy eating cum. I'd never wanted it more. I was hungry for my reward.

Brixton grabbed my head and warned, "I'm going to come."

Oh my God, yes.

He shuddered and moaned as a wave of cum shot into the back of my throat. I withdrew his cock and wrapped my lips around the head. Another large spurt exploded onto my tongue, followed by another, then another. The taste was sweet and delectable. I swallowed every drop.

"That was fucking hot," Brixton said, fully sated.

I climbed on top of him and was surprised when he frenched me fervently. Here's a guy who's not afraid of his nectar.

He relaxed, using the arm of the couch as a backrest. "You're the first person in a long time I can be myself around."

I was beyond flattered. He rolled me over and spooned my backside. What I thought was a comfortable silence turned out to be Brixton falling asleep. I was relieved that we weren't going further. I was nervous to have actual intercourse, although a little oral reciprocation would have been nice right about then. I settled for a twenty-minute catnap instead.

I awoke and found Brixton snoring lightly, his hand resting on my crotch. Our faces were inches apart. I liked the contrast of his light hair and dark eyebrows. What a beautiful, beautiful boy. I wanted to kiss him— attack him, but he looked so peaceful I didn't have the heart to wake him. I was still staring when his eyes fluttered open. He was startled to see me so close and jerked his head back, causing us both to laugh.

I rolled over and cuddled with him. It felt clingy. "How about a drink?" I asked.

"Sure," he said. "But just one more. I have a show tonight."

"Well, then I'd better make it count," I said, rising to my feet.

He stretched his arms wide. His semi-hard cock rolled from one side to the other. "Man, that nap felt good. How long was I out?"

"No idea. I fell asleep too, but it looks like we're not too far into the second half."

Brixton checked his phone for the time but started playing with it once it was in his hands.

I searched the drawers and found a couple of Red Bulls. I poured ample vodka in two cups of ice and emptied a can in each.

"Here you go," I said. "This'll jack you up."

He took a sip and then a guzzle. "Now that's what I'm talking about."

He sat up and put on his shorts.

Did I do something to turn him off? Should I have cuddled more? Shit! I went into the bathroom to grab my pants. When I returned, Brixton was at the far counter, watching the game. I planted myself on the stool next to him.

"They did an excellent job getting the bubbles out of the tinting," I said, feeling the window. "You can't even tell it's on there."

"If you're doing a job, you might as well do it right," he said, sounding quite mature.

A tiny flying insect caught my eye. It was trying to get through the glass, banging into it repeatedly.

Brixton followed my gaze. "That must be terrifying for insects. There's nothing in front of you yet you can't pass. You try and bang! You try again and bang!" He was obviously still high.

"Do you think they make it out?" I asked.

He looked at me seriously. "Not all of them."

Cheers from the crowd drew our attention.

We watched in anticipation as Richard Bennington scored the first goal. Flames shot high into the air from the goalposts.

"That was wicked!" Brixton shouted. "Are those flamethrowers?"

"Yeah. They used to shoot confetti but the local businesses complained that it was blowing from the stadium onto the street."

Brixton grabbed my Spinnakers scarf off the counter and held it high, emulating the fans below. "Bennington is awesome," he said. "Dude kicked my ass during practice."

"You practiced with the Spinnakers?"

"Of course," he said as if to say, *why wouldn't that have happened*?

"Were you down there while the crowd was streaming in?"

"Absolutely."

"Oh, man. I didn't even see you."

"That was Jimmy's doing. He didn't want it known that I was on the field. Had me in a wig. The Spinnakers sure treated me well. They gave me this jersey and my own locker. I changed with the team. How dope is that?"

"Mega dope, babe," I said trying to sound cool. "Did you meet their midfielder, Brent Edwards?" I had a major crush on Brent.

"He's a hell of a great guy. Kind of fucked with me, though. He was all like, ooh, look at the pop star go."

"Your life is just terrible," I said mockingly.

"You're one to talk. I wish I had season tickets to something."

"You could get a suite."

"Yeah, a suite, but I can't go out there," he said, motioning to the stadium. "I'm a vampire who gets moved from one enclosed space to another. I can't even go out to dinner anymore because it causes such a huge commotion. I'm usually a prisoner of my hotel room. I hate it."

"I've seen you out there. I saw you courtside at the UW/UCLA game last month."

"You watched that?"

"Of course. The UW is my alma mater."

"I bet you wish you'd missed that game."

52

"It was brutal," I said. "Why did you leave when you guys were slaughtering us?"

"Might as well be in a zoo with everyone staring at me. I commandeered a suite. I'd give anything to be able to walk around, sit in the middle and not be noticed, just to be normal."

"The thing is, by not being normal you get to make your fans feel special. You inspire them to be better people. Isn't that a decent trade-off?"

"I guess," he said. "But I sure do miss it."

"Well, you ditched the big gold chains today. That's a start."

"Don't be dissin' my game chains. They bring me good luck. We kicked your Dogs' asses that day."

Something in the distance caught his attention and he fell silent. A girl was standing outside the suite to the right of us. She was around fifteen and had an unsettled air about her.

"Looks like we have a stalker," Brixton said. "Girlfriend thinks she's sneaking past my guards."

The girl waited until the men were lost in the game before taking off over the bulkhead. She almost made it to the suite next door. One of the guards lifted her like a twig as she kicked and screamed, "Brixton, I love you!" Little did she know he was only a few feet from her face.

Brixton let out a sigh. "You know why I was attracted to you?" he asked. "Because you're not *that*."

"How do you know? Maybe I'm a crazy-ass stalker chick."

"Crazy-ass stalker chicks know all my lyrics. You didn't know any. I could tell right away you weren't a big fan."

I hesitated.

"Be honest."

"I'm not exactly your demographic."

"Ha! I knew it. Please don't become a fan."

"Deal," I said.

He laughed at how quickly I agreed. "I mean it."

"I promise. Really, I do."

"That'd be sweet," he said.

"So, where are you from?" I asked, changing the subject. I felt I was insulting his music.

"Juneau," he said proudly.

"Alaska? I thought you were from Canada."

"Why would you think that? I just sang our national anthem from the heart."

"You're uncircumcised," I said, embarrassed. "I'm sorry — that is so lame."

"Don't apologize. It's cute. You're cute. So, you're from Seattle?"

"Born at Swedish Hospital. That's about as native as you can be," I said. "Most people around here are California transplants."

"I couldn't imagine leaving California," he said.

"You don't miss Juneau?"

"Yeah, but I don't miss the weather. Besides, if you're in the music business you have to live in L.A."

"Unless you lived in Seattle during the grunge scene," I said.

"I was five when the 90s ended." We both laughed.

"Speaking of grunge," Brixton said, "I saw the spring collection at the Saint Laurent fashion show last year in Paris. The look is coming back."

"And here I was about to throw out all my flannel."

"You know, you don't act your age. You're all cool and hip and shit. I thought you were in your early twenties. I was jacked when I learned you were thirty. Boy, Dusty sure doesn't like it."

"Tell me about it," I said. "He thinks you're crossing boundaries with the handlers because they're all in their thirties."

"Is that all? I couldn't figure out what the hell his problem was."

"He's worried about you falling prey to a cougar," I joked.

"Dusty worries about everything. He's always up in my shit."

"He's just looking out for you."

"Yeah, right," he said. "So besides grunge, what other music's on your radar?"

I almost blurted out Robbie Cumberlake but caught myself — not wanting to scream out my dream idol's name. I offered up the Sisterly Sisters instead.

"Jacob Cutters was just at my house!" Brixton said. "He's fun to party with. A little grabby, though." He turned away uncomfortably.

"I bet," I said, smiling. I spun him around and bent him over. I started making up a silly pop song while grinding into his ass, "*I wanna take you in the bop bop.*"

His cheeks grew flushed. "I ain't no bottom dweller."

"Bottom dweller? Oh my God!" I said as I fell over laughing. "Are you a homophobe?"

"That's not funny," he said. "Half the people I work with are gay. You don't last long in this business if gay people bother you."

"My ex-husband bothers me."

"Why, is he gay?" he asked flippantly.

"Turns out he is," I said.

"Really? I was joking."

"Afraid so."

"How long were you in this gay marriage?"

"Ten years."

"Damn. What was that like?"

I thought about the question for a moment. "It was three minutes of sex followed by a half-hour of him crying," I joked. "Actually, the marriage was good at first. He was the right amount of safe I needed at the time."

"But the wrong amount of gay."

"Totally. I guess he blamed me for not being able to be himself, which is completely fucked because he was such a closet case. Look, I'm sorry I brought him up. He's an ass." I started to pace. "And yes, I've been tested!"

"Fuck him," Brixton said. "He should have been honest with you sooner."

"Yeah, fuck you, Dennis!" I said and flipped the bird in his direction.

"Is he here?"

"He's sitting with my brother."

"I was wondering who those guys were."

"You were watching me?"

"Of course," he said. "Your ex has a stupid-ass beard. Forget about him. So, what was that song you were singing?"

"I was just making it up."

"Seriously? That shit was tight." He sang my line, "*I wanna take you in the bop bop,*" then threw in a couple verses of his own, "*I'll seduce you with my pop pop. Let our boots do a little knock knock.*"

He spun me around and thrust against me as we sang in unison, "*I wanna take you in the bop bop.*" I could feel his hardness pressing into me. Before long, our dance turned into a dry humping session, although at that point I wouldn't call myself dry.

He started kissing my neck. His hot breath on my skin left a tingling in its wake. I turned my head to meet his and closed my eyes. He playfully nibbled on my upper lip.

"I want to fuck you," he said in a low throaty voice, his hand rubbing me through my jeans.

A feeling of trepidation released the butterflies in my stomach. "I don't have any protection," I said.

"I do."

He rummaged through his backpack and retrieved a purple box of Kimono Micro Thins.

"Ooh, they're Japanese," I said. "Konichiwa."

56

My hand was on my pants but Brixton brushed it away. He pulled the zipper down slowly. His index and middle finger slipped inside me before my pants were halfway off. My moistened lips welcomed his fingers as my clit sprang to life, commanding me to grab the box of condoms.

Brixton whipped off his shorts and spun them over his head like a lasso before sending them hurtling toward the window. He removed his shirt seductively, revealing his masculine chest and sexy, sculpted sternum. Brixton was comfortable in his skin, standing naked before me. Who wouldn't be with that rocking bod? A slight shiver shot up my spine as he steadied his hard cock. I rolled the latex sheath onto his shaft.

I stepped out of my pants and kicked them away. Normally I would be overcome with self-consciousness but with Brixton, I never felt more at ease. He led me to the couch and sat me gently on the cushion. I raised my arms as he lifted my sweatshirt over my head. With a flick of his wrist, my bra was lying on the floor, exposing my gravity-defying 36 B's. They may not be huge, but I couldn't ask for anything better for sports. Brixton kissed each breast and traced the nipples with the tip of his tongue. He explored them as if he was meeting new friends, wanting to get the 411, what they like and don't. He looked up at me for reassurance and I patted him on the head like a good boy. Thankfully he laughed.

He took his palms and pushed my tits together, stroking each areola simultaneously with his index fingers. His tongue swirled around my nipples sending me into a state of nirvana.

His confidence put me further at ease. He positioned himself on top and kissed me sweetly—a most heartfelt kiss, before entering me. Although I was well lubricated, his girth made it slightly painful.

"Are you OK?" he asked, holding still, his face inches from mine.

I nodded and said, "Oh yeah," completely enthralled by his concern. I pushed my hips forward, plunging him balls deep inside me. Brixton started thrusting cautiously at first and then gained momentum. He fucked with his whole body, everything working in unison like a finely tuned machine.

Unlike Dennis, who had me questioning every move and wondering what I was doing wrong, I was now empowered enough to allow myself to be lost in the moment and focus on the sensations imploding between my legs.

Brixton reached up and removed the tie holding my ponytail. I shook my hair free like it was still long. He pulled out of me and rolled the black ring down his shaft, stretching it around his balls. Brixton then grabbed my ankles as his cock became engorged, and pushed my legs up high.

His eyes grew wide when he saw how flexible I was. Taking the cue, he positioned my ankles behind my neck and rammed home full hilt into my quivering quim. I gasped in pain and ecstasy. He plunged vigorously and then held back, thrusting with a slow, rhythmic motion. I lost all sense of where he began and I ended; our bodies had become one.

Brixton took me in his arms and carried me to the window. He bent me over the counter and kneeled from behind. I looked back, wondering what was happening.

"There's no better view on earth," he said, lightly flicking my labia. Rising to his feet, he dove into me with his hard cock.

"Oh God, yes," I moaned.

"You're the fucking best," he said.

The crowd cheered in the foreground. We fruitlessly tried to catch some of the Spinnakers' game but couldn't concentrate on anything but our ravenous desire.

With his cock still inside me, he maneuvered us to the side of the room by the outer door. He slid out and turned me around so my back was pushed up against the wall, then hoisted me onto his waist. His thrusts were so powerful the picture next to us fell with a loud thud, shattering the glass into tiny shards. He kept right on fucking me.

The security guards outside stood to investigate the noise. The stockier of the two brought his hands to the side of his face and looked through the glass door. He was only a couple of feet from us. I think he could see past the tinting because his eyes widened and he turned around abruptly. The guard said something into his walkie-talkie, which made both men laugh.

"Let's get away from the window," I said, disembarking from Brixton and leading him to the sofa. I pushed him onto the couch and straddled his beckoning cock, clenching down firmly. He winced in pained pleasure. Those kegel exercises must be working.

His cock was custom-made for my body. The girth and length—everything fits perfectly. I angled my hips up and out until I hit the right spot. Face to face, I rode him like the cowgirl I was fast becoming. I smashed my tits against his mouth, and he soon found a nipple to suckle. I bucked that bronco hard and fierce with unbridled enthusiasm.

It turns out I was being overly enthusiastic. He came up gasping for air.

"Slow down, baby, you'll break my dick off."

"Oh, sorry, I didn't mean to hurt you."

"You didn't hurt me. All the same, let's give Boris a rest."

Boris? What kind of name was that for a cock?

He scooped me up from behind and sat me upright on the couch as he assumed his position on the floor. Labia lapping ensued. Brixton probed me relentlessly, trying to open the corners of my lubricated love triangle. He applied varying degrees of pressure to my throbbing clit with the point of his talented tongue. I was about to orgasm from

59

the soft butterfly touches but he mixed it up with more aggressive licks, causing me to see silvery stars.

I was getting close again when he pushed away abruptly and walked to the kitchen. I was slightly miffed until I realized he was heading for the radio.

"89.5," I said.

"That's what I was going for!" he said. "I love C89."

I wanted to ask how, but of course he would know all the dance stations—especially ones that ran out of a high school. I wished they were playing one of his tunes but how could you argue with Lorde's "Royals." Plus, it would be great scream-filtering music.

Brixton returned with a bowl of ice cream. I could sense the gears turning in his dirty mind. He dipped three fingers in and scooped out a handful of Pralines and Cream. Damn if he didn't gently tap it into my pussy. The cold sensation sent my legs flying. He sucked and licked me clean, working diligently to get all of the dessert out, producing a couple sugary orgasms.

Now it was Brixton's turn. He began frenetically fucking me missionary. A smile formed, then a smirk, and he gasped.

I could tell he was close. He has the best orgasm face, half lost in the moment and half with me, but 100% joy. We fell on the floor in a sweaty mess and laughed warmly.

He rose onto his elbows so he could look at me. "That was fucking awesome!"

I tried to play it off but it was the best sex I'd ever had. "It was brilliant," I admitted.

His phone vibrated. "Oh shit!" Brixton said after reading the message. "I have to leave in fifteen minutes." He tugged the condom off with a snap, tied a knot at the end and put it in his pants pocket.

I was left speechless. What the hell was up with that maneuver?

"Let's take a quick shower," he said.

I followed him like a puppy into the bathroom.

"Hey, don't mention my tat to the crew. My bullshit contract doesn't allow ink."

"That's lame," I said.

"Tell me about it."

We had to shower in a hurry.

"Next time," Brixton purred in my ear. He cupped my pussy gently with his hand and kissed me on the lips.

A harsh knock on the bathroom door jolted us back to reality.

"Let's get the show on the road," Dusty said. "The jet's awaiting."

We dressed hurriedly and walked into our room. I spotted Stephanie climbing over the bulkhead from the suite next door. She had her hair swept up into a cool faux hawk.

"Hi, Stephanie," I said as she walked in. Brixton was taken aback that I was familiar with his stylist.

"Christ, you guys," Stephanie said, getting a whiff of the room. She waved a hand in front of her face and sang Marcy Playground's "Sex and Candy."

"More like sex and honey," Brixton said.

"OK, Pooh," Stephanie said, "Get your head out of the honey jar." She cracked a window and placed a stool near the sink. "Hop on up."

I found my rubber tie by the couch, twisted my hair into a ponytail and slipped it through the back of my Spinnakers cap.

"We have to make this quick, Spider. Get your ass up here," Stephanie said, patting the seat. "What is that?" she asked, annoyed. "Is that my phone?" She ripped it from his hands. "Damn it, Brixton, how did you get this again? I've been looking for it all day." She glanced at the screen, "I told you to stay off my Twitter account."

"I didn't post anything," he said innocently.

"How did you even get into my phone? I changed my password yesterday."

"I'll sing you one of your favorite songs," he said in a feeble attempt to make amends.

"You are such a little shit."

Brixton rose from the couch and retrieved his electronic keyboard. He sat on the stool and began playing the opening to the Eurythmics song, "Jennifer." I was bawling before he hit the first verse.

"Are you OK?" Stephanie asked. I couldn't respond. "Oh fuck, was your friend named Jennifer?"

I nodded. Not only was that her name, it was the song I requested for her funeral.

Stephanie whispered in Brixton's ear, "Jackie lost her best friend Jennifer to cancer a few weeks back." He stopped playing and turned away from the keyboard. There was a slight hesitation before he walked over and took me in his arms, holding me close. Dusty looked uncomfortable and left the room.

"I'll play a happier song," Brixton said as I wept into his shoulder.

"No, finish it," I managed to say between sobs. "I think it will help."

He gave me a firm squeeze and resumed his place with the electronic keyboard on his lap. "Hang on a minute," Brixton said. He grabbed a pair of drumsticks from his bag and handed them to me. "I need you to add a beat. When I motion, hit both at the same time on the counter like this. Ti-Ti Ta Ti-Ti."

I knew the part of the song he was talking about, but how he taught me cracked me up.

"What?" he asked.

"You reminded me of my elementary school music teacher."

He kissed me on the cheek. "I saw the fear in your eyes when I handed you my sticks. Just wanted to make you comfortable."

I smiled but looked away, not wanting him to see me get all googly-eyed.

Brixton sat thoughtfully for a few seconds then struck the keys with his long, slender fingers. His voice was pitch-perfect. Whenever he changed the beat or mixed in the background vocals, he managed it with precision, never missing a note. It was as if I was watching a conductor and a musician, wrapped in one impressive package. His rendition would have made the Eurythmics proud. He performed it impeccably, expressing the emotion in his soothing voice. Near the end, he nodded at me and I hit the drumsticks against the counter, hopefully to the beat of the song. I must have been doing it right because he looked at me approvingly.

"Nice," he said.

My part wasn't much, like the guy in an orchestra who plays the triangle. Still, it blew my mind performing a song with a true artist. By the time he finished, I felt relaxed, at peace, and totally in love.

Brixton caught my eye and sat up abruptly, almost knocking his electronic keyboard to the floor. I changed my expression to one of appreciation. I hoped my dopey look hadn't freaked him out like some lovesick fan.

"Better?" he asked.

"Much."

I understood why he didn't want me to become a fan.

Stephanie began working on his hair. "You don't have time for the flat iron," she said.

"Good," he responded. "Damn thing's frying my follicles. Give me what Mick's sporting these days."

Stephanie flashed me a knowing look. "I don't have time to cut it but I can add some texture."

Whatever they're paying Stephanie, she's worth every penny. She dabbed product in her hand and twisted, sculpted, and teased his hair into shape. I watched in awe

63

as she transformed Brixton from a pop idol into a little rocker. He was smoking hot.

Dusty walked back into the room and handed me three tickets. "You're in the suite next door," he said. "I already spoke to the concierge."

"That is so sweet," I said, touched by the gesture.

"It's the least I can do to make up for my behavior last night," he said, raising his voice so Brixton could hear. "I want to apologize for that. I wanted to earlier but it would have ruined the surprise."

Wanting to apologize is not really apologizing, but it was as good as I would get from him. "We're cool," I said. "I've had a wonderful day."

"Oh, hell no!" Dusty said, catching a glimpse of Brixton's new hairdo. "Change it back."

"Too late," Stephanie said. "I'll fix it on the plane."

"The fuck you will," Brixton whispered in her ear.

Dusty closed his eyes and balled up his fists. A pained expression was on his face. "Fine."

"Thanks," Brixton said.

There was a loud knock at the front door. It was Jimmy. He had traded in the suit for jeans and a black sweater. "Ready, boss?" he asked, addressing my man.

"Hold up, dawg," Brixton said. He located his backpack and retrieved a pair of magenta-colored gloves.

"I want you to have these," he said. "It's going to be cold after the game."

The gloves were finely crafted—from the exquisite stitching to the buttery softness of the leather. "Did you get these for me?" I asked.

"I sent for them today."

"Thank you."

Brixton had been eyeing my scarf all afternoon. I removed it from my neck and placed it around his.

"Are you serious? This is crazy awesome—I love it. The Spinnakers wanted to give me the golden scarf but I didn't want it to be a big deal. This is perfect."

"Time to go," Dusty said anxiously. He glanced over at me. "You need to cross over to the other suite from the outside. We don't want to break the young girls' hearts."

"No problem," I said. Brixton leaned in and kissed me on the cheek.

Jimmy pulled him aside. "The service elevator is ten suites down, on the right. We need to make this quick."

"Oh, come on," Brixton groaned.

"I mean it. Heads down on this one. We're running."

"We'll be in the luxury hall for the suites. It's all good, bro."

I could tell Jimmy was wrestling with something. I wondered what horrible threat he was dealing with now. Brixton didn't seem the slightest bit concerned.

"We'll be OK, Jimmy," Dusty assured him.

Jimmy pleaded with his eyes; *how can I keep him safe if you don't let me do my job*?

"Let the madness begin," Brixton said. He shook his head, wiggled his body and assumed the confident stance of his pop star persona. Jimmy adorned him with two thick gold chains. To add insult to injury, Brixton lowered the back of his pants, exposing the top half his underwear.

I stared in disbelief at the degradation.

"What?" Brixton snickered.

"I'm curious," I said. "Did someone drop you when you were a baby?" The shock on everyone's face was priceless. "I'm only asking because I can see a crack in your butt." There was a slight pause before Brixton and his entourage burst out laughing.

I walked over to the counter, took ownership of the Grey Goose, and said triumphantly, "I'm out of here. Goodnight, everybody." I left the room without looking back.

"I like her," Stephanie said as the door was closing. "She's bricky."

Once inside the suite next door I started giggling to myself. I couldn't believe I had been so bold.

"Let's bounce," I heard Brixton say through the paper-thin walls. How much had people heard? The girls in the hall spotted him the moment he exited the room and erupted into high-pitched screams of "Brixton" and "I love you." The shot of the soccer field on the TV switched to a closed-circuit feed of Brixton as he worked his way out of the building. He was in full rock god mode but was charming and patient, posing for pictures and signing autographs.

I waited until the crowd dissipated before making my exit to retrieve Randy and Dennis. I peered into the hallway. The coast was clear.

I rode the escalator down to the club level. When I opened the door to the stadium a blast of cold air swept across my face. I slipped on my new gloves—the inner lining was lush mink, which surrounded my hands in warmth. Sewn into each palm was a dark blue teardrop. I placed my hands together and the two patterns formed a perfectly shaped heart. It was silly, goofy and so damn sweet.

Dennis exploded when I reached our seats. "Where have you been?" he demanded.

"None of your fucking business," I said.

"This is bullshit," he fumed, crossing his arms like a pouty toddler.

I should have prepared for this behavior but I was floating on clouds. "Come on, Randy," I said, ignoring the asshole.

"Can't we watch the game?" Randy pleaded.

"Let's go," I said firmly. "Now!"

"Whatever you want, sis."

Randy followed me out of our section, leaving Dennis behind. I would have made a scene if I had stayed one more minute.

"I'm sorry, Randy. I can't be around that blithering idiot right now."

"No worries. Let's get a drink and chill out. There's a beer garden on the north end of the field."

"How about we watch the game from Brixton Webber's suite?" I said and handed him a ticket.

"Look at you," he grinned.

"Don't get too excited, he's already left."

"I don't care," my brother responded with total indifference.

I felt Dennis' eyes follow us as we climbed the stairs to the club level. "Wait," he cried as he raced after us. "I'm sorry."

The Next Day

An intense urge to throw up woke me from my alcohol-induced coma. I jumped out of bed into a falling stumble, barely reaching the toilet. There's no glamorous way to say it: I puked my fucking brains out.

When I felt I could safely leave the bathroom, I crawled back to bed, knocking my head against my MacBook. The cool metal soothed my throbbing skull. I closed my eyes and fell fast asleep.

I awoke an hour later to a semi-bearable existence. My stomach was no longer nauseous, and the stabbing pain in my forehead had subsided. I found my Mac and surfed the Net before landing on Brixton's Twitter account. There was no mention of his weekend in Seattle, which I have to admit hurt a little. I'm not sure what I was expecting, perhaps some kind of coded message. Something like, "Best time of my life spent in Seattle. Love you."

I lost interest in the Internet and drifted off again. When I came to I felt a pleasant tingling between my legs. My fingers must have found my happy place while snoozing because I was swollen and soaking wet. I stroked my pussy with my right hand and tapped my trigger with the tip of my middle finger. I don't know what it is about being hungover but it makes me horny as hell. I fantasized about Brixton tenderly flicking my clit with his talented tongue. I oscillated between hard pressure and light, feathery strokes until my body convulsed in a mind-bending explosion.

Still in a daze, I texted Dusty and asked him to thank Brixton for everything. He immediately called back.

"Hey, Jackie. We get hacked by the press constantly. I can't have you texting me. You need to be cool."

"Oh, shit," I said, realizing I had made a terrible mistake.

"You'll know if Brixton wants to see you," he said abruptly.

"I'm sorry," I said, but the phone was dead.

Pipe Dream

There had been no word from Brixton in the week since he turned my world upside down. My mind was awash in an endless loop of Brixton-induced fantasies. Each day I awoke waiting for a call or at least an email but all I received was nothing. My desperate-sounding text must have screwed everything up. Christ, what was wrong with me?

I had promised Brixton I wouldn't become a fan, but I needed a connection with him. It wasn't long before I gave in and watched his movie, *Web of Life*, to try to gain perspective of who he truly was. From there I moved on to the Net and found a few interviews and television appearances. It turns out he's a bit of a hellion, getting into scuffles with the paparazzi, shooting his mouth off at inappropriate times, and hanging with bad crowds. Basically, he was acting his age, but you wouldn't know it the way the media blew up the stories to epic proportions. It was obvious they were out for blood.

At night I would look for new pictures. Sometimes all I had to type was the letter "B" into the search box and his name would appear. One letter. That blew my mind.

There were plenty of images of his sweet little ass, mostly shots in his underwear with his pants practically falling off. Unfortunately, there were few pictures of his bulge. My favorite shot is one taken without Brixton's knowledge out on his back patio. His hand is in his underwear, which is low enough to show his pubes poking out from the waistband. Many a night, I fingered myself to that picture, replaying our time together. God, I needed him.

Happy Hour

It was Thursday, late afternoon, and Lidia and I were about to head into O'Asian for drinks. We were in their courtyard rock garden—a wonderful oasis in an otherwise sea of concrete. Lidia was knee-deep into her second cigarette. I'm not a smoker but don't mind sitting with her when she partakes.

She had her cell phone out and was playing around when she thrust it in my face. Her look was forced deadpan, but a slight smirk gave her away.

"What the F is this?" she asked.

I laughed. I'd had the same reaction when I first saw the photo. It was Brixton walking the streets of downtown Juneau on his birthday, dressed as a husky with dog-ears sticking out from his hair. He wore realistic blue and white contacts, a painted black nose, a spiked leather collar on his shirtless torso, furry snow boots, and a bushy tail that stuck out from his black leather pants. The boy looked ridiculous.

"Somebody lost a dare," I chortled.

"Either that or he's clearly tripping," Lidia replied.

"Sounds like he had fun at his birthday party anyway."

"What was it, his sweet sixteen?" Her snarkiness was dialed to eleven.

"Very funny, *biatch*." She knew how old he was.

Lidia took a drag and blew out a smoke ring, then used her fingers to try and shape it into a heart.

The restaurant was far enough from work that we had to take the bus tunnel. I realized why she had picked the place as we walked through the door. Daniel, the cute waiter who used to work at the Bellstrom Café, was tending bar.

73

I shook my head at Lidia.

"What?" she said. "I love a sexy voice."

We sat at a table across from the bar. Daniel didn't notice us right away—he was mixing a row of drinks. His black hair was shorter than the last time I saw him, and his glasses had larger frames, giving him a preppy look. My old fantasy fuck had turned into a frat boy. He raised his head after spotting me. A gleam of wishful conquest sparkled in his eyes.

I gave him an innocuous smile. The dumb shit stopped in the middle of his drink order and headed straight over.

"This day just gets better and better," he said. I forgot what a tall drink of water he was. "I'm stoked to see you, girls."

I always thought Daniel was too young for me, but twenty-one didn't sound so bad anymore. "Hello, Daniel," I said, embarrassed. I had every reason to be. When we were both working at Bellstrom he told me how much he wanted to fuck me. I was flattered, maybe a little turned on, but the boy was completely inappropriate. Still.

"You're even prettier than I remember," Daniel said.

"Slow it down there, cowboy," I said. I guess I still hadn't forgiven him.

"Come on. I was young."

"It was two months ago, Daniel."

"Nobody's perfect. Let me make it up to you with a righteous cocktail," he said, sounding like an idiot. "It's a good one."

"Works for me," Lidia said.

I tried to ignore them both.

"I'm sorry," Daniel said. "I admit I was out of line. But give me a break. Look at you. What guy wouldn't want to fuck you?"

"Go make the drinks, barkeep," I said dismissively.

"Don't be like that," Daniel said. He headed to the bar, glancing over his shoulder. I pretended not to notice, but I did. His biceps pressing through his tight baby blue shirt were a sight difficult not to behold.

"Barkeep?" Lidia laughed. She opened a menu and held her reading glasses to the page like a magnifying glass. "Their appetizers rock, and it's happy hour. Most everything is four bucks."

"Gotta love that," I said. "Oh man, bacon-wrapped scallops. There goes my diet."

We weren't halfway through the menu when Daniel returned with purple drinks in thick stemless martini glasses.

"You'll love these," he said.

I took a sip. "Mmm, this *is* good."

"Pomegranate Splash," he said proudly.

Lidia tasted hers. "Oh yeah, keep 'em coming."

"Oh crap, my order," Daniel said, looking back at the couple waiting patiently. "I'll bounce over later."

I smiled politely.

Once he was out of earshot Lidia said, "You *should* fuck him."

"So, are you and Paul doing better?"

She laughed at my subject change. "It's still tough."

"Really? You guys were doing so well on Saturday. I've never seen Paul so happy."

"He was just feeding off how much you lift me up."

"You're my BFF. What can I say?"

"You're mine too," Lidia said. "But Paul and I aren't quite there yet. I thought I was sad when he was always home and we were broke. I guess maybe I was happier after all. Now that the housing market has picked up, he's always away. I love that his business is booming but it's straining our relationship."

"The money must help some, huh?"

"Yeah, it's a blessing. We can buy Ellie a few things we've been putting off. Haven't been laid in a month, though."

"Paul's been holding out?"

The blaring chorus from "Call Me Maybe" erupted from my purse. I really needed to change that ringtone. When I saw the number I felt a rush of adrenalin surge through my body. "Hi, Dusty," I said, trying not to sound too excited.

"What's up, Badness?" Brixton said.

"Brixton!" I responded enthusiastically.

"Nice," Lidia said.

"You up for a ride on my tour bus?" he asked.

"Hell, yes," I said without hesitation. "When?"

"How does now work for you?"

I froze. I'm not usually game for last-minute plans. "That works perfectly," I managed to say.

"Sweet. I'll send someone to drive you to the airport. I hate to cut this short, but my show's about to start. Here's Dusty. He'll take care of the details. Can't wait to see you."

I melted.

Dusty filled me in on the plan. He didn't sound happy about me coming, but he was cooperative. I put my phone away and sat back, speechless.

"Well," Lidia said.

"Well, nothing. I have to get home," I said, standing up.

Lidia pushed me back down. "Oh no, you don't."

"What?" I asked, trying to be coy.

"Where are you going?"

"Chicago. I have to pack before the limo arrives." I cringed, hoping I didn't sound arrogant. "Please don't tell anyone. His fans would freak if they knew he was with an older woman. It would be over."

"Come on, Jackie, it's me." Her face beamed with pride. I leaned in and gave her a big hug.

I pulled back abruptly. "Can you cover my shift tomorrow?"

"Not a problem," Lidia said.

"You're too good to me."

"Go," she said. "Get your Jackie O."

I made my exit while we were still laughing. Halfway out the door, Daniel accosted me. "What the hell? You just got here. Don't leave me hanging, Jackie."

"Something suddenly came up."

"Tell me about it," he said, adjusting his crotch.

"Get over yourself," I snapped. The little shit grabbed my ass in response, but I worked my way free and headed for the door.

The Flight

I was happy to see that my brother wasn't home. This one would have been hard to explain. Not that there was time for details. I needed to pack fast.

Dusty had mentioned that Brixton wanted me to dress sexy. This contradicted everything I'd read about him and how he doesn't like his dates to look too provocative. I had a feeling Dusty was trying to set me up. It's too bad because my closet was chock-full of sexy lingerie that had backfired on my feeble-penised husband.

Both times I had been with Brixton I was in casual sports attire, which seemed to work wonders. I picked a couple of outfits that would be flirtatious without the appearance of trying. It was an overnight bus ride, so I grabbed a pair of warm pajama bottoms and tossed them in my pack.

I changed into my favorite black panties and bra, then slipped into a comfortable black hoodie. Blue jeans and black tennis shoes completed my look.

Carly Rae Jepsen's ringtone chimed from my purse. It was the driver calling. I told him to meet me by the boat ramps. That was far enough away that my neighbors couldn't snoop. I left a note for my brother, letting him know I was spending the weekend with Lidia.

I locked the door and bounced down the steps from my house. Across the water, the setting sun cast a golden glow upon the buildings of downtown Seattle. We were a few weeks into daylight savings time and I was enjoying the later sunsets. Spring had arrived—it couldn't have come soon enough. The past winter had been particularly gloomy.

A ferry was disappearing into a low fog bank in the distance. The familiar sound of a deep and prolonged foghorn made me smile. I love watching the ferries cruise the tranquil waters. The waves pushing away from the hull resemble a hundred centipede legs moving the ship along.

A cream-colored stretch limo signaled to turn into the parking lot up ahead. I picked up my pace. When the chauffeur called, I was at his window, both of us with phones to our ears. He grinned, exposing deep laugh lines, and stepped out to open my door.

"Welcome, Ms. Notter. My name is Sam."

"Call me Jackie," I said as I eased into the car.

This was no airport limo. It was a top-of-the-line Mercedes with soft leather seats that cradled my body. I leaned back and took in the opulence.

"Make yourself a drink, Jackie. We'll be there in no time," Sam said over the intercom.

I had already found the vodka and the little cans of cranberry juice. I made a double and popped a Xanax to calm my pre-flight jitters.

I was well into my drink when Sam turned off the freeway. I fumbled around until I found the call button, "Aren't we going to Sea-Tac?"

"No, Ma'am. Boeing Field."

I sat back, confused. There were no commercial flights from there.

The car raced along Airport Way to the east side of the runway and then pulled into a lot. Sam came to a slow, controlled stop next to a small Learjet.

"You have got to be kidding?" I said out loud. The door opened before I regained my composure. I hurriedly tried to finish my drink but Sam stopped me.

"No need to rush. Take it with you," he whispered.

Someone was approaching from the jet. I was thrilled to see that it was Stephanie. She was wearing a tight black leather motorcycle jacket. Her hair was choppy, messy, and straight out of Passion Magazine. She had a self-assured gait that reminded me of one of the cool kids from high school.

"Hey, Stephanie!" I said.

"What's up, Jackie?" We embraced like old friends. Holding onto her put my nerves at ease, although it could have been the Xanax kicking in. "Go make yourself at home," she said.

"That plane right there?" I asked, pointing at the Learjet, still not believing what I was seeing.

"Yep. Hurry up. We're cleared for takeoff."

Sam retrieved my backpack from the trunk and bid me adieu. Was I supposed to tip him? I glanced back at Stephanie and figured she'd take care of things.

I climbed the plane's steps to the landing, where a tan gentleman in a captain's uniform greeted me. He was exceedingly handsome in an old-school Hollywood kind of way.

"Hello, Ms. Notter. Welcome aboard. My name is Purvis. I'll be your captain this evening." He slipped my backpack from my shoulder. "I can store this for you."

"Thank you, Purvis," I replied, suppressing a giggle. His name was killing me.

I tried my best to blend in. This was an entirely different world—a glimpse of luxury normally reserved for the upper crust. What was I doing here?

The cabin of the plane was stunning. The walls and seats were upholstered in bright white leather, the floor a plush gray carpeting. Blue neon lights added a futuristic tone to the decor. It was a smaller jet with four seats—two sets facing one another, each with a shared white console. I was standing in the lounge area, which housed a small kitchen and bar.

"I love your plane," I said to the captain.

"It's your plane, Jackie. Make yourself at home."

"Don't mind if I do," I said, eying the vodka. I topped my drink off before taking my seat.

The co-pilot shut the door as soon as Stephanie stepped aboard. She chose the seat next to me.

"Captain Purvis is a seasoned pilot, right?" I asked.

"Did he say his name was Purvis?"

"Yeah."

"He's just screwing with me. I gave him that nickname cause he's such a perv."

"Oh man, that's rich."

"He's Captain Roberts. And don't worry, he's one of the best."

We taxied toward the runway and waited for our place in line. The force of the engines slammed me against my seat as the plane shot out of the city like a rocket. This was the first flying experience I'd had where I wasn't paralyzed with fear. The takeoff was more exhilarating than scary.

"Have you ever been in a private jet?" Stephanie asked.

"First time. This is beyond words."

"It is at that," Stephanie said, pouring Cognac into a glass. Her demeanor was slow and casual. I don't know why I kept being reminded of high school. It just felt like I was finally hanging out with the popular kids. Except in this world the cool girl wasn't a total bitch.

"I'm glad you made the flight. Brixton's had a shitty couple of days. He just wants to get the hell out of Chicago."

"Are you talking about the game last night?"

"You saw it?"

"A little. What was up with the crowd booing him like that?"

"Wasn't it brutal?" Stephanie sighed.

"I don't understand why they treated him so poorly."

"Drunk, jealous fucktards."

I repeated what I said to my brother when we saw it happening. "Maybe they were saying Boo-rixton."

82

"You're awesome. It hurt the kid, but that's not what brought him down. [Name Removed] did a number on him today at lunch. She royally screwed him up."

I laughed. "[Name Removed]?"

"Yeah. Bitch went for the jugular. Brixton had promised to stay away from drugs, and then he goes and gets caught in that damn video. She was trying to help lead him down the right path but he took it so personally." Her face grew serious, "You didn't bring him pot, did you?"

"Oh heavens, no. I wouldn't even know where to get it." Christ, did I just say, Oh heavens no? I sounded like such a nerd.

"Good. He needs to learn to deal with his problems without using a crutch."

"It's the only way for someone to grow," I said, redeeming myself.

"He'll be OK now," Stephanie said, patting my leg and lingering a bit on my thigh muscle. "Sorry." She took a long pull from her glass. "Brixton was right. You have a tight little body. What's your secret?"

I was caught off guard and sucked part of my drink down my windpipe. I loved how forward she was. "My secret?" I asked once my coughing fit was under control. I wasn't about to tell her of my metamorphosis back from the brink of Dennis. Luckily, a story popped into my head.

"At work a few years back, I overheard two guys from marketing call me a butterbutt."

Stephanie laughed.

I continued, embarrassed, "It sure lit a fire under my ass, so to speak. I tried the gym for a while but didn't like it. My saving grace was the kettlebell. I found the best DVD workout. If you want I'll burn you a set, but you don't need it, you look great."

"Anything to keep me out of the hotel gyms. *Butterbutt*," she said. "That's funny."

"Yeah—now!"

"I'm sure they weren't talking about you."

"Maybe, but my ex had destroyed my confidence by then." How did that slip out? In my family you keep your problems to yourself.

"Jackie," Stephanie said, leaning over and placing a reassuring hand on mine.

"Nothing I can't handle," I said, then kicked the conversation back to her. "So why aren't you on tour with Brixton? Doesn't he need you?"

"I was visiting my professor from college. He has a brain tumor. Stage 4 cancer."

"Stephanie, I am so sorry. Are you guys close?"

"He was my first love."

"Wait, what?"

"I went the reverse route at Berkeley. When all the girls were running from the frat boys I found love in a man. Weird, huh?"

"My husband turned out to be gay, so weird is my middle name," I replied.

"And I turned out to be a lesbian. So, there you have it. But don't get me wrong, Jon was my soulmate. The romance lasted only a few years but was the most loved I've ever felt." She paused for a long moment. "He's also the reason I'm infatuated with the Stones."

"So, you're not together now?"

"It's complicated. I had a girlfriend when I went back to take care of him. She couldn't handle it. The bitch up and bolted."

"Kind of a shitty thing to do," I said.

"You got that right." We clinked glasses and Stephanie disappeared in thought.

I took advantage of the silence to check out the spectacular view. We were flying high above the clouds. The last remnants of the sunset were slipping away.

"I'm in a Learjet," I said.

"That you are, Jackie."

"So, has Brixton said anything about me?" I shouldn't have asked but I needed to know where I stood.

She smiled. "Of course. He hasn't called because he's playing it cool. It's a stupid guy thing."

My heart was beating out of my chest. Could he like me as much as I liked him?

"He seems to trust you, Jackie. That's a rarity in his life. Everyone wants something from him. But you, he thinks you're cool. Says you're a dude. He means that in the best way."

"I hung around my brother a lot when we were growing up. The girls were too interested in boys."

"I hear you," Stephanie said. We both chuckled.

"All I can say is, with him, you're in for a wild ride." She said this with a devilish grin.

I didn't like the sound of that. All rides eventually come to an end.

"You should have seen the impact you had on him. He was a new man. Went from being a major stress case to not having a care in the world."

"And it was because of me?"

"Yes, it was because of you."

I felt myself blush.

"I want you to know he's never asked for someone to be brought backstage. It's just not him."

"That means a lot," I said.

"It should. You have something, Jackie. You're real."

Her statement struck me as odd. Real was the last word I would use to describe myself. I've always felt the need to put up a front.

"He feels he can be himself with you."

"That is so sweet."

"You have no idea. Everyone expects him to be the coolest guy in the room. It wears him out."

"I totally get it. Some days I'm not in the mood to deal with customers, so I put on an act."

"Exactly. He powers through those days by playing different characters."

"Is walking around with his ass hanging out one of his characters?"

"That one's all Brixton."

"Doesn't it drive you nuts?"

"Please. I've seen him naked more than his mother. It's his penis I'm tired of seeing. I swear sometimes he flashes me on purpose."

"I can see how that would get a little much for you."

"Just reminds me why I'm a lesbian."

"There was a long period when I wished I was one," I said. "I tried it a couple of times but it never stuck. The emotion wasn't there, which made things worse. The last thing I needed was something that was just physical." I stopped myself. "I'm sorry."

"Don't be sorry. People open up around me. It's a gift—or a curse, depending on how you view it. Whatever the case, it was the reason they hired me. Dusty wanted someone Brixton could confide in. It's worked out for both of us."

"Dusty didn't send you to find out about me, did he?"

"Absolutely not. I wanted to get to know the girl that allows Brixton to be himself. But."

"What?"

"I did want to check you out," she admitted. "You had the same haircut as a model he has a crush on, and the sports look he loves. It was too much of a coincidence."

I was steamed. Dusty *had* tried to get me into clothes Brixton didn't like. But it was the hairstyle that sparked my curiosity. Is that what drew him to me?

"My friend talked me into that haircut. It would be like Lidia to pick the one Brixton liked. Come to think of it, she was really pushing that style. The sweatshirt, though, was all me."

"Honey, I know. Took me all of five minutes to figure out you're legit. But you can't be too careful in this business."

"No worries. I would have done the same thing," I said. "Speaking of trust, who the hell called his mother and ratted me out?"

"I have no idea. Brixton sure was pissed. He called an all-hands meeting the morning of the Spinnakers game. Told us he can't work with anyone he can't trust. So far no one has left. He settled down once you guys hooked up again." She giggled. "I thought Brixton was going to get us kicked out. You kids were going at it so hard the walls in our room shook. I kept having to turn up the TV."

"He was amazing," I said, somewhat embarrassed. "The best I've ever had."

"Wow, I wasn't expecting that." She looked as if she wanted to ask me something.

"Why is a 30-year-old just now getting laid properly?" I responded before she had a chance to speak.

"Well, yeah," she said.

I sat silently, hoping she would drop it.

"Come on, Jackie. I can tell you're hiding something behind that big smile."

I felt cornered but at the same time safe with her. My first thought was to deflect the conversation and bury my problems, but she didn't seem like she would put up with that. I took a deep breath. I tried to speak but couldn't find my voice. I'd never told anyone besides my mother what happened. Not one other person. It was a few moments before I could get the words out. Even then, I was shocked that I had done so.

"My stepfather molested me when I was ten," I managed to say.

"Oh my God, Jackie."

I took a long drink. "I told my mother after a few months."

"Good for you."

"Yeah. A lot of good it did me. She slapped me across the face and called me a liar."

"What the fuck?" Stephanie said wide-eyed. I looked away.

"She refused to believe me, my own mother. It took a year to build the courage to stand my ground. I told the bastard that I was going to the police if he laid one more finger on me. He threatened me, he threatened my family, he even threatened my dog, but I held strong. It was the scariest thing I've ever done."

"Please tell me it worked."

"Well, it stopped. That night, my mom, brother, and I sat at the dinner table waiting to eat. He came in with a shotgun and blew his head off."

Stephanie sat in stunned silence.

"Part of his ugly brain slid onto our dining room table when he fell forward. I remember laughing uncontrollably and running. I ran and ran until I ended up at my grandparents' house. I stayed with them for the rest of the summer."

"Where was your real father?" Stephanie asked.

"He died of a heart attack when I was five."

"Good Lord!"

"Yeah," I said. "I had a pretty screwed-up childhood. Needless to say, I have trust issues with men. Please don't tell Brixton any of this," I pleaded.

"Oh, honey, I wouldn't do that," she said, kneeling between my legs and holding me tight. Her caring nature opened the floodgates and I had a good cry.

"Drain that fucker from your head," Stephanie said. "Let him go."

The harder I cried the better I felt. I cried until I ran out of tears. Stephanie knew when to let go.

"For years I did anything to keep out of the bedroom," I said, drying my eyes. "Sports became my lover. Well, until I met my husband-to-be. Dennis was so harmless. He was wonderful at first. That didn't last long, though. The bastard ended up denying me everything I needed, sexually and mentally. He wouldn't even go down on me. Brixton was the first guy to do that. An 18-year-old. Can you imagine?"

"Yes. I heard your screams from my dressing room."

"How is he so good?"

"Brixton has to be the best at everything. He reads books and studies articles. Where he gets his best techniques is talking with other stars. He learned a trick where he mashes the clit, pretending it's a kernel of corn. I taught my ex the move. It creates this wave of energy that wakes up every part of your body."

"He did this thing where he flicked his tongue up and down in this vibrating, pulsating motion. That's the one that brought on the screaming." Just thinking about it made my clit tingle.

Stephanie laughed long and hard. "I taught him that one."

"Figures," I said.

When our laughter subsided, she became serious once again. "Have you gone to therapy?"

"No. I've never talked about this until now."

"Oh honey, you have to. I see a therapist and I'm damn glad I do. You won't regret it."

"I'll think about it."

"Don't think about it, do it," she said, wiping mascara from my cheeks. "Let's get your face cleaned up."

"Yes, please," I said.

"Do you mind if I work on your hair before we start on your makeup?"

"Not at all."

"That model I was talking about changed her style. I want to mess with Brixton. Give you her look again."

"I don't want to freak him out."

"I just love you. Trust me—it'll be fine. I only need to take an inch off and straighten part of it. Don't worry, Cristal is an idiot."

"Her name is Cristal, like the champagne?"

"Believe me, you have *nothing* to worry about."

That did make me feel better.

Stephanie gave me a neck and scalp massage while she washed my hair. I swear she was manipulating the energy in my body, pulsing it away from her fingers.

The cut didn't take long, but I liked the result, especially after she gelled and spiked it.

I was admiring my new hairdo when out came a small, black velvet bag from a side compartment. It was makeup time. Stephanie dabbed on concealer, then a touch of blush, followed by a light dusting of bronze powder. Next, she focused on my eyes. Stephanie whipped out a gold eyelash curler and pressed it on my lashes. Her left arm rested on my thigh as she meticulously applied mascara on my top and lower lashes.

"Not too much," I said as she began to apply gloss to my lips.

"Don't worry, this is nude. Can't be too much."

She finished and gathered all the products, slipping them in my purse. I hid my excitement.

"You're gorgeous."

I checked myself in the mirror and beamed. The hairstyle was fresh and young and my makeup subtle. "Thank you," I said, placing my hand over my heart. "For everything."

"My pleasure."

I walked back and retrieved our glasses. Stephanie just wanted water. I made myself another drink, but only a single.

The co-pilot opened the cockpit door. He was small and wiry but looked like he could hold his own in a fight.

"Hello, Jackie, I'm Stewart. We'll be making our final descent in a few minutes. I hope you enjoyed the flight."

"I had a lovely time. Thank you, Stewart."

"You're welcome." He looked at the bar longingly and returned to the cockpit.

The plane was taxiing along the runway in Chicago when Stephanie motioned to the window. "There's Brixton's plane," she said, pointing to a 737 parked in front of an open hangar. "After Georgia and Florida, we have one last stop in New York and then we're off to Europe."

I was surprised that his name wasn't on the plane.

"Nice ride," I said.

"Would you like to see it?"

"Hell, yes."

Our jet stopped just shy of the hangar. I stumbled going down the ramp. Purvis reached out to catch me but I found my footing.

"Hey, Stewart," Stephanie said. "Would you mind letting us on Spider One? I want to show Jackie around."

"Not at all," he said. "I'll get the keys."

Stewart walked over to the hangar toward a room in the back. Purvis was busy inspecting an engine on our plane.

"Spider One?" I asked.

"Brixton came up with that after watching *'Air Force One.'* He loves making fun of himself. I think it's because no one else will."

We climbed the steps at the back of Brixton's plane and followed Stewart aboard. He flicked on the lights and headed to the front, leaving us to ourselves. The interior was more luxurious than the previous jet but had a similar color palette.

"I love the interior. It's so…"

"Cheery," Stephanie said.

"Yes, cheery. That's the word."

"We try to stick with bright white; it seems to lift his mood. You need to keep the talent happy."

"He has a beautiful plane."

"Oh, it's not his. We're leasing it for the tour."

I noticed a definite class distinction in the cabin as we made our way forward. Each section was roomier and more lavish than the last.

"His bedroom is the best part." She opened a door and turned on the light, revealing a private room with a full-size mattress. The place was immaculate. Having seen the disaster that was Brixton's dressing room, I assumed someone else had straightened things up.

"What a life," I said.

"Hey, your ride's here," Stephanie said and turned out the light. I looked onto the tarmac and saw the familiar black Range Rover.

"Thanks, Stewart," she yelled back to the cockpit as we walked out the door.

"Anytime," he said.

"Hello, Stephanie," the limo driver called out.

"What's up, Terence?"

"Nothing much, my sister. You must be Jackie," he said to me. "So nice to meet you."

"Well, me too," I said. Well, me too? What the hell was that? "Oh damn, my bag." I didn't want to lose it a second time.

"It's already in the car," Terence said.

"Walk with me," Stephanie whispered as she moved us into the shadows. "Don't take this the wrong way. You're an incredible woman, but promise me you'll see a therapist. A good one will do wonders for you. Keeping all that inside allows your stepfather's abuse to continue."

I lied and said I would schedule an appointment. But the last therapist I saw blamed all our marital problems on me as if it were my fault. Mine! Fucking prick.

Stephanie put her arm around my shoulder. "In the meantime, I have a trick to chase your internal critic away."

"I could use that," I said.

"It's easy. Whenever a negative thought pops into your head, say to yourself, 'That is not the person I want to be.' It will squash that demon to a pulp. It's as simple as that."

"I'll try it. Thanks, Stephanie."

"Say it for me."

"Now?"

"There's no better time. Come on. That is not the person I want to be."

"That is not the person I want to be," I said, feeling vulnerable.

"How easy is that? I love it. Get to a therapist. You'll learn how to forgive the people who have wronged you. Forgiveness is the key to happiness. With that, nobody owns you."

"It's not that easy."

"Trust me. You can learn how," she said.

I promised her I'd try.

"I hate to lay this on you now," she said. "I wanted to talk about it earlier but things got heavy. There's a death threat against Brixton that you should know about."

"Dusty said there are four."

"There are now five. In an Applebee's in St. Louis, a woman overheard a conversation. Two rednecks were talking about abducting Brixton and…" Stephanie swallowed hard, "dismembering him. It wasn't just hate talk; they were as serious as a heart attack. The sick bastards were gone by the time the police arrived."

"When was this?" I asked, horrified.

"Two days ago. Be careful."

"I will. Don't worry," I said. "Does he know about this?"

93

"Absolutely. Dusty tried to talk him out of taking the bus, but once Brixton gets an idea stuck in his head it's hard to change his mind. He's a stubborn little shit."

"We'll be safe," I said. "I promise."

"Take this," she said and handed me a folded paper. "These are the police sketches of the two guys."

"Thanks," I said and put it in my purse. We gave each other a big hug.

"I like you, Jackie."

"I like you, too, Stephanie."

Tour Bus

"We'll be there in no time," Terence said and rolled the divider up. I was in a talkative mood. I had hoped for it to stay down.

I opened the notepad on my phone and wrote Stephanie's phrase for chasing negativity away. Remembering the police sketches, I reached into my purse. The first guy looked average and unassuming. His accomplice made my flesh crawl. It wasn't his short, white, spiky hair that creeped me out. Or even his severely pockmarked face. It was his eyes. They were dead, void of emotion. I put the sketches away hurriedly. I wasn't in such a talkative mood anymore.

A half-hour later we stopped outside a secluded parking lot. The monstrosity of Brixton's tour bus dwarfed two police cars and a small crowd. I couldn't believe I was about to see my man again. I flipped on the overhead light to gather my belongings.

"Please turn that off," Terrence commanded. I complied but didn't understand.

"You're not getting out here," he said. "We need to ditch the paparazzi first." He picked up his cell and made a call. "We're here. Yes, sir. Safe and sound."

The bus started with a rumble and exited the lot. Officers held the crowd back the best they could. Camera flashes lit up patches of the area, illuminating them from night to day. As soon as the bus was clear another officer blocked the exit with his cruiser. A motorcycle broke free from the pack and jumped over the curb. A cop in the street raced after him, sirens blaring. We eased onto the road and followed behind. Up ahead I saw that the motorcycle had been apprehended. A block later we were nabbed.

Terence showed the officer his credentials and explained that we were with the tour bus. Soon we were on our way, with a police escort, mind you. It took another fifteen minutes to catch up with the bus on the freeway. When it came into view the divider rolled down.

"Jackie, it's go time. The bus will pull onto the shoulder. When it does, you need to hop on and get that mother rollin'. But," he punctuated with his index finger, "Mr. Webber has a couple crazy-ass stalkers right now. If anyone shows up besides that cop car, get your ass back in here, pronto. We need to keep you in one piece. Literally. You have to be calm and you have to be quick."

"I can do this," I said confidently, but my pounding heart said otherwise. We passed the bus and gained significant ground before pulling over. As soon as we stopped I jumped out with my bag and ran back about fifty yards. I felt safe with a cop in the vicinity but it was still intense. The bus came to a screeching halt and the side door flew open. I ran to catch up as Brixton thrust his hand out to pull me in. His body was backlit, producing a halo effect illuminating his golden locks. He wore a black hoodie, similar to mine, except his had numbers on the front and was unzipped low, exposing his pecs. He was so handsome he came off as unworldly. If his Superman song isn't about him, it should be.

The door slammed shut behind me as the bus lurched forward, knocking me off my feet. We ended up in a heap at the top of the stairs.

"Oh my God, that was exciting!" I wrapped my arms around Brixton.

"I like your new do," he said.

"Stephanie styled it on the flight over."

"Oh, thank God," he said, relieved.

"What?" I asked. But I knew what he was thinking. I don't know why I let Stephanie cut it like his model crush.

"Nothing. Don't let her talk you into going brunette. I like you blonde."

He gazed into my eyes. I couldn't look away. We stared at each other and began kissing passionately. I reached for his neck, bringing him closer as his hands caressed my breasts.

The liquor had loosened me up. Breaking free from his lips, I held my arms high so he could lift my sweatshirt over my head.

"Are you sure?" he asked. "I don't want to go too fast for you."

His concern threw gas on the fire. "I've never been more sure."

I unzipped his hoodie and slipped it over his shoulders—his eyes watching me the entire time. Brixton unbuttoned my jeans as fast as he could. I helped him shimmy them off, at the same time kicking my shoes free. He unclasped my bra in a matter of seconds, freeing my breasts. I tried to get his pants off but his belt buckle was like none I had ever seen. Brixton released the three prongs and lowered his jeans halfway.

He wasn't wearing underwear. His impressive cock stood tall, reaching to the sky. I slid down the stairs until my face was inches from it and grabbed hold. His excitement warmed my palm. I stroked the shaft then caressed the head with the tip of my tongue. I outlined his frenulum with small circles, which made him gasp. Steadying myself, I inserted all seven inches of him into my mouth. It hadn't been a dream how perfect he fit. I sucked his cock greedily.

Brixton was enjoying himself but needed to satisfy me. He pulled out of my mouth and hoisted me up on the landing. With a wicked grin, he began with something new, pressing hard on my clit with his tongue. It was the smashing corn move Stephanie had talked about. The pressure caused pulses of electricity to radiate across my pelvis. I opened my eyes wide and wrapped my legs

97

around his back. Stephanie was right; a wave of energy woke every part of my being.

He nibbled on my clit with intermittent flicks of pressure. This sent me into a whirlwind and my head pulsated with heat. He kept the pace, drenching his face in wetness. I was embarrassed and tried to sit up, but he pushed me back and dove in even harder. Now, I was begging him not to stop, although the pressure was becoming unbearable. Soon, it was. I eased him off, but he was having none of it. Waves of heat concentrated around my lower body until my clit felt like it was sparking. Ripples of ecstasy shot out from my pores as a glass-shattering scream escaped from deep inside. My clit was like a pounding heart in AFib, pumping in and out as my orgasm contracted wildly. I rode his tongue until I couldn't take it anymore and pushed on his head for release. His dripping face was glazed in a well-earned satisfaction.

"I want to be inside you," Brixton said through gasps.

He didn't just assume he could take me. He was asking permission. I'd never been so worked up in my life.

"Do you have protection?" I asked.

"In my jeans."

I tossed him his pants and he retrieved a condom from the front pocket. I was on my back as he was preparing to enter me. He held my gaze and carefully pushed himself inside me. There was an immense pressure even though I was as wet as possible. I let out a moan of pain and pleasure.

"I missed you," Brixton said.

"You and me both, tiger," I said.

He thrust with a rhythmic movement that encapsulated every part of his being. I wrapped my arms around his back, driving him in as deeply as possible. It felt so right, so perfect. The moment seemed to last forever.

"Let's get away from the drivers."

The door to the cab was right next to us. My face turned crimson, realizing they heard everything.

I was thrilled at how easily he lifted me to my feet. He led me into what he called the chill room. A comfortable couch sat across from a large flat-screen TV. Further in were more chairs, a small kitchen and a wrap-around dining room table. The lights were dim but the bright, modern white of the furnishings illuminated the room. The look reminded me of the plane.

"Everything is so cheerful," I said.

"Yes! Oh my God, you get it. My last bus was dreary. I don't need wood and earth tones. I'm down to earth enough. I need modern. I need bright. I need you." Our lips were drawn together as his hands caressed my face.

"Want to have a little fun?" he asked. "Do you trust me?"

"Unequivocally," I said.

Brixton spun me around and bent me over the couch. I braced myself on my tiptoes. He kicked my legs out wider and drove into me. I caught my reaction in the mirror and looked away. He grabbed a handful of my hair and demanded that I watch myself. The roughness could have seriously backfired but it didn't—I wanted him even more. Staring at myself getting fucked was a strange experience. It should have made me insecure but instead gave me strength.

Brixton finally allowed me to lean back enough to see his face. He raised his eyebrows deviously, then bent over and kissed my forehead.

"Let me show you the rest of the place," he said, pulling out of me.

I followed him to the kitchen on legs of Jell-O. He sat me on the cold granite counter and entered me.

"Music. Sisterly Sisters," he said in a monotone voice. The music switched to one of my favorite songs.

I loved that he remembered I was into them. "You have a good memory," I said.

"You won't find many singers who don't. Look who gets voted off American Idol first—the ones who forget the lyrics."

I stared into his eyes while he fucked me. He didn't turn away.

In mid-thrust, he opened the fridge, grabbing two cans of Reddi-Wip. I was intrigued. I'd always wanted to lick whipped cream off a guy, something I confessed to my husband, so of course the asshole kept me from it.

"Whip-it?" he asked, handing me the can.

I laughed at how wrong I had been. "Why not?"

We let all the air out of our lungs and inhaled the nitrous, draining the cans of the wondrous gas. I tossed the empty into the sink and waited for the effect. Brixton was thrusting harder and harder when the wah, wah, wah of the high kicked in. I leaned my head back and let it drop to my shoulders. We laughed as the world vibrated around us.

The high receded quicker than I would have liked. He collapsed onto the dining room table and slid down to the seat. I positioned myself on top of him and rode strong. He gave me control and I felt powerful. *I* was fucking *him*.

After a few minutes he motioned for me to get up. He took my hand and led me to the hallway where the bunks were. There were two sets of three stacked on one side and a set of three on the other. Brixton opened one of the doors and I climbed in and turned onto my back. It was a tight fit. My man worked his way toward me and forced my legs up by the ankles until my feet were planted on the ceiling. He used the leverage of the cramped space to his advantage, driving into me with deep, rhythmic thrusts.

"Is this bunk yours?" I asked, my head bouncing on the mattress.

"*Please*," he said. "Do you want to see my room?"

100

"Of course."

"Let's not, just yet. This feels really good."

A slight tingling sensation was spreading below. I couldn't believe it. I might actually come. I'd never had an orgasm with a man inside me.

A rush of warmth filled me from my toes to my clit. My swelling vulva coaxed him in deeper with each powerful thrust, as my love button twitched and expanded until I felt like one giant clitoris. Fires of lust emanated from my core as the heat pushed its way to the surface, erupting into a pure, unadulterated orgasm that left me sweaty and shaking.

Brixton could not have been happier. He had made me come without his tongue.

"On to my room!" he commanded.

We climbed out of the bunk.

"Oh wait," he said. "One more room first."

He opened the door next to the single set of bunks. It was a bathroom with a shower. The space was tight but we made it work. I sat on the counter facing him while he drilled into me standing up.

"Is this the Sisterly Sisters' greatest hits?"

"Just a few of my favorites from each of their albums."

"I love this song."

"Sometimes in Bliss" had helped me get over Dennis. The line that I used to sing in anger came up. I belted it out, "*I don't really feel like going homo.*"

Brixton laughed. "Let's get out of here." He led me down the hall and into his room. It was beautiful. There was a queen-size bed against the back wall and a desk with his electronic keyboard. His acoustic guitar was in the corner. He threw the comforter and top sheet aside and jumped on me missionary style.

"Pull out when you're about to come," I said. "I want to watch."

"I will."

He stretched his legs out and thrust faster and faster. I was getting close. "Wait for me. I'm almost there!"

Brixton kept the pace diligently and brought me to orgasm again.

"Whose pussy is it?" he demanded as the contractions receded. I couldn't tell if he was serious or playing around.

"It's yours, Brixton. It's all yours."

He plowed in deeper a few more times then pulled out and ripped the condom off. With two quick strokes he shouted, "Peanut butter!" His orgasm face was a blissful paradise. The first shot hit me on the cheek. He came and came until my belly was a glistening pool of semen.

I was trying to comprehend what he had said. Who yells out peanut butter? It was so silly and off-the-wall that it gave me a bad case of the giggles. He joined in, falling on top of me. Our breathing slowed in unison as we calmed down.

Brixton rolled off me and lay on his back—his abs now shimmering with cum. He brought a washrag from the bathroom and cleaned us both meticulously. That's when it hit me. He doesn't trust me with his cum! Now I understood why he put his used condom in his pocket when we were in the Spinnakers suite. Did he think I would shove his cum in me to get pregnant? What the hell kind of person does he think I am? I wanted to confront him but didn't feel like dampening his spirits.

"You're in a good mood," I said. I was glad I had made him happy. "Stephanie said you'd had a bad couple of days."

"Yeah, they sucked, but Eileen called and made everything alright."

"Eileen DeGenius?" I asked.

"Fo' shiggidy."

I felt deflated; it wasn't me who had made his day.

"Eileen's my favorite person in the whole world. I just love her. She had me turned around in a half hour.

102

She's amazing." He stopped, realizing how much he was gushing over her. "And then you showed up and made my day. Thanks for rollin' out here so fast. You're the best."

"Nice save," I said.

"You liked that?" he said, laughing. "Seriously though, I'm glad you came."

"With that talented tongue how could I not?" I quipped. "I did have to shuffle a few things around but it was no big deal. I sensed something in your voice when you called. Not every day is an up day."

"Tell me about it. I can't always be as cool as my fans think I am. That was until Stephanie taught me how to play different characters when I'm feeling low."

"My friend Jennifer and I used to play this game where we were the coolest people in the world. Usually, we did this at concerts, but sometimes we played it at the beach." I left out the part where we played the game high. "The key is, as the coolest person in the world, people should like you. You're not an ass."

"Exactly!" he said. "You know, that game doesn't have to end with Jennifer. Maybe we can play it together sometime."

"I'd like that," I said.

"I would, too."

Out of the blue, he asked if I had any sleeping pills.

"Don't get into pills, baby. They'll mess up your career. Look at Elvis." I could tell by his blank stare that he didn't understand. "Look at Heath Ledger."

"I'm not gonna mess with the tides."

"The tides?"

"Highs and lows. Uppers and downers. And yes, I know who Elvis is. I just need a good night's sleep."

"That's what Heath said." I paused to let that sink in. "I don't have sleeping pills, but I do have Xanax, as long as it's a one-time thing."

"Says the woman who has Xanax."

Having lost the argument, I dug in my purse for the bottle.

"Yes!" he said raising his arms in the air in triumphantly.

I was trying to get one pill, but three fell into my palm. Before I could scoop two back, he snatched the bunch and swallowed dry.

"Dude! Not cool."

"Don't worry, we have seventeen more hours to ourselves," he said and winked. "We can sleep in as late as we want."

The pills did the trick. He was off in la-la land within ten minutes.

"You know, my life isn't normal," Brixton slurred.

"I know, babe," I said and kissed his forehead. I spooned him from behind. His smooth, flawless skin made my clit tingle.

I was drifting off to sleep when a buzzer sounded over the intercom, snapping me back to reality. It rang a second time from the chill room. I jumped up to investigate and was startled by a large man approaching from the dark hall. I froze, not sure what to do.

"Hold on," the man said, "I'm with Brixton."

I looked around for something to wear and spotted Brixton's T-shirt.

"I need some ID," I said firmly. How was I to know he wasn't a stalker?

"Of course, Jackie," he said, reaching for his wallet. I didn't need to look since he knew my name, but I checked his credentials anyway. His name was Rory McKay. It was a fine Scottish name that went well with his red hair. He had a large Wally Walrus mustache that was one part ridiculous and two parts awesome.

"I'm sorry to disturb you. A suspicious car has been following us."

"A blue sedan? That's a cop."

104

"He's long gone. This is a new tail. I need you and Brixton to get into his safe room." Rory lifted the back of the kitchen bench, revealing a metal door. He turned the handle and lifted. The light in the safe room came on automatically. The room was larger than the bunks but not by much. I could tell by the mess that Brixton liked to hang out down there.

"I'll try to wake him, but he's out cold," I said.

"Shit, I'd rather leave him be," he said. "Brixton hasn't been sleeping well. He needs his rest. Let's at least get him on the floor."

I followed Rory into the bedroom. Brixton was sleeping on his stomach with his bubble butt facing us. I threw a sheet over him. Rory doubled up the comforter at the foot of the bed.

"Grab his feet," he said. "We need to get him out of the line of fire."

I lifted his legs carefully.

"What the hell?" Brixton said, but fell back to sleep when he was on the floor.

"Let's turn him," I said. "Which direction is the car? I'll wrap myself around him for protection."

"I can't have you take that risk, Jackie."

"No time," I said. "Come on, help me."

"OK. The guy is right behind us. The bed should offer protection, but if shit goes down, we're getting you in the safe room."

We rolled Brixton onto his side. Rory instructed me to keep the light off. "And don't look out the window," he added. "I'll be right outside your door."

I slid up against Brixton and wrapped my arms around him with my head protectively above his. Although uncomfortable, it was the best position to offer the most cover.

I had been sitting still for so long my neck was cramping up. The piercing sound of a police siren made me jump, kinking my neck even worse. Red and blue lights flooded the room. The bus changed lanes and sped up until we returned to cruising speed. I took a peek and saw a car pulled over in the distance.

Rory knocked on the door. "All clear, Jackie. Have a good night."

"Wait, hold on," I called. "We need to get him back on the mattress."

I woke up to an empty bed and stretched noisily before rolling over. The clock on the nightstand said 10:02 a.m.

Brixton was in his underwear, playing an electronic keyboard at his desk. The headphones left him oblivious to my awakening. His back muscles flexed with each key pressed, bringing to life the notes I couldn't hear. I snatched his shirt off the floor and put it on. He flinched when I slid my hand down his chest from behind.

He dropped his earphones to his shoulders. "Hey, girl. Did you have a nice sleep?"

"It was wonderful. That's the most comfortable mattress I've ever been on."

"I know, right? Took them six mattresses to find one I liked. Can I get you anything?" He started to get up. I pushed him back in his seat.

"Play for a little longer?" I said. "I need to pee."

"Sure," he said and put his earphones back on.

Brixton had wrecked my vagina the night before. The time it took for me to go was absurd.

I was washing my hands when the aroma of fresh gourmet coffee beckoned me. I headed to the kitchen. With cup in hand, I made my way back to Brixton.

"I'm sorry, did you want a cup?" I asked.

"I have one," he said, lifting it.

I noticed he had a strong erection pushing through his underwear. I reached down and rubbed him through the fabric.

"Can you play me something?"

"I don't know. I can't have you become a fan. You know that."

"I'll suck your cock."

"I have the perfect song," he responded, comically fast. Men are so easy. "I need to set the beats first. Hang on a sec." He pushed a couple of buttons and played a drumbeat on the keys, then looped it and hit save. With that set, he began singing The Talking Heads, "Road to Nowhere." It was a perfect song for a lazy road trip. I went down on him in rhythm with the music.

Brixton finished the song and leaned back to focus on the moment. He raised his cock to meet my mouth and thrust so hard his ass rose off the seat—a move Dennis used to do when he wanted a little something extra. What the hell, I thought. I wet my finger and slid it up his ass.

"What the fuck!" He jerked backward, accidentally kneeing my breast on the way down.

Unbearable pain shot through my chest. I ran to the bathroom so he wouldn't know how badly he hurt me.

"I'm sorry, Jackie," he said, knocking. "I didn't mean to hit you. You just shocked me."

"No, I'm sorry," I said, peering through the semi-open door.

"It's no big deal, baby. You have to get out of there," he said, looking embarrassed. "You made me have to poop." The innocent way he said it made me laugh.

He turned on the bathroom radio as I shut the door behind me. I grabbed my coffee and headed to the chill room to give him some privacy and me some recovery time. I embraced my tender breast and waited for the pain to subside.

I heard the door open and moved my arm to my side.

"There you are," Brixton said. "Come back to my room. I need to finish." I wasn't in the mood anymore but forced myself to rally.

He sat on the bed and I kneeled before him. Brixton lasted a solid half-hour. I was toying with him, bringing him to the edge then backing off until he was begging to let him come. I brought my hand into the mix and stroked as my mouth rubbed vigorously against the head.

"Oh my God, yes," he shouted. His balls danced in my palm as he unloaded into my mouth. I swallowed in a gulp of relief.

We lay next to each other, listening to the road noise. Without looking, he laced his fingers through mine. I wanted to apologize for the mishap with his sphincter. Then again, it would be best to pretend it didn't happen.

"Did you leave room for breakfast?" he asked.

I responded with playful shock but relented. I was starving. "Sure."

He reached over and pressed the intercom.

"Hello," Rory answered in a groggy voice.

"Good morning," Brixton said. "Would you mind making us breakfast?"

"I can make it," I said. "Ask him if he's eaten."

"Scratch that—Jackie's making us something. You hungry?"

"Famished."

Brixton put on flannel pajama bottoms with a pattern of little microphones that at first glance looked like penises. I handed him a cotton wife beater. I'd seen enough pictures of him to know his preference. My bottoms were adorned with cocktails glasses and olives.

I found an assortment of fresh meats and vegetables in the fridge. There were enough ingredients to make omelets—my specialty.

Rory wanted a Denver omelet, and Brixton a ham and cheese. I made mine with a plethora of mushrooms.

The boys were almost finished when I took a seat. I had insisted they start without me.

"That was the best omelet I've ever had," Rory said. He sat back, content in his seat. His plate was bare as if he had licked it clean.

"It was the tops," Brixton said. There was a look of satisfaction in his eyes.

"You're welcome, boys." I took a bite. I don't know if it was me or the quality ingredients, but my omelet was delicious.

I looked at Rory between bites. "If you don't mind me asking, who was in the car following us last night?"

"Just some kid coming back from his night job. The cops said he was keeping up with us so he wouldn't zone off to sleep."

"What?" Brixton said, catching up with the conversation. "When did this happen?"

"Last night, while you were comatose. Jackie did a fantastic job protecting you."

"It was nothing," I said.

"It was very brave," Rory said, patting my hand.

Brixton looked as though he didn't know what to think. I hope I hadn't freaked him out.

"I have wonderful news for you, Spider," Rory said, saving me. "Guess who showed up at your hotel in Atlanta this morning?"

"Macklemore?"

"What? Macklemore? No, your stalkers. They're in custody."

Brixton's smile grew, his lip quivered and tears pooled in the corners of his eyes. "Thank you," he managed to say.

"This one was all Jimmy. I swear the guy has eyes in the back of his head. Spotted them in the parking lot."

I put a hand on Brixton's leg and squeezed. He gave me a lingering kiss on the cheek. "Looks like I get to keep my head."

The dark comment brought silence.

"I'll get out of your hair," Rory said. "I'm going to catch some Z's."

"You can sleep in a bunk if you want," Brixton said.

"We have our own up front."

"Really?"

"A bathroom, too. Where did you think we slept?"

"I guess I never thought about it. Can I take a look?"

"Of course. It's your bus."

"Coolness," Brixton said and stood up. "Hey, Rory..."

Rory sighed. "What do you want?"

Brixton grinned. "The danger's gone. Can we stop at one of those old-time burger places for lunch?"

"The danger is never gone. You know that. But sure, we can stop for burgers. You've earned it."

"I mean really eat at a burger joint. Not me eating on the bus or behind the security fence. But eating out in the open with the people."

"You remember what happened the last time we tried this."

"Come on, it's Friday afternoon. The kids will still be in school."

Rory didn't say anything. He was fighting with the idea. "I'll have to check with Jimmy."

"Please," Brixton begged.

"All right," Rory said, still not happy about it.

"Fan-fucking-tastic," Brixton said, bobbing his head back and forth.

His enthusiasm made me giggle. "Hurry back," I said. "It's shower time."

"I can stay," he said.

"Go, check out the cab. I'll get the shower going."

"Let's bounce," he said to Rory.

110

I made my way to the bathroom. I wanted to do some prep cleaning to make sure I was fresh. I was surprised at how fast the water heated up, and how much pressure there was.

Brixton was soon squeezing his way in next to me. He looked at my breasts, then at my face.

"Can you hand me the shampoo?" he asked, motioning to the bottle of Pureology. I was going to compliment his choice of product but didn't want to be uncouth.

Brixton washed my hair, working the lather in from the front, massaging my scalp to the back of my neck, his fingers kneading the same as Stephanie. She had taught him well. My knees weakened. Next was a fingertip spider-move across the top, followed by a temple massage.

It was my turn. I slid up behind him, focused on his scalp, massaging the sides of his head, and then worked my way upward.

"That feels so good," he said.

I caressed his head for five minutes before giving in to the urge to run my hands through his long, healthy tresses.

With the water off, we washed each other's back. I stayed clear of his ass but he was all up in mine. He sure seemed to enjoy washing my chest. I can honestly say my breasts have never been cleaner.

"Your face is just as beautiful without makeup," he said.

It was the best compliment I've ever had. I was beaming.

He was methodical in his vaginal cleansing techniques. I tried to wash his cock equally well but ended up just stroking him.

After our shower we sat naked in front of the bedroom mirror, styling our hair. Brixton's penis was soft and relaxed, same as the mood.

"Go real light on the makeup," he requested. "Like you did for the Spinnakers game." I loved that his example was the one I did.

He reached for a pair of black silk pants that looked like he was about to parachute in from the 80s.

"Can you let me dress you?" I asked, hoping I wasn't overstepping my bounds.

He hesitated. "I don't know. I haven't recovered from the last time did that."

"The dog outfit?"

"Yeah," he said, embarrassed.

"My friend Lidia showed me the picture," I said. "I was wondering what you were doing in that getup."

"I lost a bet with my high school friends. You can't back out of stuff like that."

"You looked ridiculous but cute. Must have been one hell of a bet."

"It was stupid. They bet I couldn't get a room at the Hotel de Ville in Paris. I've been to every country in the world. I knew I could. Turns out the Hotel de Ville is City Hall. So I had to dress like a stupid dog and walk around my hometown. I acted like it didn't bother me, but man was that embarrassing."

"I can't believe people are making fun of you for that. You were being a good friend."

"I know, and so does the media. We couldn't have explained it clearer. But the truth isn't what they're after. Those bastards have it in for me."

"I'm not like them. I would never do anything to hurt you."

"I know that," he said, giving me a squeeze.

"Then let me dress you. We're going out in the Deep South to a burger joint. Let's give them the boy next door. You want to blend in, don't you?"

"Of course," he said, conceding. "I get final say."

I searched through his clothes for something unassuming. "Do you have shorts?"

"I have these," he said, handing me a pair of dark blue chinos.

"Perfect. Oh my God, and with these shoes." I held up his white Reeboks.

"Those are my workout shoes. How about these?" he asked, holding a humungous pair of sneakers.

I wanted to say no big shoes but shook my head unapprovingly instead. He grabbed black socks. I took them from him and handed over a pair of whites. He pulled the socks high; I slid them down for a less dorky look. In the back of his closet, I found a simple white T-shirt with thin, horizontal red stripes.

"Ha, I knew you'd pick that one." He slipped the shirt over his head and shook his hair out. The style wasn't exactly boy next door because he was so freakishly handsome, but it was close. Why he doesn't dress like that all the time is beyond me. Get rid of the thug apparel. At this stage, he has nothing to prove to anyone. All it does is add fuel to the media's fire.

I put on a short halter dress and headed to the chill room. The stereo wasn't responding to my voice commands, and none of the remotes worked. Brixton sat beside me and retrieved an iPad from the end table.

"Music or TV?" he asked.

"Music, definitely."

"I'm kind of into reggae right now. Do you mind?"

"I'd keep that to yourself," I said. "They'll send you to rehab."

"Ha, probably."

"Can you download Pato Banton's 'Never Give In'?" I requested. "He's awesome."

Brixton had a peculiar look on his face. "How do you know Pato?"

"My brother gave me a CD. Said I needed some happy music."

"You can't get happier than Pato. Man, I wish I had some herb. I should have had you smuggle some aboard."

"We can have fun without it." I looked around and spotted a basketball video game. "I love this game."

"You are so in for it," he said. "No one can beat me. I'm the b-ball master."

"Bater," I joked. "I have to warn you, I played this a lot after I quit my basketball team."

"Why would you quit basketball?"

"The girls kept blowing out their ACL's. I didn't want it to happen to me."

"Women shouldn't play basketball," he said, taunting me. "Prepare to have your ACL's blown."

"Oh, it's on!" I said.

At first, he held back, but as soon as he figured out how good I was he grew serious. Brixton had skills but mine were stronger. I took him with two three-pointers in a row.

"Fuck!" He paced angrily back and forth and walked into the kitchen. His tantrum made him look ridiculously young, which took me aback. He returned and sat down, all tough, "Best two out of three."

"What? No."

"Two out of three," he said sternly. I should have let him win. Damn it! Stephanie told me he has to be the best at everything he does.

"It was luck," I said.

He thrust the controller in my hand. "Your ball."

I had fun the next two games, but holding back felt forced. I shared in his celebration when he won the match. I wasn't faking that; he made an amazing three-point shot at the buzzer.

"In your face," he said, pointing at me. I laughed. Having to be the best at everything isn't that bad of a flaw, although it wasted a large chunk of our time.

I think he realized that he was acting like a dick. He put my head in his lap and stroked my hair.

I kept the conversation on him but steered it in a positive direction. "So, do you write all of your songs?"

"I love that you don't know anything about my music. My problem isn't writing songs; it's being unable to stop. Yesterday I wrote a song about peanut butter."

"That's adorable."

"Well, it started that way:

Peanut butter is all I need
Peanut butter is good indeed
Slathered up with jelly, 'nutter
Nothing better 'cept smoking weed

"The rest kind of fell apart from there. But writing that simple verse put me in a better mood." He paused. "Until my lunch with [Name Removed]."

"[Name Removed]," I said, thrilled. I didn't want him to know that Stephanie and I had talked about his talk show friend.

"Yeah, she's my bud. Although, yesterday, she was in major mothering mode. Drove me crazy. She wants me to be the 14-year-old angel she met years ago. Girlfriend's pissed that I'm smoking weed."

"I probably shouldn't do this," I said and grabbed his iPad. After a quick Google search, I excused myself to use the bathroom.

Brixton glanced at the page. "What the fuck?"

I had brought up an article where [Name Removed] admitted she used to do cocaine.

"Oh, she is so getting it," he said, picking up his phone.

When I returned, Brixton was laying into [Name Removed]. I held back to give him space.

"No, you listen to me. You made me feel like shit yesterday. What? I know you didn't mean it but you did. No. No. No." He quietly listened. "I'm nineteen. I'm going to make mistakes. You can't hold that against me. I'm still a good guy." She talked for a long time before he could

115

end the conversation. "Don't worry. I love you, too. Bye," he said and hung up.

I sauntered into the room and Brixton gave me a warm smile. "Thank you."

"Anytime," I said.

"One favor serves another," he said, incorrectly. "I know just the thing." He picked up his phone and made a call.

"Hey, Jacob. What's up? Ha ha. In your dreams. No, my girl Jackie wants to say hi." He passed me the phone. "Jacob Cutters," he whispered.

I couldn't believe I was about to talk with the lead singer of the Sisterly Sisters. Jacob's my hero. What a trip.

"Hello," I said nervously.

"Hey, Jackie. What's shaking, hot stuff?" I was expecting his voice to be flamboyant, but he was down-to-earth.

I wanted to tell Jacob that we were having a Darty like his new song says, but chickened out. "We're chilling on Brixton's tour bus. Just the two of us. What's up in your world?"

"I'm havin' fun, laying down some sic vocals."

"Sweet. I thought I heard a new song a few days ago. I was psyched, but it turned out to be some other group. What's up with that? Did you write it for them?" Shit, why was I talking about another band?

"I know the song. Yeah, we had nothing to do with that."

"Are you going after them? It's crazy how they copied your sound."

"Imitation is the sincerest form of flattery."

"Serious? I'd be pissed."

"What am I going to do? Start screaming that someone stole my purse? Certain times you have to step back and check yourself. Lawyers bring on a world of darkness. Who needs that?"

"You're pretty awesome."

"I know," he said, making fun of himself. "So, you knocking that big cock of his?"

"Oh my God. Hang on a second." I covered the mic and turned to Brixton. "Can I tell him we had sex to his songs last night?"

He shook his head no.

"I'm back."

"I heard everything you said. Spill it, sister. How big is he? Say when. Six inches? Seven?"

"Stop," I said, meaning he needed to stop talking.

"Seven. Nice. Thanks, girl. God, I'm jealous. You enjoy it."

"Absolutely," I said. "It was fun talking to you."

"You too. Put the boy on."

I handed the phone to Brixton.

"Yo, Jacob. What? Thirty. Yeah, that is sweet," he said and looked at me. "No! I'm not sending a picture of my cock. I have to go. Talk to you later. I'm not mad. I'll call you when I get back in town."

"Thanks," I said, kissing him.

The intercom buzzed. "Hey, Spider," Rory said, "I found the perfect hamburger joint. Sit tight. We'll be there in five."

"Cool. Thanks, Rory."

Within minutes we were easing into the lot of one of those old-time hamburger stands—the kind with an inch thick of paint on the building. The sun was shining, but there were trees to offer shade if Brixton wanted it.

We came to a stop and Rory told Brixton to hang tight. He motioned for me to come up front. I met the driver, a nice fatherly figure with gray hair. Rory and I exited the truck from the passenger side. Even though it was early spring the humidity hung densely in the air. Summers must be unbearable. The driver stepped outside and checked the surroundings.

"Why don't you save us a place in line," Rory suggested. He strolled to the window and spoke to a

117

heavyset woman at the counter. Her eyes grew wide and she handed over the loudspeaker microphone.

Rory held the button and the speakers squealed. "Ladies and gentlemen. You may be wondering whose tour bus that is parked over yonder. I'll let you in on a secret. Inside the bus is teen idol Brixton Webber." A murmur spread through the small crowd. "If I can get your word that no one will take pictures or videos, and that nobody will make a big deal of this, I will have him come out and eat with you. No pictures. No fan-fare. No texting people and inviting them over. No disturbing his Aunt Carol."

Did he call me his aunt? Brixton laughed from inside the bus.

"Please treat him like a normal person. If you do that, he'll sing a couple songs for you when he's done eating. Maybe sign an autograph or two. Sound like a plan? Raise your hand if we have a deal."

There was unanimous agreement. The people shuffled around aimlessly. "Go back to your tables. He'll be here for a while."

Satisfied but still looking worried, Rory walked over to the bus and unlocked the door. Brixton stepped out wearing Gucci sunglasses that didn't go with his outfit. I'd forgotten to accessorize him.

A goofy-looking man clapped but his friend put a stop to it. Brixton joined me in the back of the line.

"You can come on up, sweetie," the woman at the counter motioned.

"I never get to stand in a line. Thanks, but this is right where I want to be."

There was a couple in their early twenties in front of us. The man turned around and said, "I'm Stephen, and this is my girlfriend, Julie."

"I'm Brixton. This is my Aunt Carol and my bodyg... my friend, Rory."

The couple could not have been more pleasant. I felt like I was in a Norman Rockwell painting. All that was absent were the kids stuck at school. Boy, would they be upset that they missed him.

Brixton asked Stephen if he would trade sunglasses.

"Hell yes," he said, handing over his old aviators. Brixton's look was complete.

I decided to skip healthy food for the day and ordered a bacon cheeseburger. Brixton ordered the same and threw in a corn dog for good measure.

We sat with the driver and Rory at a sunny table off to the side. The driver was a silly man with crazy stories about his life in Kentucky. I felt bad that I hadn't offered him an omelet.

Our lunch arrived surprisingly fast. I had a feeling they pushed our order ahead of the others. My burger was insanely delicious. The smoky essence of the bacon and the succulence of the sweet onions drew me in. Our group became silent as we savored the feast. A good meal will do that.

Something remarkable happened during our time there. Whenever a car pulled up, the rules were explained to the new person. No one brought out their cameras. No one used their phones. They let Brixton be normal. The joy in his eyes spoke volumes. It inspired him to relive childhood memories of playing in the woods behind his house. I shared the story of Jennifer and me as kids stealing Easter candy off the graves of dead children. The look of horror from the older men in our group was hilarious. We laughed about that for some time.

Brixton leaned back and soaked up the rays. The vampire was getting his long overdue sun.

"We need to get going before school lets out," Rory said. "There's maybe a half-hour."

"Can you grab my guitar, Aunt Carol?" Brixton said to me sarcastically. Rory handed me the keys.

119

The crowd cheered when I exited the bus with his six-string. The moment was surreal but I kept my cool. I handed the guitar to Brixton, who had moved to a picnic table by the bus. He put the strap around his neck and checked the tune of the strings.

"You can take pictures. I don't mind." A sea of cell phones appeared. I moved out of the way so I wasn't in any of the shots. "Please don't call anyone. If people show up, we'll have to jet."

"You got it, Brixton," a man yelled out.

"What do you want to hear? Doesn't have to be one of my songs. I can play most anything."

Another man shouted, "Freebird!"

Brixton let out a sigh. "Except Freebird," he said.

"When Doves Cry," someone else requested.

"Wow, that's an old one. I've only heard the song— I've never played it. But I'll give it my best shot."

He stared at the guitar's frets, deep in thought, then raised his head. "I can't play the beginning. I'd need an electric guitar. Here goes nothing."

Brixton played the song from memory, lyrics and all. The song was haunting, sending chills through my body. I had no idea he was *that* talented.

Halfway through his rendition, a car backfired in the parking lot. Rory and our driver jumped into action. Rory drew a gun from a concealed holster and covered Brixton's front. Our driver had his back with his gun out ready to use.

"It's just Jenkins," a man called out. "His car backfires."

Brixton caught my eye and laughed. Soon everyone joined in.

"How about a couple more?" he said. Rory was nervous but didn't intervene.

A woman shouted out the name of a song I didn't recognize. Brixton was equally perplexed.

"What, you don't know country?" a man hollered.

120

"Sure, I know country."

He began playing "Friends in Low Places." The crowd was singing the chorus in no time.

"I get to pick one now," Brixton said. "I wrote this next song with one of the coolest peeps I know. Don't worry this isn't on your kid's albums."

I didn't know what he was singing until he reached the chorus, "I wanna take you in the bop bop." He had made a song of my silly little lyric. I was a bit shocked that he was singing it in front of such a wholesome crowd but flattered too.

After his performance, Brixton made a point of meeting everyone. He posed for as many pictures as possible before Rory sent us on our way.

The crowd waved and chased after the bus as we drove out of the parking lot. Then came a high-pitched "Waaaait!"

"Stop!" Brixton commanded over the intercom.

A girl of about ten ran up to the side of the bus, crying.

Brixton opened the door. One look at him and she fainted—just fell right over.

"Carmen," a dark-haired man said, running to her side. I recognized his buzz cut as the driver of the backfiring car. It was Jenkins.

Brixton picked the girl up and carried her inside to his couch. Jenkins turned out to be her father. He waited at the top of the stairs.

The girl came to, screaming. Brixton put his finger to his lips and she obeyed.

"What is it, my birthday?" she asked.

That cracked him up. He motioned to her father, holding his hands up like he was taking a picture. Jenkins pulled out his phone and Brixton and the girl posed.

The girl spotted me and said, "Who are *you*?"

"I'm his Aunt Carol," I said halfheartedly.

"You better be," she snarled.

I looked at Brixton and mouthed, *what the hell*?

"I'm sorry to do this, honey, but we have to roll. It was nice to meet you, Carmen."

Brixton's memory amazed me. There's no way I would have remembered her name only hearing it once.

Her father practically had to drag the girl away.

"Wait, hold up," Brixton said. He returned from the cab with two concert tickets in his hand. "I want you to have these." The girl screamed again.

Jenkins noticed where the show was playing and sighed. "I can't afford the gas. I've been out of work for a few months now."

"Daddy, please. I'll die if I don't go."

"Well, I don't want you to die," Brixton said. "Don't move." He joined me back in the chill room and opened a hidden safe. From a stack of hundreds, he counted out ten.

"I can't accept all this," Jenkins said. "It's too much." He pocketed one bill and handed the rest back. Brixton tried to get the man to keep all the money but the father had his pride.

"You're a good man," Jenkins said.

Brixton offered the girl one last hug. While doing this he slipped the rest of the money in her pocket.

Rory opened the cab door. "Get a move on it, Spider."

The father had to pry his daughter's hands off Brixton. The bus rumbled to a start, and as soon as she let go, we were off.

"That was one of the best times I've had all year," Brixton said. "How incredible was that? They let me be normal."

"They sure did," I said. "I hope this doesn't sound petty but how come you were so nice to that girl after what she said to me?"

"Don't let anything my fans say get to you. She didn't mean it."

"You're very sweet."

"So how did you like your song?"

"I can't believe you played it."

He slapped my ass. "Let's take a nap. I'm spent."

"Sounds like a plan, Stan," I said.

We stripped naked and climbed under the sheets.

"Thanks for dressing me down," he said and planted a soft kiss on my lips. "You were right."

I woke up to an empty bed again. Before searching for Brixton, I lay on my back for a few minutes, enjoying the rocking of the bus. I found him in the chill room with his keyboard, writing notes.

"Hey baby," he said. "Come join me."

I sat down and rubbed his leg. "What are you working on?"

"A song I'm writing for Adam Lambert."

"Look at you."

"I was inspired by one of my gay fans. This kid emailed me, saying he didn't want to live anymore. I called and talked to him for hours. His parents are hardcore Christians. To say they weren't taking his sexuality well is the understatement of the year. My mom's religious but she's cool with the Bible—uses it in positive ways. I was shocked at how he was being treated. Family is supposed to come first. I told him they're the ones with the problem, not him. He promised to tough it out until he graduates. I sure hope he does. He was a cool dude. Hearing that shit messed me up royally for a few days, though. I had to transfer all my anger into a song."

"I want to hear it," I said.

"I don't know."

"Come on."

"OK, but keep in mind it's not finished."

He picked up his iPad and clicked on a song called "I Love the Sinner." It kicked off with deep church bells morphing into a dark techno beat. Even before the lyrics began I could feel the pain:

Mom... Jesus... is in... my bedroom.
Mom... Jesus... is in... my bedroom.

Get your god out of my bedroom.
Fire and brimstone, it's all doom.
Won't let you kick another boy out of his room.

Don't use the Bible as a weapon.
Don't point your Bible at me.

Your hate is deadly. Your hate is wrong.
Your hate will only make me strong.

Religious evil. Religious sin.
You love the sinner but you hate the sin.
Do you love the black man but hate his skin?
My patience is wearing it's wearing thin.

I love the sinner. I love the sin.
I love the sinner. I love the sin.
I love the sinner. I love the sin.

Get your god out of my bedroom.
Fire and brimstone, it's all doom.
Won't let you send another boy to his doom.

You act as though you're better than me.
What have you done that we can see?

We're all his children.
You pick and choose.
You segregate.
You make up the rules.

124

Your hate is deadly.
Your hate is wrong.
Your hate will only make me strong.

Religious evil. Religious sin.
You love the sinner but you hate the sin.
Your ugly mouth is a firing pin.
Why do you judge me for loving him?

I love the sinner. I love the sin.
I love the sinner. I love the sin.
I love the sinner. I love the sin.

Get your god out of my bedroom.
Fire and brimstone, it's all doom.
Won't let you send another boy to his tomb.

The most extreme Christians are the least Christlike.
All they do is judge and fight, fight, fight.

You're supposed to love your fellow man.
Treat them with kindness.
Give them a hand.

The kids today will make you see
Just how good people can be.

Religious evil. Religious sin.
You love the sinner but you hate the sin.
What is this 1940's Berlin?
You'd be a better person finding love from within.

You're the freak. You're the tool.
You're the one I need to school.

"That kicked ass," I said. "Has Adam heard it?"

"Not yet. I hope to meet him when I get back to London."

"He's going to love it," I assured him.

"I hope so. You ready for some fun?"

"Always."

He jumped up, cleared the couch of remotes, then pushed a button. The sofa folded in and away, adding a few extra feet to the room.

"What are we doing?" I asked.

He held out his finger to tell me to wait. "I'm crossing boundaries here. Don't let this go to your head, girl. We're just dancing." He turned on the TV and from his iPad cued a video.

"Robbie Cumberlake has been nice enough to loan me his choreographer. I had to fire mine."

"What happened? I loved your dance moves at the show."

"Let's just say he was more focused on his subject than his subject, if you know what I mean."

"Oh my," I said, feigning shock.

"Marty is working with me when I get to Georgia, but I want to learn a couple of the moves so I can perform the new solo tonight."

I kept my cool but inside I was jumping out of my skin. This was a fantasy I'd acted out a hundred times in my room as a little girl. "Can we dance to the song first?" I asked. "Without the choreography, so I can get to know the beat."

"Absolutely," he said. "First I'll teach you how to loosen up your body. I have the perfect song." He put on Deee-Lite's "Groove is in the Heart."

My brother and I used to dance to that as kids. "I love this song." How did he know this? Had he been reading my Facebook page?

I didn't need help getting my sober legs going. Lady Miss Kier's dance moves came right back to me.

"You're awesome," Brixton said. He knew how to move to the song, which surprised me since he wasn't even born yet when it was a hit.

Dancing with him, I felt the mystical connection we'd had at the concert. We weren't dancing close enough to touch but our minds were intertwined. I was starting to get turned on.

"How do you know that song?" I asked.

"It was my choreographer's favorite," he said. "You are so fucking hot." We made out for a while and then he put on his song. It was the Superman tune from his concert. The funky beat sure had me dancing at the show.

He paused the music. "We can't do this," he said.

"What's wrong?"

"See how you're looking at me. You can't become a fan."

I wanted to joke that I'm not twelve but thought better of it. "We're just dancing."

"OK, but you keep your head." He put the song back on and grooved to the beat. I followed his lead and made moves that flowed with the song. Brixton was a fun dance partner. He would recognize when I was trying something new and laugh or praise me. That freed me up to have fun with our dancing. What I liked best was how he sang along to his own song.

Sweat was beginning to soak through Brixton's T-shirt. His athletic musk stirred my juices. I would have taken him right there but I *had* to learn his new dance moves. I just had to. It would almost be better than sex.

"Play the video," I demanded.

"Fine."

"Hello, Brixton," Marty addressed him from the screen. He had a tightly cropped beard and wore a fedora like Cumberlake. "If you have time it would help to learn these steps before you get to Atlanta. The choreography is tight in "Superman" but not in the best way. We're funking it up white boy style and bumping up the hero

127

action that leads to your flying moment, which, I have to tell you, is badass. What we're bringing to this dance is something I call musicality. I'll take it slow. To start, there are six eight-counts. I'm going to show you the first four. Then we'll regroup and learn the rest. Let's do it."

"I'm ready," Brixton said to the screen.

"Reach out and grab some air," Marty instructed. "Step back with your left foot. Slide the right back over and point, then kick back. OK. Let's try that all at once."

Brixton pressed pause and backed it to the beginning of the lesson. I was already lost, but by the fourth time we both had it down. Within an hour, he had the whole set memorized. I expected the dance to look like Cumberlake, but it was all Webber.

"You'll blow the crowd away with this. How long do you have this guy?"

"One week."

"That's not long."

"I know, but Marty says it's plenty of time. Can you watch me and the video to make sure I'm doing it right?"

"Sure thing."

"Be tough. It has to be tight."

He restarted the video and I stopped him three moves in. "When you bend over here you're not leaning far enough to the left. Rewind the video. See how he gets his right shoulder up?"

"Yeah. Keep it coming." He practiced the move over and over until it was ingrained.

He began the routine again but I was too horny to concentrate. I sidled up behind him and grabbed a handful of cock. He pressed pause. "You need to focus. This is important."

"I'm sorry."

"It's all good, baby."

Brixton nailed the routine after ten tries. That seemed fast to me. He practiced a few more times, then fell onto the couch, dripping in sweat. I sat next to him while he toweled off.

"I'm curious about something," I said. "How come you grab your cock so much when you're performing? Are you trying to be like Michael Jackson?"

"I wish. Michael was the best in the business. Do you really want to know?"

"Yeah."

"You know how hot it gets in the crowd? Well, heat rises. Around the third song this wave of the most wonderful smell." He stopped talking. A guilty smirk emerged.

"What?"

"You don't want to know."

"I do."

"For the rest of the show all I can smell are girl parts. It never stops. I have a special pair of underwear that tucks my boner back but it still gets loose. I grab myself to flip it out of the way. Every time we're planning a new tour I throw out The Moist Tour as a name, but I always get shot down."

"Christ, that would sell out fast, even if I do hate that word."

"Moist?"

"It's awful. I don't know what it is about it."

He stuck his hand up my skirt and into my panties. His fingers were glistening when he brought them out. "I love it," he said.

"We'll have to take it slow," I said. "You really gave me a pounding last night."

"No problem." He flicked on the intercom. "Hey, Rory, what kind of stretch are we looking at here?"

"A couple more hours, Boss."

"We'll be in my safe room if you want to hang out here."

"Cool. Thanks, man."

"I just realized I've never asked what you do for your bread and butter," Brixton said as he unlocked the safe room. "Sorry, that was a bit rude."

"Please," I said. "I never brought it up because it's not very exciting. I'm a salesperson at Bellstrom."

"It sounds hard," he said.

"It is," I agreed.

"Don't sports stars shop at Bellstrom for their large shoes? I bet you get them in there all the time."

"We used to. Not so much after our basketball team was sold to Oklahoma."

"Ouch, sorry. I forgot about that."

"No worries. Soccer almost fills the void."

"You're such a sports girl. That is so hot."

I loved how much it turned him on. My husband was the exact opposite. He only looked at the newspaper's sports section to use it to start a fire. Although I always suspected that was more to piss me off.

"Ladies first," he said.

I climbed down the ladder and landed on the mattress. Brixton closed the hatch and the room went dark. He turned the lights back on and pressed a button that sent a breeze our way.

"I hope this doesn't sound creepy," he said. "I checked your house out on Google Maps. Rolled around your block with Street View. It looks like a great place to live."

"Now who's the stalker?" I joked. "I couldn't imagine living anywhere else in Seattle. Being on the beach rules."

"It suits you," he said. "How about a back rub?"

"Sure. I'm pretty good."

"I bet you are, but I meant for you."

I can't remember the last time a man gave me a back rub. "Marry me," I said jokingly. Luckily he laughed.

We both stripped naked. Brixton turned me over onto my stomach and straddled my ass. The plush velour blanket felt like a thousand kisses upon my skin, but was nothing compared to his talented fingers.

I'm not sure if he was doing it on purpose, but I could feel his goods rubbing against my body ever so slightly. This was becoming the best massage I'd ever had. What amazed me the most is he never touched me sexually. The closest he came was a feathery graze as he brushed past. Even when he turned me over and worked on my front he focused on the massage. Someone had taught him well. He rubbed every part of my body except my feet. That was odd but I didn't say anything. I was beyond relaxed, almost out of my body.

"Don't get up," he said as he flopped down next to me. "I like to come to my safe room and fly on my magic carpet. You game?"

"Sure," I said but had no idea what he was talking about.

"It's like meditating except you're not grounded to the earth so you feel as if you're flying. Are you scared of the dark?"

"I won't be with you here."

"Good, this room is pretty much a sensory deprivation chamber." He shut the lights off and we were in the blackest black I've experienced. There was not a sliver of light.

"You OK?"

"I'm cool. I've never seen dark like this."

"You'll get used to it. I'll talk you through this," he said gently. "Start by relaxing your head. Let it sink into the mattress. Continue working the stress out through your neck, down your body. Now shake your hands out and let your arms sink. Work your way along your chest to your toes, letting go of any stress, any weight."

I had never meditated before but his technique was working. I felt tingly and light as I wiggled out the last bit of tension from my toes.

"Your body should be completely relaxed now. Let your eyes drop back as if you're looking at one of those 3-D magic pictures where an image appears."

My eyes sank into position and I was brought to the edge of dreamland. It was like a door unlocking.

"For me, this is the key to meditation. It's all in the eyes. They're the window to your soul. All you need to do now is let the road noise block the voices in your head. If that doesn't work, picture rocks on your beach tumbling as an endless wave drags them back." He grew silent.

The road noise was enough to quiet my thoughts. I pictured myself in space, floating weightlessly. A smattering of stars began to appear. Soon, I was surrounded. The Earth was nowhere in sight. Streams of color flashed by like a smoldering haze moving sideways. The smoke transformed into clouds as I drifted above them. A breeze added to the effect. I slipped into the center of a billowy cloud and fell asleep. A thunderous knock woke me up.

"Fifteen minutes, Champ," Rory said.

The lights came on blindingly. Brixton adjusted them to a reasonable level.

"I fell asleep," he said. "Sorry about that. I was hoping we could fool around. Next time."

"I'm not complaining. That was a trip. What the hell?"

"Sensory deprivation. It's better than acid."

"I was flying, "I said.

Brixton leaned in close. I breathed him into my lungs and offered myself in return. With the lightest of touch, he caressed my upper lip with his mouth. I licked his lower lip. He bit mine playfully then presented the tip of his tongue. I swirled my tongue around his and then retreated, drawing him further into my mouth. Our bodies were intertwined as if we were rolling around in the surf. I didn't want the moment ever to end.

But it did have to end. With my bag packed, I relaxed in the chill room with Brixton, watching the Atlanta neighborhoods move past our window. A small mob of teenage girls swarmed the bus as we closed in on the arena gate. Brixton lowered the window halfway so he could brush the tips of the girls' outstretched fingers. I was inches away from them, hidden behind the tinted glass. Their screams followed each attempt at contact. Once inside the gate, he slid the window back in place.

"I dig you, Jackie. Last night was one of the best times I've had in years."

"Same here," I said, at a loss for words.

"Sorry to do this but there's a shit storm of fans around. I need you to hang back for a while."

"Not a problem," I said.

"I'll get someone to fetch you." He kissed me and headed for the door.

"Wait, do you have my ticket?"

"Oh crap, I do." He withdrew a folded piece of paper from his pocket.

I opened it up and saw that it was a plane ticket. "No, my concert ticket."

"Baby, you can't go to the show. You're my normal. My anchor."

I had been looking forward to seeing him perform again. As much as I tried, I couldn't stop the tears.

"I thought Dusty told you. Shit!"

Rory came bursting through the front. "Your family's coming this way."

"Fuck!"

"Come with me," Rory said, pulling me to the cab.

"Wait," Brixton said.

Christ, finally.

"Your bag."

I ducked into the driver's bathroom and quietly sobbed so no one would hear.

133

Silence

Brixton's next stop was New York. He was all over the news, but not in a good way. The first incident was a Twitter post that made its way to CNN. The Tweet was a picture of him surrounded by Hasidic Jews in full Sabbath garments. His caption was what caused all the outrage. He had written, "Look at me and the Jews." It was an innocent comment from a naive Alaskan boy, but people sure used it against him. Not even Dusty could calm the furor, and he's Jewish. But that was nothing like the trouble Brixton caused at the 9/11 Memorial. He was filmed at the edge of a fountain, laughing uncontrollably. This wasn't just any fountain. Brixton was caught laughing at the footprint of one of the fallen towers. The media latched on hard to that one. They were brutal.

A week had gone by with no contact. I was surprised that he hadn't called for emotional support. A sense of panic was creeping in. Had he heard me crying in the bathroom? Did my 'Marry me' joke linger in his mind? Was he having second thoughts? It took him a week to contact me the last time we hooked up, but that was different. We had just met.

My doubts were about to manifest into a horrific reality. Lidia and I were sitting on a large piece of driftwood on Alki Beach, staring at a picture in *Us* magazine. There, as big as life, was me at the picnic table with Brixton. It was one of those "Stars — they're just like us" pictures. From the angle, it appeared that the photo was snapped from inside the hamburger shack.

"So, Aunt Carol, how does it feel to be famous?"

I read the title: "Brixton sharing lunch with his Aunt Carol and two bodyguards." I was in more trouble than I thought. I bet his mom forbade him to see me. The tears began to flow.

"Oh, honey. It's all right," Lidia said. "It doesn't even look like you."

"We're through," I managed to say. "I was a secret."

I gathered my belongings and slouched back home, where I spent the next two days in bed.

As the weeks went by nothing could patch the hole in my heart. I felt like a shell of a person.

Not even Stephanie would return my email. I had screwed up enough times at work to learn to keep my emotions in check. I didn't call Brixton's handlers. I didn't send more emails. I didn't want to make things worse.

It was the beginning of another hollow day when my brother knocked on my bedroom door.

"Jackie, phone for you."

"I don't want to talk to anyone." I'd been ignoring Lidia and hadn't entertained the thought of playing volleyball with my team.

"I think it's that guy who drove us to the Spinnakers game."

I grabbed the phone from my nightstand. "Jimmy?" I said, trying to keep my cool.

"Hey, Jackie. Sorry for the silent treatment. We've had a stalking problem. I need to clear something up. Can you get on your computer for me?"

"Sure. What's this about?"

"Just, please, get me access."

Jimmy walked me through an app that gave him control of my mouse. He opened the settings icon and highlighted my IP Address.

"Do you mind if I go through your email?"

136

"Not at all. Let me log in." I took control and brought up Gmail. My email address was already populated in the login box. He stopped me while I was filling in my password.

"Do you have another email address?"

"That's it. Well, except for my Bellstrom email."

He arrowed over to my Internet history and selected a couple of specific days. I panicked, hoping they hadn't been times I was perving on photos of Brixton.

"There's no way it was her," he said to someone in his room. "She wasn't online at the time."

"Jackie, is there anyone else in your house who would be contacting Brixton?"

I lost it. Everything made sense now. "My fucking ex-husband lives downstairs. You met him when you picked us up for the game."

"Is he on your same Internet plan?"

"Yes."

Jimmy read off Dennis' email address.

"That's the prick."

"Jackie, your ex has been stalking him. It's nothing serious, but when we traced it to your house. Well, you can imagine our conclusion."

I was shaking with rage. "Fucking asshole! He's a dead man."

"Come on now. Pull yourself together. You can't mention this to him. No one can know that you're with Brixton."

That calmed me down slightly. "I need to go for a walk. Can you have him call me?"

"You bet. Everything will be fine," he assured me, then hung up.

I was overcome with anger and a colliding sense of relief. I headed outside toward the beach with thoughts of confrontation on my mind. In my fantasy, Dennis answered the door of his apartment and I slapped him as

137

hard as I could. The force was strong enough to knock his head against the doorframe.

"Crazy bitch," he said, rubbing his temple.

I stared him down. "I'll fucking kill you."

Dennis let out a high-pitched scream and slammed the door shut. He's lucky it was just a fantasy.

I walked along the shore away from the city, scanning the sand and pebbles for treasure. Red sea glass worn smooth by the tide caught my eye. I'd never found red. It was a sign.

I heard a Facebook IM notice ping on my phone. It was from Stephanie: "I am so sorry for not returning your email. I will never let you down again."

Hours later, an unfamiliar number popped up on my phone. I answered right away.

"What's up, Badness," Brixton said.

"Oh my God, it is good to hear your voice."

"I am so, so, so sorry. Please don't hate me."

"I don't hate you. It just hurts that you couldn't trust me."

"It was a huge misunderstanding. I'm just as pissed as you. I miss you so much."

"I miss you too. Why didn't you call? We could have straightened this out in a minute."

"Things seemed different than they were. It's all cool, baby. Want to come see me?"

"Of course I want to see you. When?"

"Tuesday. I'm going on a sailing trip in the BVI. My friend Cory will be held up in L.A. for a few days. You can take his place until he arrives. We can play that game where we're the coolest people in the world."

"I would love that." I had no idea where the BVI was but I didn't care.

"I need you to promise me something. It's still a boys' trip. Eli is being super cool about letting you come. I need you to swear that you won't stop us from doing anything stupid."

"Should I be scared?"

"Very. It's one of the only breaks we get."

"I can be a dude. Jennifer didn't name me 'Badness' for no reason."

"You represent well," he said. "Keep in mind this is two, three days, max. When Cory arrives, you have to get right on his seaplane. No fighting it. No tears."

"No problem. I just want to see you."

"Me, too. In the meantime, why don't you step outside?"

"Are you here?" I said ecstatically and headed for the door.

"I wish. No, I bought you something to make things right."

In my driveway was a dark blue convertible BMW Z4 with a large white bow on the trunk.

"Brixton, this is too much."

"Nonsense. What is too much is the hell you and I had to go through the last few weeks."

"I don't know what to say."

"You don't need to say anything. It's all good. Especially the color. They call it deep-sea blue metallic. How perfect is that for the beach?"

"It's beautiful."

"I want you to know I didn't skimp on anything. Everything in that car is top-of-the-line. Well, except the engine—that's stock. I don't want you killing yourself. I really like you."

My knees gave way. I leaned on my new car for support. "I like you too, Brixton."

"Stephanie will call to arrange your flights. I'll see you in a week."

"Can't wait."

A man in a BMW jacket stepped out of a parked 740i sedan. "Hello, I'm Jordon. Are you Jackie Notter?"

"That would be me," I replied.

"Fantastic." He produced a stack of papers from a manila folder. "This shouldn't take long. I need you to sign here, here and here."

I completed the paperwork and he handed me the keys, followed by a cashier's check.

"That should more than cover the taxes." The check was for $10,000.

My head was spinning. It was all too much. "I hope I can afford the insurance."

"If you don't mind my asking, it depends on how old you are."

"I'm thirty."

"No problem. It'll be about $140 a month if you don't have any priors."

"Really?"

"They say twenty-five is the age when the price of insurance drops but it's thirty. I'm surprised your rates haven't lowered already."

"They may have. I don't pay too much attention to that stuff. Thanks again."

"My pleasure," he said. "Let me show you a few of the features. First off, you have a keyless entry. Touch the door here."

The car unlocked like magic.

"The ignition is the same way. You can keep the key in your purse. As long as you're in proximity, you can unlock it and start her up."

I lowered myself into the driver's seat. The dashboard was space-age-modern. Tears of happiness ran down my face. I had been thinking of ditching my car this summer. Even with the bump in insurance, not having a car payment would save me a couple hundred a month. It was like getting a raise. This was the sweetest thing anyone had ever done for me.

I played with the buttons that controlled my seat. Different sections lifted, moved, or inflated until I had it all out of whack. Jordon helped me get it right. He even set it so a single button brought everything back to my position.

I was glad to see that it was an automatic. The car purred when I turned the engine over. I loved the sound: deep and throaty.

Jordon waved goodbye and was off. I was startled by a knock at the window. It was my brother.

"What is this?" Randy asked.

"Someone likes me," I grinned.

"I can see that. Let's go for a ride." I knew he wouldn't ask questions. That's not his M.O.

"After you wash that grease off your fingers."

Randy hated it when I told him to wash his hands. I didn't care. Who would want those greasy fingers all over their new dash?

He returned cleaner but not as much as I would have liked. I relented and let him into the passenger seat. Randy played with the stereo and stumbled onto the navigation feature. "No more excuses for being late," he said.

For having a stock engine the car was plenty fast. The ribbon flew off when I peeled out of my driveway. I felt like a teenager with my first car. Still, I couldn't get past my anger toward my ex.

"I want Dennis out of the house!" I told my brother.

"I know you do, Jacks, but we can't afford it."

"We could rent out his apartment."

"Not for the amount he's paying," Randy said. "What's he done this time? I can have a word with him."

"You can't talk to Dennis."

"You're scaring me. What did he do?"

I wanted to tell him about Brixton but I couldn't. "Nothing. He just scares me. I don't think he's stable."

"What? He's a pussy-cat."

"I can't move on with him around."

"That, I can understand. I'll see what I can do. The housing market is going crazy right now. We're close to refinancing. Maybe we can buy him out."

"That would be wonderful."

"In the meantime, I'll make sure you get Dennis' spot in the garage."

"Thanks, this car wouldn't last a week on the street."

"Best car gets the garage. That's the rule. It's a sweet ride. Can I drive?"

"In a bit."

The first thing I did after returning home was Google BVI. I was ecstatic to see Brixton was taking me to the British Virgin Islands. Luckily, Dennis talked me into going to the Olympics when it was in Canada. I'd be screwed if I hadn't ordered a passport for the trip. I guess the bastard was good for something. All I needed was the perfect swimsuit.

Dennis

The sun shining in Seattle is a wondrous rarity. Lidia took full advantage of the warm day with a trip to my beach. Her six-year-old daughter, Ellie, was in the backseat looking adorable in her pigtails and terrycloth clam diggers.

My weekend with them had been pure bliss. I'm not ready to have children, but Ellie had revved up my biological clock. I could spend hours with that kid. Her innocence, honesty, and enthusiasm warms my heart.

I should have waited until I was home to check my messages but I hadn't looked all day.

"Are we boring you?" Lidia asked.

"Of course not. I just want to make sure everything is copacetic for my trip tomorrow."

"Whatever, Ms. World Traveler."

"Oh, shit! My phone's off."

"Swearing," Ellie said from the back seat.

Lidia held out her hand and I dug in my wallet for a quarter. I couldn't find any so I snagged one from the stack in the console.

It took a minute on the charger for my phone to power up. There were four messages from my brother, which scared me to no end. I played the last one first.

"Where the hell are you, Jackie?" Randy said. "You need to get down here."

My heart was racing. I clicked back to his first message.

"Jackie, meet me at Harborview. Dennis was jumped. Call me."

"Good Lord," I said. "Dennis had the shit kicked out of him."

"Swearing."

143

"Not now," Lidia said to Ellie. She took a moment to respond. "What happened?"

"All I know is he's at Harborview."

"Shit."

"Swearing," Ellie said louder. Lidia dropped two quarters into the swear bag.

"Do we have time to stop for smokes?" she asked.

"Sure," I said, spacing out the window. Was Dennis going to screw up my trip? I almost felt guilty for having such a selfish thought. I called Randy's cell but it went straight to voicemail.

Lidia turned into the 7-11 on Admiral Way. I unbuckled Ellie from her car seat and we all went inside. Ellie led me to the candy aisle, skipping along happily. She was allowed one item. Her choice was a bag of peanut M&Ms. We met up with her mom at the front counter.

"I'm really into 7-11 speed," Lidia said, scanning the selection of energy and diet pills. "It's the poor man's cocaine." She grabbed a packet of pills and pointed out her smokes to the clerk.

"How do you say thank you?" Lidia asked the man as she entered the PIN for her debit card.

The clerk looked at her with a queer expression. "Thank you?" he said, confused.

"No, how do you say it in your language? Oh, I know, *gracias.*"

"It's *dhanyabad,*" the man said, irritated. "I'm from Nepal."

I gave Lidia a horrified look of embarrassment. Ellie laughed so hysterically we had to leave the store. Once out of earshot the three of us cracked up the entire way home.

We sat in my driveway for a few minutes, composing ourselves. Lidia followed me to the back of the car to retrieve my bag.

"Do you want me to drive you to the hospital?" she asked.

"No, I'll be fine."

"OK, but call if you need help with Dennis, I'll take care of things."

"Thank you so much, and for the weekend. I had a wonderful time."

"It's always a pleasure."

"Bye, Auntie Jackie," Ellie said and raised her arms to be picked up for a hug. I gave her a squeeze and kissed her forehead.

"I love you, Ellie."

"I love you, too."

Dennis' apartment was dark. I headed upstairs, hoping Randy was home. The door to my room was shut, which was unusual. I stopped dead in my tracks when I saw a figure in my bed. The body stirred and Dennis propped himself up on the pillow. He had a splint taped to his nose and black and purple shiners underneath both eyes.

"What the hell are you doing in my bed?" I snapped. Years of anger flooded to the surface. I couldn't stand Dennis invading my personal space. His recent stalking of Brixton only added to my hostility.

"Please, Jackie," he sobbed. "I need you."

Hearing that felt like an added twist of the knife. "I needed you in our marriage!"

"I turned out to be gay."

"You were always gay! And besides, that's no excuse for being an asshole."

He began to whimper.

"Come on, Jacks," my brother said from the doorway.

"You know what, fuck it. I'll go," I said.

"Jackie," my brother pleaded.

"No, it's for the best. I can stay with Lidia for the week. I'm sorry, Dennis. I shouldn't have reacted like I did."

"Please don't go," he pleaded.

"I have to." I reached into my closet and produced the Gucci carry-on Brixton sent me. I must have packed a dozen times since my man called. The only thing left to add were my toiletries. Dennis watched me the entire time, looking like a sad puppy.

I sat down on my bed before heading out. "I'm sorry you were jumped. Are you going to be all right?"

"I think so. It's been horrible, Jackie. Why would someone do this to me? I was just walking along the beach. It's not like I was prancing around in *short* shorts."

"It's not your fault, Dennis."

"That means a lot. Thank you."

I hadn't heard gratitude from him in a long time. I leaned in and gave him a hug. He winced when I touched his side.

In the hallway, Randy silently pleaded for me to stay, but I shook my head and left the house. Once outside, I sent him a text. "Call his mother."

BVI

Brixton hooked me up with a massive ocean-view suite at the San Juan Ritz-Carlton in Puerto Rico. I'd arrived late the night before, so I didn't have time to enjoy my room. When I woke up, I headed to the hotel gift shop to buy the fabulous sunhat I had spotted in the window. The last-minute purchase made me late for my flight. Not that it mattered—my noon reservation was with a private charter.

I stepped into the warm Puerto Rican sun, where a limo was waiting for me. Within five minutes I was at a marina.

"Is Brixton picking me up?" I asked the driver.

"Brixton Webber?" the man exclaimed with a thick Cuban accent.

Oh shit. He wasn't part of his staff. "I wish. No, I'm here to meet my brother."

"All I know is I was supposed to drive you to this marina. And that, madam, is what I have done."

"Well then, thank you for the ride," I replied.

The driver sent me on my way, refusing to accept a tip. He assured me that everything was taken care of. I removed my hat so I could take in the tropical surroundings. The buildings were painted in soft pastels with matching terracotta roofs. Palm trees towered from above. The marina had four long docks filled with every boat imaginable. I tried to spot Brixton's sailboat but didn't see one that matched his style.

A handsome Latino gentleman walked out of the main office to greet me. He had short, choppy black hair and a couple days stubble. From the look of him, I'd say Ricky Martin was missing a brother. The man was that beautiful.

"Good morning, Jackie. I'm Carlos. I'll be your pilot today."

"It's a pleasure to meet you," I said.

"We're ready to go if you are."

"Let's do it," I said.

Carlos led me to a seaplane tied to the end of the dock. I'd lived my whole life in Washington State surrounded by water and not once had I flown in a seaplane. This was a fantastic surprise.

I entered the plane and chose a seat in the first row, behind Carlos. He looked disappointed.

"Jackie, please. Come be my co-pilot."

"Really?"

"I insist. I'd give you a captain's hat, but I don't want to mess up your beautiful hair."

"Aren't you the charmer," I said, flirting back.

The takeoff was strange. It didn't feel like we were going fast enough but the plane lifted out of the water and we were off to the BVI.

"Would you mind taking the wheel?" Carlos asked after we leveled off. "I smell that the coffee is ready."

"Sure," I said, not entirely comprehending what he was asking.

"Pull back to climb and push forward to descend. I'll be right behind you." Without further instruction, Carlos left the cockpit. What the hell?

I reached out, pushing the wheel in a panic and we plummeted. It took a few harrowing seconds before I steadied her off. Carlos' laughter could be heard over the hum of the engine.

"Cream and sugar for me," I yelled back at him.

Carlos spent the first part of our trip teaching me how *not* to be afraid of flying. I had wanted to take a Xanax, but he convinced me I wouldn't need it. He walked me through the scary bumps and noises, explaining each sound in detail. What put me at ease was learning that no matter how far you drop during turbulence you're still flying.

"Can we cruise lower?" I asked. The brilliant sapphire blue water was calling me.

"No problem," he said. "Why don't you begin the descent."

I held the wheel firmly and gradually pushed forward. When we were getting too low, I pulled back, but the wheel was locked.

"I have you," Carlos assured me. "Keep going."

We were flying so low the pontoons were practically skimming the ocean. It was exhilarating.

The radio crackled and an urgent voice broke through. "This is the United States Coast Guard. To the seaplane flying along the waterline, please identify yourself. Over."

"Oh shit," Carlos muttered. "This is Captain Rivera. I apologize for flying so low. My passenger thought she spotted a whale. We'll ascend to our cruising altitude. Over."

"Copy that. What's your destination? Over."

Carlos motioned for me to bring the plane up. The Coast Guard had us in their sites and he was still letting me fly.

"Tortola Customs. I'm flying in Brixton Webber's guest. Over."

"Proceed. Out."

BVI Customs was a breeze with Carlos at my side. The agent, Manny, was his little brother. He didn't even ask my destination.

We were back in the air, circling the largest catamaran I had ever seen. Our landing was unexpectedly smooth. I thought it would be rougher being in the open water. Brixton stepped onto the side of his catamaran to ready the lines. He was shirtless, wearing only a pair of turquoise shorts. His hair was a tousled mess. The beginning of a tan adorned his chiseled upper body. I was home.

Carlos cut the engine and lowered himself onto the plane's pontoon to catch the line. He had timed the drift perfectly. We came to a slow stop against the bumpers of Brixton's boat. I hugged Carlos before boarding the catamaran.

"Thank you so much. It was quite the flight."

"That was all you, Jackie." He turned to Brixton. "Don't fuck this one up. She's a keeper."

"I know," Brixton said and helped me up the steps to an outdoor table with wraparound seats. We were making out before Carlos cleared the water. I couldn't stop playing with the sparse patch of beard on his chin. It was adorable. The big gold chain he was wearing, not so much.

"Let me show you to our cabin," he said, retrieving my bag.

The living area of the catamaran was enormous. Across from the sliding glass door was a large dining room table, and to the right, a beautiful kitchen.

I was taking in my surroundings when a man with an English accent called out from a side doorway. "What's the holdup, mate? Come back to bed. My toger's no longer a stiffy." Eli Strut, from the English boy band FreakOn walked in stark naked. I froze.

"Damn it, Eli. This isn't funny. Her ex-husband is gay."

Eli fell to the ground in hysterics. His naked body wasn't as muscular as Brixton's but it was well defined. He had a collection of black tattoos on his torso. They seemed to be placed randomly without much forethought. My gaze lingered longer than it should have on his huge member. It was flaccid but still quite an eyeful. Brixton maneuvered me around him.

"Come on, Brixton," Eli said. "I was just kidding."

"I know, Eli."

Brixton and I had the right-side hull to ourselves. The bedroom was in the back, and at the pointy end there was a bathroom with a full shower.

"Can you give us five?" Brixton hollered.

"Abso-bloody-lutely," Eli said. I heard the sliding door to the back deck close.

Brixton set my travel bag on the leather couch. "Let's get you in a swimsuit."

I unzipped my bag and retrieved the two bikinis I'd bought for the trip. He started kissing and undressing me simultaneously. I was soon naked. My man looked me over hungrily.

"I missed you," he said.

"I've been counting the days," I admitted.

He placed a hand under my chin and brought my mouth to his. We kissed longingly as he inserted a finger inside me. My swollen vulva was enlarged like a blossoming orchid. I moaned as the passion in his kiss became all-encompassing.

"We have to stop," Brixton said. "I can't make Eli a third wheel. We can fool around tonight."

"I'm not sure I can wait," I pleaded.

"We have to," he said.

He zeroed in on the bikinis and picked the one I thought would be his second favorite: a coral bandeau top with a matching low-rise bottom.

Once dressed, Brixton took my hand and led me to the back deck. Eli was sitting at the table wearing board shorts and a black headscarf that tucked his hair back.

"Sorry about that, love," Eli said. "I was just fooling around." His slow, comforting way of speaking drew me in like a warm embrace. Not to mention he was exceptionally gorgeous. I could see why his fans loved him so much.

"It was a nice welcome," I said. "I'm Jackie."

"Eli," he said, extending his hand. "Everything I've heard about you is true. You're quite lovely, my dear."

151

"Thank you," I said, blushing slightly.

"Time's a-wasting," Brixton said, "let's get the sail up."

"Where's the captain?" I asked.

"I'll get him," Eli said and raced to the main cabin.

"Please don't," Brixton said.

Eli returned with a captain's hat and placed it on Brixton's head. He looked regal with it on.

"*You're* the captain?" I asked.

"At your service." He removed the hat as he bowed. It ended up on my head. Brixton climbed the steps to the cockpit and took control. He motioned for Eli and me to join him. With a turn of a key the engines rumbled to life and we were off.

"So, how much do you know about sailing?" he asked.

"Not much."

"Really?"

"Sadly, yes," I said.

"What the hell, woman?" Eli said. "I've been to Seattle. You have so many lakes. And the Puget Sound."

"My family is more into powerboats," I said.

"Well, sailing can be dangerous," Brixton said. "If I shout, it's to protect you from losing a finger. I'm not yelling at you. I will never yell at you, I promise."

"Much appreciated," I said.

"Let's do this," Brixton said. "Eli, loosen the main downhaul line." Brixton handed me a black rope. "I want *you* to raise the sail."

I looked at him like he was crazy.

"You'll be fine. Wrap the line around the winch three times clockwise."

I followed his instructions easily.

"Now press the button at your feet, keeping the line tight as you haul it in."

I pressed the foot pedal and the sail began to rise toward the sky. "No way, this is exciting."

"Watch your line, Eli," Brixton commanded. He wrapped one arm around my waist and held me close — his eyes never leaving the sail. I stopped when I thought it was up but he had me go another couple feet.

Brixton turned us into the wind until the sail was full. I was expecting the boat to lean but apparently large catamarans don't do that. He shut off the engines and the low rumble morphed into silence. We picked up speed until we were flying across the water.

The dramatic opening of "Sail Away" by Enya began to play. Brixton cranked the volume and he and Eli belted out the chorus.

I was overcome with emotions. Something about being propelled by the wind, in such a gorgeous setting, made me tear up. This was what life should be like.

"I cried the first time the sails went up too," Brixton whispered.

"This is the only place where I have absolute freedom," Eli said, putting an arm around Brixton. "I love you, man."

"I love you too, buddy."

Brixton leaned back in the captain's chair. He looked relaxed and at peace — like there was no place he would rather be. There's something about a man at the helm of a ship.

We'd been cruising for an hour when Brixton had Eli drop the sail.

"That group of mammoth rocks in front of us are The Indians," Brixton said.

"The snorkeling here is brilliant," Eli added.

"Why don't you give Eli a hand with the buoy?"

"Come on, love," Eli said, "I'll show you how."

I followed him up the side of the boat past a line of scuba tanks. We stepped onto the trampoline mesh at the front between the two hulls. Eli took my hands and we jumped up and down like free-range children.

"Do you fancy cooking shows?" he asked.

"Love 'em. *Chopped* is awesome but my favorite is…"

"*Top Chef*," Eli and I said simultaneously.

"Come on, guys," Brixton interrupted. "Get ready."

Eli saluted him. "Tying up a catamaran is different than a sailboat," he said. "We have to tether a bridle line from each hull to the buoy or the boat will hydroplane."

"Bridle line, like on a horse?" I asked.

"Exactly." He flipped open a compartment behind us and retrieved a boat hook. "Grab the line on the left and bring it over the railing."

We stood on the mesh as The Indians grew closer.

"It's getting shallow," I yelled back to Brixton.

"I would be careful when questioning the captain," Eli said. "He knows these snorkeling waters like the back of his hand."

"I'm sorry," I said.

"It's all good, as you Yanks say."

There were five boats tied up at The Indians. Eli pointed with the boat hook to an open buoy, guiding Brixton in. He leaned over the railing and snagged the ring at the top of the buoy as it passed under us. Eli then slipped his line through the ring and I did the same. We tied our lines and were done. I couldn't believe how easy the whole process was.

"You're awesome," Brixton shouted to me. I felt myself blush but couldn't disagree.

I was heading to the back of the boat when I noticed a large cabin cruiser descending upon us. I was about to yell that no buoys were available but spotted Jimmy at the helm. His angry eyebrows looked hilarious, especially with the sunburn on top of his head.

"Hi Jackie," he yelled, waving.

I waved back, grinning.

The boys secured Jimmy's boat to ours and I rushed aboard to give him a bear hug.

"Thank you for clearing my name," I whispered. "You're my hero."

"You have no idea," he said.

What did he mean by that? Was he talking about Dusty? Was that shithead still out to get me? For my sanity I let it go.

"I'm glad you were there for me," I said and gave him a peck on the cheek.

"Danny, can you come over here a minute?"

A thin gentleman my age made his way across the deck. His meticulously trimmed beard and perfect mani/pedi shattered any doubts about his sexual orientation.

"I want you to meet my boyfriend, Danny."

"Jimmy," I gushed. "You scamp."

"It's nice to finally meet you," Danny said.

"I'd say likewise but I had zero idea Jimmy was gay. Not a clue."

"In my line of work you have to fly under the radar," Jimmy said.

"I completely understand."

"I have a big favor to ask. Can you do me a solid, Jackie?"

"Of course. Anything."

He lowered his voice. "This trip is a nightmare for security. Spider and Strut get *way* out of control. Can you be their voice of reason?"

"I would, Jimmy, but Brixton already made me promise that I wouldn't."

"Shit. Maybe a little?" he pleaded.

"I'll try."

"Any help would be appreciated."

"It was a pleasure," I said to Danny, as I stepped over the railing to the catamaran.

Brixton was at the back of the boat, rummaging through a compartment under the wide lounge seat. "I bought you a pair of flippers and a mask," he said, holding them up. They were black with neon-pink accents.

"Love 'em," I said, with no intention of ever putting them on. "I don't mind if you guys want to go scuba diving," I said, hoping to sidestep my fish phobia.

"No way. I want to snorkel with you," Brixton said. "Besides, we're waiting for Cory before diving to a pirate shipwreck."

"Cool," I said, inwardly panicked.

"Yeah, cool until we spot a reef shark," Eli said, taunting Brixton. I guess my man was afraid of something after all.

"Let's get your bling off," Brixton said, ignoring him. "We don't want to attract barracudas." He looked me over. "You're not wearing any jewelry."

"Nope."

Brixton removed his obnoxious gold chain and placed it on the table.

"Look at that. He *is* white," Eli said. "I've never seen someone so pale trying so hard to be black."

"What are you talking about—trying?"

"Alright, Tupac," I said. "Hang on a sec while I take off my mascara."

If I had an inkling that I would be going in the water, I would have worn waterproof makeup. Oh well. While below deck I popped a Xanax to help cope with the fish.

I returned fresh-faced but felt vulnerable with no makeup.

Eli gave a wide, toothy grin and began fawning over me. "I love a girl who doesn't need makeup. You, Jackie, are a natural beauty."

"Hey, dial it down, Romeo," Brixton said, clearly jealous.

"That hurts. I would never steal Jackie from you. However, I might steal you away from her." With that, he gave Brixton a peck right on the lips.

Brixton's face turned beet red. "Don't worry. Eli's purpose in life is to embarrass me."

"I'm just an attention whore," Eli said.

"A chef in the kitchen and an attention whore in the bedroom," I said.

"It's like you know me. "Why don't the two of you snorkel together? I'll go with the poofs." He grabbed his gear and headed to Jimmy's boat.

Brixton led me to the swim deck and sat down with his feet in the water. "There can be a bit of a current," he said. "Don't panic if you get caught in it. Just swim sideways. Even if the tide drags us out they'll come get us. I guarantee we won't be out of sight."

"Are there really sharks and barracudas?" I asked as I hesitantly slipped my feet into the water. My fear of fish had shifted into overdrive.

"I've only seen one shark. But there are barracudas. They look scary but for the most part they're harmless. If you see one, just back away slowly. Speaking of scary, how is your ex doing after getting jumped?"

"I never mentioned what happened to Dennis." I rose to my feet, backing away from him. "Did you have him beat up?"

"Jackie! I would never do anything like that. I read about the attack in the West Seattle Blog."

I found that suspicious. I couldn't imagine Dennis approving something so personal. Especially since he still hadn't told his mom that he was gay. But I didn't want to ruin the trip so I conceded. "I'm sorry. That was a shitty accusation. It was just so out of the fucking blue."

"It's all good," Brixton said, motioning for me to sit back down. He washed my mask in the seawater and spat on the lens as a defogger. "I should let you know, Eli hates the f-word. Especially when women say it."

"That's good to know. I like him. You have a great friend there."

"He's my best friend," he said. "We're the same height."

He slid his mask over his face and I followed him into the sea. The water was surprisingly warm and crystal clear. I could see all the way to The Indians. But that meant the fish were also visible, and there were hundreds. I started breathing heavily, almost to the point of hyperventilating. Brixton noticed and came to my rescue, guiding me to the surface.

"You need to slow your breathing. Think of it as meditating. Relax your body and concentrate on inhaling and exhaling slowly."

I reluctantly submerged my head and tried to relax, but there were too many fish. That's when I noticed the coral. It was amazing. Not brightly colored like you see in the stores, but gigantic. There was brain coral the size of an ottoman, and finger coral that must have been six feet wide and reached majestically toward the surface. The visual distractions were so plenteous I almost forgot about my phobia.

As we made our way around the first rock, I felt better about the fish. I relaxed my arms and let them float freely behind while kicking with my fins. Brixton and I were drifting along when a massive school of long, thin, fluorescent green fish rushed toward us. There must have been a thousand fish surrounding my body. I wanted to come up for air but would have freaked out more with fish swimming blindly around me. Brixton laced his fingers through mine and my fear dissipated. We tooled around, hand in hand, in absolute serenity. I felt like a mermaid in love.

The current at the far end of The Indians grew stronger, making it strenuous to maneuver around the last rock. We were exhausted when we reached the back steps.

Brixton handed me the built-in showerhead. "There's no need to shampoo your hair when you're sailing," he said. "The sea salt is all the product you need. You'll love the freedom."

"I already am," I said.

After a quick rinse, I toweled off inside the galley's sliding door. "I really appreciate the invite," I said, but Brixton couldn't hear. He was soaking his head.

I was hanging out in the kitchen when Brixton appeared in the doorway with a towel wrapped around his waist. He stepped onto the wet floor, and his feet slipped from under him. His head hit the doorstep with a mighty thump.

"What the fuck?" he screamed at me. "You wipe up your water."

I was in shock and stared at him, dumbfounded.

"I didn't mean it, baby."

"Two hours ago you said you'd never yell at me," I cried. "What the fuck, indeed?"

"That was the captain in me yelling," he said, trying poorly to justify it. "Do you know what would happen if I had to cancel my tour?"

"I'm sorry. Next time I'll be more careful."

"No, I apologize," he said, getting up. "I should have had you dry off on the deck where it doesn't get slick." He found a towel in the kitchen and wiped the floor.

"Come with me," I said. "I'll make you forget about your pain."

"Nice," he said, rubbing his head.

I sat on the couch in the bedroom with Brixton standing in front of me, his towel still wrapped around his waist. With a flick of my wrist the towel dropped to the floor. His magnificent cock arose tall and eager. I grabbed hold and looked up at him. The perspective was enticing— his member in my face and Brixton gazing down at me with anticipation.

I had just taken him into my mouth when the swim-deck shower turned on. Eli was back on the boat.

159

"Better make it quick," Brixton said.

"You asked for it."

I vigorously pumped his shaft back and forth in a spiral motion while simultaneously sucking on the head. I was like a wildling attacking her prey. He lasted barely a minute before groaning and exploding in my mouth.

I slapped his butt playfully and handed him a pair of shorts from the bed. "Sorry about hurting your noggin," I said.

"Let's call it a draw for what I did to your ex."

"That's not funny," I said, tensing up.

"I was just joking, baby."

"Maybe you didn't do it but one of your handlers?"

"Really? Come on."

We reemerged outside to find Eli drying off by the party table. He glanced at Brixton and snickered. "That was fast."

How the hell did he know? I looked over. The window above our bed was open.

"It was all her," Brixton said, smiling at me.

"Nothing like a nice gobbie in the afternoon," Eli said.

Brixton laughed. "That's Cory's word. He has the best Australian names for things—like brekki for breakfast."

"Chockie," Eli said, pointing at a candy bar.

"I heard the Australian accent comes from their settlers being drunk all the time," Brixton said.

"That explains rather a lot," Eli responded.

"Wait, are you talking about Cory Sinclair?" I asked.

"That's our boy," Brixton said.

"Cory almost had to skip the whole trip but he was eliminated from *Star Dancers* last week," Eli said.

"He didn't take a dive for us, did he?" Brixton asked, shocked.

"Not Cory," Eli said. "I thought he was going home with the trophy. He was probably too young for the old codgers."

"How old is he?"

"Seventeen," they both said.

"Wow, he looks older."

"He's actually the most mature of the three of us," Eli said.

"That's saying a lot," Brixton added. "When Eli was 17 he dated a 32-year-old."

"Yeah, Caroline received so many death threats it ended up destroying our relationship," Eli said. "You're wise to keep your affair a secret."

As if I had a choice.

"It's for the best," Brixton said.

"Easy for you to say," I replied.

Treasure Island

Brixton started the engines and brought us into Bight Bay. The harbor was packed with sailboats, catamarans and cruisers. Aside from the restaurant at the end of the bay, there wasn't a structure in sight. The hilly landscape consisted of rocks and bushes. Jimmy chose two outer buoys on the far right. Being on the very end added a protective barrier for our boat.

"Welcome to Treasure Island," Eli said after we tied up.

I was confused. The name was different on Brixton's map. "I thought this was Norman Island."

"Technically. But this is the island that inspired Robert Stevenson to write Treasure Island — the story of Long John Silver. Real pirates used to hide their booty here. That's Willy T's pirate ship over yonder. We're partying there tonight."

"Jimmy's going to let Brixton party?"

"Not much he can say. The drinking age in the BVI is eighteen. They're making a VIP area for us on the upper deck, and I believe our own rum bar."

"I'm more of a cosmo girl," I said.

"Not down here, sweetheart. It's all rum. Speaking of which, I think I'll have one."

Brixton was already in the galley setting up the bar.

"Pusser's?" I said, reading the name on a bottle.

"It's the only rum to use for a painkiller," he said.

"The drink of the Virgin Islands," Eli added. He handed me a metal cup that read "Pusser's Marina Cay Painkiller's Club," with the ingredients listed on the back: rum, pineapple juice, cream of coconut, orange juice and ground nutmeg. It sounded dangerously delicious.

Brixton whipped up three painkillers with a flourish. He'd made them before.

"Drink up, me hearties," he toasted, with an exaggerated pirate swing to his raised arm.

The cocktail was delicious, unlike anything I had tasted. "This is wonderful."

From the corner of my eye, I caught the intimidating figure of an enormous black man in a life jacket climbing up the back stairs. Water was dripping off his towering frame.

"S'up, Tyrone?" Eli said.

"Living the life, sir," he responded. It was odd hearing a British accent from such a hulk of a man.

"This is Jackie, Brixton's girlfriend," Eli said.

I tried hard to contain my enthusiasm. It was the first time I was referred to as his girlfriend. All the same, I didn't want him to get freaked out so I said, "Whoa, slow it down there. I thought we're just fuck buddies." I winced, remembering Eli hates the f-word.

Brixton stared at me; his eyebrows raised in surprise. "You're the coolest girl I've ever met."

"It's a pleasure," Tyrone said and wrapped his gigantic hand around mine. His shake was soft and gentle. "Have you thought about what you would like for supper? Jimmy said there are too many young blokes at Pirates Bight for it to be safe. You can dine here or on Willy T's."

"Are you *mad*?" Eli said. "You can't sneak onto a pirate ship in broad daylight. Don't worry about dinner. I'm making burgers after I ring my Mum."

"Thanks, mate. I'll get out of your hair then. Jackie."

"Tyrone."

Eli found his cell phone and relaxed out on the back deck.

"Eli calls his mother every day," Brixton said. "He's a total mama's boy."

"That is the sweetest thing I've ever heard."

164

"He'll be on the line for at least a half-hour. Let's go make out."

Let's go make out. It was so high school. But then again, I did want to kiss my man.

Our tongue wrestling left me weak in the knees. He is such a creative-romantic. We could just be holding hands and he'd figure out a way to make it exciting. I was falling hard for him.

Brixton was on top of me in our bed. He eased off, holding himself up by his arms. "I need a refill. How about you?" he asked.

"Yes, please." I wanted more of our alone time but reluctantly followed him to the kitchen.

Eli had moved to the salon and was stretched out on the wraparound seating of the dining room table. "I have to go, Mum. I love you."

"Do you mind if I tour your side of the boat?" I asked after he hung up.

"Not at all."

"Make mine a rum and diet coke," I said to Brixton. "Single shot."

"Don't you like the painkillers?"

"A little too much."

Unlike ours, the other hull had a bedroom on each end with a bathroom and laundry room between them. Eli, being a true gentleman, picked the smaller bedroom in the front. The color scheme was the same nautical blue and white as ours.

"How large is this boat?" I asked as I joined the boys in the galley.

"She's a 46-footer," Brixton responded.

"That's huge. Doesn't it scare you to drive it?"

"Not at all. Serenity handles like a breeze."

I'd noticed the charter company's paperwork sitting on the navigation table earlier. "They must have required a hell of a deposit to charter this. I couldn't rent a car until I was twenty-five."

"Funny that you say that," Brixton grinned. "Last year was the first time we went out alone. They refused to let me have a boat because I was too young. Pissed me off so bad I bought Serenity to add to their fleet. I'm about to close on purchasing their charter company."

"Why not just go somewhere else?" I asked.

"I don't like to lose."

"That's healthy," I said, rolling my eyes. Brixton laughed.

Eli had moved to the back and was tending to the barbeque. "Can you fix me another painkiller?" he asked.

"Of course, my friend," Brixton said.

"Thanks, mate."

"Hey Jackie, would you give these to Eli." He handed me a stack of hamburger patties.

"Is there bacon and cheese inside these?" I asked.

"Totally. Eli makes the best burgers."

"I can't wait."

"Eli," I said, stepping onto the back deck, "I have your patties."

"Can you set them on the table? I can't get this bloody thing lit."

Brixton opened a compartment below the seating for the outdoor table. He gave Eli a knowing look as he flipped a lever next to the propane tanks.

"Bugger, I forgot about the shutoff valve." Eli gave his friend a playful squeeze to his waist.

Brixton balled up a sheet of tinfoil from the table and threw it at Eli, accidentally hitting him in the nuts.

"Tell them…" Eli said, falling over dramatically like he was dying, "that it was his ball that hit me."

With the veggies and condiments prepped and the patties cooking, Eli took a moment to relax with us at the party table.

"Did you happen to see that bullshit video of me laughing at the 9/11 memorial?" Brixton said.

"How could I not?" I replied. "You were all over the news. What the hell happened?"

"Trey Morris happened. He kept whispering the funniest things in my ear. The man meant no disrespect to the 9/11 victims. It's just impossible for him not to be funny."

"I didn't hear anything about that in the news," I said. "It was all just attack, attack, attack."

"And you won't hear the truth; the media hates me. Trey did everything he could to get through to them. But they already had their story."

Eli looked at him earnestly. "You have to stop feeding the media's narrative. You think you can beat them but you can't. If I were you I'd focus on keeping a positive face. That's all I do."

"Easy for you to say. You're the *new* thing," Brixton responded. "They'll turn on you too."

"I know, man," Eli said. "You don't deserve it, though." He excused himself to go to the loo.

Brixton took over the cooking duty as soon as Eli was out of sight. I wanted to tell him that was a bad idea. You never mess with another man's grill.

Eli returned with a spring in his step but stopped abruptly. "Don't you dare press down on that patty," he said, scolding Brixton. "Get out of my kitchen."

"Whatever, Chef Ramsay."

"Why would you want to squeeze the flavor out?" Eli said, yanking the spatula out of his hand. "You know how tasty these are."

"Sorry, I'm getting buzzed."

"It's all good, my friend."

"Want to know who helped the most during my 9/11 media storm?" Brixton said.

"Who?" I asked, wishing it had been me.

"Carrot Top."

"Carrot Top?" I laughed.

"Yeah," Brixton said. "He called out of the blue. Turns out Scott is a hell of a nice guy. He explained how he handles all the negativity that gets thrown his way. Walked me through a couple of things I could do to get through it."

"How do you even know who Carrot Top is?" I asked.

They both said in unison, "Family Guy."

"God bless cartoons," I said and made a mental note to talk about Family Guy if we ever run out of things to say. It was bound to happen with an 11-year age difference.

"Screw the media, straight up their bloody arses," Eli said. "Speaking of arses, you should get your buns ready."

I had a feeling we were in for a solid night of partying. As a peace offering to my body, I put a lot of veggies on my burger.

I took a hungry bite and the flavors of bacon and sharp cheddar danced across my taste buds. "You weren't kidding—this is the best burger I've ever had."

"I can't take all the credit," Eli said. "Danny found a bakery yesterday. Those are his buns." We all looked at each other and giggled.

I was nearly finished with my burger when a little burp from the Coke snuck out of my mouth. "Pardon me," I said.

That sent Eli over the edge. I didn't understand what was so funny but his laughter was infectious.

"In England we say *excuse me* after a burp. *Pardon me* is for a toot." We all broke into hysterics.

Brixton was leaning back, laughing skyward when something up front caught his eye. He stared, transfixed.

"Come with me," he said as he climbed along the side of the boat. I rounded the corner and was struck by the rays of God shooting downward from the clouds.

He sat on the trampoline deck and I took a place at his side. Eli soon joined us, sitting on the other side of his friend.

The magic started after the sun slipped below the horizon. A pinkish-red hue filled the evening sky. The sunset was perfectly framed in the mouth of the bay, offering a magnificent show.

Brixton reached over and slid his fingers into mine. His touch sent my heart racing. Brixton's too. I could feel his strong pulse against my palm.

"I need some time alone with Jackie before we head to the bar."

"We have to go into this night guns-a-blazing," Eli replied. "You can't show up to a party with your chamber empty."

"Fine. We can wait," Brixton said, frustrated.

Eli brought his face right up into Brixton's crotch. "It's going to be all right," he shouted at his dick.

"Do you have a girlfriend?" I asked Eli. All this touchy-feely stuff was making him a little suspect.

"Hey, I was just playing."

"I didn't mean it like that," I lied.

"I have thousands of girlfriends," he said. "Some just haven't met me yet."

The sunset was draining of its color and Eli was getting antsy. "Let's have another drink," he said and made his way to the back.

"I'll have another painkiller," I said.

"That-a-girl," he said.

I ducked into the bathroom to touch up my makeup. All I needed was a smidge of eyeliner and some blush. My hair already rocked from being blown by the wind. I wasn't about to change that.

I joined Brixton at the outdoor table. Eli popped out of his cabin with three oversized Pixy Stix.

"Race you," he said.

169

"Oh my God, no," I said. I couldn't imagine putting that much sugar in my body while drinking.

"It's on," Brixton said. He grabbed a stick and tore the top off.

They both downed the powder in one pour. My stomach turned from just watching. Brixton threw his empty plastic tube down and shouted, "Done!"

Eli was a close second. "I am so Pixy-tripping," he said. As funny as it was, I felt old at that moment.

I was assigned to Jimmy's dinghy for the ride over to Willy T's. Brixton and Eli rode with Tyrone. They were lagging behind our boat. Eli was hiding his unruly mane behind a red Jack Sparrow scarf. Brixton wore his loose and free; it was flowing wildly in the wind. The boys seemed so carefree. I wish I had that kind of happiness.

Willy T's looked like a pirate ship. It was an old steel-hulled vessel moored about a hundred yards from shore. We were the first of our gang to land at the dinghy dock.

The middle section of Willy T's housed an outdoor kitchen. In the back of the ship was the bar, packed with people drinking and dancing. Disco lights shot off in all directions. Once aboard the ship, Jimmy led me to a staircase guarded by an intimidating biker dude.

"Hey, Jack."

"Jimmy. How's it hanging?"

"Good, my man. This is Jackie. Can you take care of her? Get her up top. I have to tend to the boys."

"Absolutely." Jack produced a stack of wristbands and slapped one on me.

I wanted to wait for Brixton but Jack ushered me up the steps to an open deck above the bar. The crowd in the VIP area was Hollywood beautiful. I didn't recognize a single person.

"What is this, a handsome convention?" I said to no one in particular. I glanced over the edge as Brixton and Eli were climbing out of their Zodiac.

A girl yelled out, "Holy-mother-fucking-shit!" It didn't take long for the crowd to erupt in screams. Brixton and Eli raced up the stairs, their faces fraught with disappointment. They wanted so badly to blend in and party anonymously with everyone. Thankfully, the upstairs crowd didn't make a fuss, although every eye was on them.

"Let's get this modeling show started," Eli said, and everyone laughed. He could have said anything and they would have responded with hysterics. We made our way through the crowd to our reserved table.

"That didn't work out so well," Brixton said.

A woman in her early twenties popped her head up over the side and screamed at the boys. Someone, probably our security, snatched her away comically fast.

"I will shut this night down if that happens again," a man said over the loudspeaker. "Don't test me."

"We can still have fun. Drinks!" Eli commanded.

"I can go get them," I said.

"There should be a waitress here," Brixton said. "Speak of the devil."

The devil turned out to be a spunky girl in a pirate hat. Her tits were riding outrageously high as if they were filled with helium. "Welcome back, boys," she said and handed over two Pain Killers from her tray.

"Hey, Holly," Eli said.

"Would you like one?" she asked me.

"I would love a Pain Killer," I said. "But just rum and Diet Coke from here on out."

"You've got it, Aunt Carol."

"Really?" I said to Brixton.

He just laughed.

Holly pilfered a third drink from her tray and handed it to me.

A strong beat filled the air. Eli jumped up and yelled, "Let's dance," like Kevin Bacon in *Footloose*. The crowd leaped to their feet, summoned by their god.

Everyone was dancing with everyone. The atmosphere was comfortable—not your normal meat market vibe. I was drawn to a group of Brazilian models and lost track of the boys. I scanned the room for Brixton but couldn't find him. Instead, much to my horror, I spotted Cristal at the top of the stairs. She was gorgeous, by far the most beautiful woman in the room. I was happy that Stephanie had arranged to get my hair styled. It would have been embarrassing to still have the same style as his crush.

I watched in horror as Cristal sidled up to Brixton seductively. Her hands explored his lower body, as mine turned into fists. Brixton, bless his heart, passed her off to Eli and made his way over to me like a dog with his tail between his legs.

The way the Brazilians moved their bodies so freely was enticing. They danced from their hips, sexually thrusting and gyrating their whole body. Brixton and I tried to keep up the best we could. The dancing was liberating. I felt alive.

Jimmy's boyfriend, Danny, was off in the corner, his eyes fixated on our empty table. I was about to ask him to join us but realized what he was doing. Jimmy was having him watch our drinks so no one would slip anything in them.

Brixton stormed off the dance floor and back to his seat. Confused, I followed his lead.

"What the bloody hell was that about?" Eli asked as we joined him.

"Those Brazilian dudes kept grabbing my cock."

"It's when the gays *stop* grabbing your todger that you need to worry," Eli wisecracked. As if to mess with him, he lovingly reached out and fixed a section of Brixton's hair that was out of place.

Cristal found her way to our table and plopped herself on the other side of Brixton.

"Why don't you join me," Eli said, motioning to the seat next to him. "I feel as if I'm talking to a panel."

"A what?" Cristal said and moved around to his side of the table.

"A panel. Like the panel of judges on *American Idol*."

"Oh, ha ha, that's funny," she said, although I could tell she had no idea what he was saying. Stephanie was right. Cristal was an idiot. And her laugh was awful, guttural—like a goat.

"What agency are you with?" Cristal asked me.

"I'm not a model," I said. "Although I was Ms. Washington."

"Serious?" Brixton said.

"No," I laughed.

Eli perked up. "If you *were* in a beauty pageant, what would your one wish be?"

"World Peace," I said without thinking.

"For how long?"

"One hour," I said. The absurdity of my response made the boys laugh. Cristal joined in but once again she was lost. Brixton and Eli were practically rolling on the floor. I've never been around guys that laughed more than those two.

"You have the best hair," Cristal said to the boys.

"I want to cut it so bad," Eli said. "But everyone says it will ruin my career."

"Isn't it your face that makes you?" I asked.

"That's what I say," Eli responded. "No one listens."

"I think it's pretty," Cristal said.

"Why don't you go for a movie role?" Brixton said. "Something that calls for short hair."

173

"You, my friend, are a genius." Eli stretched over the table and kissed Brixton on the forehead.

An older man with a weathered tan sat down at our table. He was overly confident as if he owned the ship. I soon found out he did.

"What's up, Howard?" Eli said.

"Nothing much, my friend. Nothing much."

"This is the Captain of Willy T's," Eli explained to me.

"Who knows for how long," Howard added. "With that Jack Sparrow scarf you're sporting, there may be a mutiny on the horizon."

"Johnny gave this to me. It's from the first *Pirates of the Caribbean*. Would you like it?"

"That was a gift for you," Howard said. "You need to hold on to that thing, dude."

"No shit," Brixton said.

Howard pulled a homemade vape from his pocket. He loaded it with ground-up pot. "Want to get high?"

"Yes, please," Brixton said.

"This is mellow weed but the vape kicks it up a notch. You won't be disappointed."

When it was Cristal's turn to take a hit, she stuck her finger on the bowl and burned herself. "Ouch, drugs aren't supposed to hurt." Her stupidity made us all laugh.

The high was a creeper, a little too much at first, but then it reached a nice plateau, leaving me with a strong sense of confidence.

I leaned over to Brixton and whispered, "Can we play the coolest people in the world?"

"Honey, we've been playing that all day."

I stared into his eyes, giggling.

"Well, this ship can't run itself," Howard said. "Enjoy your evening."

As Howard was leaving, he slipped Eli a Ziplock full of weed. Eli showed it to Brixton slyly and offered a thumbs up.

174

Howard stopped at the table next to ours. "You're going to delete that picture of Brixton on the vape or you're leaving," he demanded.

"Of course," the woman replied. "I'm sorry."

"That goes for all of you," Howard said. "No pictures!"

Eli grabbed my arm. "What's on your wristband?" He turned the plastic bracelet toward him. V.I.Pirate was emblazoned in bold black letters.

"That's awesome," I said.

"I don't understand," Cristal said. We ignored her.

"I want one," Brixton said.

"You're a walking V.I.P. pass," I responded.

"Oh, I get it," Cristal said.

"I'm snagging a bracelet," Brixton said. "Right after I take a leak." He motioned for Jimmy. Tyrone was called over the walkie-talkie and told to man the stairs.

Cristal leaned in close to me. "Have you ever peed standing up?" she asked.

"Can't say that I have," I said, laughing.

"I tried it today. If you pull your clit up you can aim the stream just like a boy. It's all in the hips."

I liked how free she was with her thoughts.

"So, do you think I have a chance with Brixton tonight?" she asked.

Both Eli and I yelled, "No!"

"Well, you don't have to be rude about it." A full minute later it hit her. "You're not his aunt, are you?"

I didn't know what to say.

"I won't tell," she said, patting my hand. "I'm so jelly I'm jam."

Brixton returned with a look of wonder in his eyes. "Did you see the leather vest on their security guard? I think he's in a gang."

"We should start one," Eli said.

"Totally," Brixton said. "What would we call ourselves?"

"How about The Giggle Poos?" I said, drawing the name from thin air. This sent the boys into hysterics—the name fit.

After they had calmed down, Brixton grabbed Eli's wrist and slapped a V.I.Pirate band on to match his own.

"I guess I'm cool now," Eli said. "So, what's up with Holly's tits tonight?"

"I know," Brixton responded. "They defy gravity. I bet tits look the best in space."

"I don't know," Eli said. "Those melons would be flapping all over her face."

"No, they're wide," Brixton said. "They'd work in space."

"You have great tits," Cristal said to me. "They're perky. These big things get in the way of everything." She jiggled them around like a juggler.

"Can we talk for a second?" I asked Brixton. He followed me to the back of the ship.

"What's up, baby?"

"Stephanie told me about your crush on Cristal."

"No, no, no," he said backpedaling.

"It's OK," I assured him. "I was curious if you wanted to have a threesome. I'm not really into that sort of thing but I'd do it for you."

"You are seriously the coolest girl in the world," he said. "Thank you for offering, but to tell you the truth, meeting Cristal kind of turned me off. She's not the sharpest knife in the drawer if you know what I mean. It's your clever mind that I like. Well, that and your body." He winked and led me back to the table.

I planted myself next to Brixton, happy as could be. "So, what kind of last name is Strut?" I asked Eli.

"My real name is Stuttgart."

"Like the town in Germany where they make Porsches?"

"One and the same. There is something to a name. I do love my Porsches."

"What kind of car do you like?" I asked Brixton.

"Really?" he said.

"What?"

Cristal looked at me like I was the stupid one. "His initials *are* BMW."

I looked at her confused, wondering why she emphasized are instead of BMW.

"Don't worry," Brixton said. "I like that you didn't know that."

Cristal was now hot on Eli's tail being all touchy-feely. I could tell he was uncomfortable with his best friend's crush hitting on him.

"What in the bloody hell is that?" Eli said, pointing off to the side. As everyone's attention was diverted, he stripped naked.

Wearing only a shit-eating grin, Eli ran to the back deck and hurled himself into the sea.

"What the fuck?" Brixton said. He tossed his phone to me and snatched Eli's underwear off the floor. Jimmy tried to catch Brixton but missed by an inch as he leaped after his friend. I gathered the rest of Eli's clothes and looked over the side for the boys. The water was so congested with people who had jumped in to be with their idols that Jimmy couldn't safely follow. The stragglers still on board were shining flashlights into the sea, illuminating Eli and Brixton, hoping to catch a glimpse of nudity. Camera flashes shot into the night like strobe lights. Howard was screaming at people to stop taking pictures.

Jimmy ran for the stairs, with me on his heels. We raced across the floating dock to the back of the boat, where Tyrone stood, yelling for people to make room.

"You need to learn to swim without a life jacket," Jimmy yelled at him, then dove in.

"Get back!" Jimmy was screaming and throwing people out of the way like rag dolls. I couldn't locate Brixton. I was panicked until I saw Jimmy pull him out from under the water, coughing and laughing. Jimmy dragged Brixton to the dock as Eli swam behind. Before they climbed out, Brixton helped Eli into his underwear.

"That's it, you're done," Tyrone said. Someone had to be the bad guy.

"Come on, mate. I'm not drunk drunk," Eli said.

"That's exactly what a drunk drunk would say," Tyrone replied.

Howard ambled over with a T-Shirt for Eli. "You earned this."

"Hell yes," Eli said, holding the shirt up for Brixton to see. I learned later that if you jump off the top naked, you get a free T-shirt.

Brixton was clearly jealous. It was one of the few things he couldn't buy.

The crowd booed as Eli was ushered to the dinghy. Brixton was right behind him. Tyrone shuttled them out of there in a hurry.

I waited for Jimmy as he consulted with Willy T's security. "How about giving us a 15-minute head start?" he asked.

"No problem, boss."

"I hate this trip," Jimmy said as we pushed off from the dock.

Danny and I locked eyes and smirked. I caught sight of Cristal in my peripheral but acted like I didn't see her. She was frantically trying to get my attention as we raced away.

"Grab that plastic cup off the floor," Jimmy said to me. "Hold it over your flashlight as a lantern."

Jimmy's makeshift lantern worked remarkably well. We motored to the opposite side of the harbor from where our catamaran was moored. I had no idea where he was taking us. At the far end of the bay I lost track of Brixton's Zodiac. It had disappeared.

"OK, turn the light off," Jimmy said. We made our way back to our boat in the darkness. "That should shake them off our trail."

Back at Serenity, Brixton took my hand and helped me aboard. Jimmy and Tyrone hooked the pulley lines onto the dinghy and hoisted it out of the water.

"If you promise to keep the lights off we'll leave you to yourselves," Jimmy said.

"No problem," Brixton said. "Sorry for the fire drill."

Jimmy just shrugged. I think he was relieved to have the boys back on the boat but didn't want to give them an inch.

Eli returned from the bathroom a short time later. It was just the three of us now.

"Why did you have to go and mess everything up?" Brixton asked. "I was having fun."

"You're just jealous of my T-shirt," Eli said. He pulled it off and threw it at him. Brixton tossed it aside and headed to the galley in a huff.

"I thought what you did was brilliant," I told Eli. "You couldn't have his old crush pawing all over you."

"Is that true?" Brixton asked, poking his head through the sliding door.

"Of course, mate. I wouldn't do that to you. Besides, Cristal is kind of a 'tard."

"Sorry I got all salty," Brixton said. "What can I do to make it up to you?"

"How about everyone gets starkers?"

"I'm not that sorry."

"Dude, come on," Eli said. "It's just nudity." With that, he stripped. Eli's unruly bush was prominent in the darkness. I was glad I hadn't shaved completely.

"What the hell," I said and threw my clothes off.

Seeing me naked was too much for Brixton to handle. I could see Boris rising under his shorts.

He adjusted himself. "All right, but I'll have to wait a bit."

Once Brixton's erection subsided, he removed his clothes. I missed that beautiful body. I couldn't hold out much longer.

"Another round of drinks," I said and headed to the kitchen.

Eli whispered, "You weren't kidding. She has a smoking hot body."

I returned with a tray of rum and Coke's, still beaming from the compliment.

"This isn't so bad, is it?" Eli asked, referring to being in the buff.

"Not at all," Brixton said. He stumbled to the swim deck and peed off the side.

Although I was drunk, I never thought I would have the courage to do what I did next.

"I think it's bullshit that boys are the only ones that can pee standing up. I'm going to see if Cristal's trick works."

I walked to the swim-deck parallel to Brixton, but even with all the booze I had consumed I was having second thoughts. Brixton and Eli moved behind me, staring, waiting. I pulled up on the hood of my clitoris and began to pee. I had to arch my hips to get the stream to rise but damn if I wasn't peeing like a boy. "Oh my God, this is awesome," I said.

When I finished, Brixton and Eli were lost in silence, both with raging hard-ons. I couldn't help looking at Eli's cock. He was enormous. Nine inches, maybe ten, with the circumference of a soup can.

"Holy shit, Eli," Brixton said. "It's a monster."

"It's a curse," Eli said.

"Don't be a cock martyr," Brixton said.

"Serious, yours is flawless, B. Perfectly proportional." Eli leaned over and stroked Brixton's member a few times. Brixton didn't get upset; he just politely removed Eli's hand.

I reached for the outdoor showerhead and rinsed off my particulars, aware that Brixton was watching me the whole time. I let the water linger as it rained pleasure upon me.

"That's it," Brixton said. "Bedroom. Now!"

"Mind if I watch for a bit?" Eli asked.

Brixton shot me a look of apprehension, begging "no" with his eyes but I thought it would be fun to tease him. Besides, it was Brixton who didn't want Eli to be a third wheel. I took their hands and led them both to the bedroom.

"You're only going to watch," I said to Eli and had him relax on our couch.

I walked Brixton backward to the bed and forced him down. The mattress was on risers so his feet dangled over the edge. I was fully aware of the show I was giving Eli. Men do love the view from behind. Brixton stared up at me with drunken eyes; his cock pressed firmly against his defined abs. When I grabbed the shaft, his balls shifted in anticipation.

With the ferocity of a lioness I went down on him hard and true, but he wanted his turn. He twisted me off him and rolled me onto my back. His mouth was on me like he hadn't eaten in days. We fought mightily for control and finally settled into a 69. The only problem was I kept getting distracted by the pleasure I was receiving.

Brixton caught sight of Eli stroking his cock while watching us.

"That's it," Brixton said. "Out."

"Fine," Eli said. "Your bloody Internet damn well better be working."

I laughed as he slid the door shut.

"Yeah, you liked playing that game with me?" Brixton said. He raised me up by my belly to a kneeling position and smacked my ass—harder than I think he meant to. I tensed up and pushed the bad thoughts away.

Eli knocked on the door. "You all right in there, love?"

"I'm good," I said. "Thank you."

"Sorry," Brixton said. "I was just playing."

"I know, babe."

My mind was racing. Why would Eli feel the need to check on me? Had Brixton hurt his ex? What the hell? I guided his head to my crotch and tried to remain in the present moment.

He went to town, drunk and greedily. Brixton was as patient as he was determined, and determined he had to be because I was pretty hammered.

I knew I was getting close but couldn't quite relax enough to let myself go. Finally, I felt something blossom from deep inside me. I could tell it was worth waiting for as a slow-rolling wave of ecstasy began to build. I felt my orgasm mounting from head to toe as I came in a seismic lightning rod of pleasure.

Brixton made me come two more times before he was ready to enter me. He spun me around and pushed me forward, so I was kneeling over the bed as he fucked me from behind. It was inebriated, sloppy sex and I enjoyed the hell out of it. The alcohol had numbed any pain I would have felt. I kept begging him to go faster, harder. He pounded into me with the strength of a stallion, shaking me to my core.

"Let's do it standing up," I said.

"Oh, hell yes."

He brought me to a wall and we slid into each other, face-to-face. There was a shelf above my head that was strong enough to support my weight. I hung on tight as he thrust with all his might. He was biting my neck but the pain was pleasurable. Brixton moaned louder and louder as he edged toward climax. I dropped to my knees.

"In my mouth!" I demanded. "In my mouth!"

I heard Eli whisper, "Holy shit!" from outside our door — the little peeper.

Brixton ripped off the condom and erupted in a torrent of satisfaction. All the pineapple juice he was drinking made his cum taste as sweet as honey. Savoring the flavor, I kept it in my mouth before swallowing my prize.

I played with his deflating cock, waiting for the last remnants to emerge. Moaning for more, I licked up each dollop with the tip of my tongue. When there was nothing left, I rolled his penis around in my hand, tracing the contours, exploring his natural state. I rubbed my face against it like a purring cat sidling up to its master.

"That was dirty fun," I said, still holding onto his member.

"The best kind," he responded.

I flopped onto the bed as Brixton stumbled to the bathroom. He didn't return. I found him passed out on the toilet. His Twitter account was open. He had been saying goodnight to his fans. I appreciated that he didn't do that in front of me. I woke him up enough to get him back into bed.

I was exhausted but his drunken snoring made it impossible to fall asleep. Eli popped his head into the room. "If you turn him on his left side he'll shut up."

"Thanks, hon."

"No, thank *you*."

The Caves

I woke up feeling like my skull was being crushed in a vice. The only remedy was a couple of ACC's, but they were all the way in the bathroom. I slid out of bed quietly to not disturb Brixton, but once on my feet realized he was already up and about.

I played on his iPad while waiting for the wonderful combination of aspirin, codeine, and caffeine to kick in. It wasn't long before I found myself at the West Seattle Blog to check on his story. I felt bad for looking but I was having a hard time shaking my suspicion that he had something to do with Dennis being jumped. The post that Brixton claimed he read was nowhere in the list of current stories. My heart pounded as I scrambled to the bathroom and threw up.

Donning a long nightshirt, I stepped into the galley to confront Brixton. Eli was lying flat on his back against the wraparound seat of the dining room table. He looked almost as bad as I felt. I sat down, holding my head.

"I have to go, Mum. Love you," he said and put his phone away.

"Hey, Eli," I mumbled.

"Good morning, sunshine." He scooted up in his seat. "Put on your suit. We're going swimming. It will take that hangover right away."

I smiled, realizing where I was. I changed into my second new swimsuit, a black tankini. Eli approved.

"Where's Brixton?" I asked after searching the deck.

"Out digging for buried treasure."

"Yeah, right." I laughed.

"No, really."

"Good Lord. How much money does he need?"

185

"$100 million," Eli said.

"That was oddly specific."

"It's all the wealth he keeps. He's disgusted by the ginormous amounts of money the rich are hoarding. Everything over $100 million gets siphoned into Brixton's foundation. At this point he's given away more than he's worth. The guy's a bloody saint."

"How come I've never heard about this?"

"The media never talks about his philanthropy."

What troubled me is, after hearing this I still couldn't shake my suspicion of him.

"Speak of the devil. Here comes our fearless captain."

Brixton and Tyrone were in our Zodiac heading to Jimmy's boat. They both had their shirts off. Brixton was wearing a black pirate scarf with his long blond hair flowing out the back. Tyrone was rocking a pirate's hat and a childlike smile.

"Ahoy there," Eli said.

Brixton waved at me. He was so distracted he ran right into Jimmy's boat. After dropping Tyrone off he powered over to us.

"Sorry I keep disappearing," Brixton said as he was tying the dinghy to our boat.

"Don't worry about it," I said, waving my hand away.

"It's nothing personal," Brixton added. "I don't need much more than six hours of sleep. My brain gets restless if I stay in bed too long."

"I'd sleep ten hours a day if they'd let me," Eli said. "We were about to go for a dip. Care to join us?"

"I'd love to," Brixton said. "Emergency exit?"

"Emergency exit," Eli agreed and opened the plexiglass portal in the floor of the galley.

He dropped through, followed by Brixton. I grinned and lowered into the void, plunging into the warm sea below.

The morning light illuminated the water a brilliant blue and sent rippled-projections across the boat's underside. The water was clear enough that I could see twenty feet to the bottom like it was inches away. What thrilled me most was the lack of fish—none were in sight.

The azure water reflected in Brixton's eyes, turning them into sparkling sapphires. We snuck a kiss while Eli swam laps along the boat's length. The space was a haven for the boys, far away from their screaming fans.

"I like your hair wet," I told Brixton.

He rolled his eyes.

Eli popped up behind us and splashed around like a contented puppy.

"Did you find your treasure?" I asked.

"Not even a speck of gold. I think it's in a cave that has collapsed. Speaking of caves, I want to take you to the best one on the island. If we go right away, we can make it before too many peeps are up."

"I'm game," I said, not realizing it was a cave that could only be accessed from the sea.

"You're not scared of the dark, are you?" Brixton asked.

"A little."

"Even better," Eli said. "Let's go."

We swam to the back steps to grab our snorkeling gear and left in the Zodiac.

As we drove toward the outer edge of the cove, I spotted Jimmy waving in the distance. "Jimmy's calling for you," I said.

"Oh shit," Brixton said, bringing us to a stop. He gestured for him to join us.

Jimmy was not pleased. He jumped in his dinghy and took off after us. Brixton drove around the bend where several dinghies were tied to a buoy line.

"Nice," Eli said. "Hardly anyone here."

Jimmy glided toward our Zodiac and gave Brixton a look of intense frustration.

Brixton started to explain but Jimmy said, "Don't speak. Just don't."

"Sorry," Brixton said.

I caught Eli's gaze as he slipped on his flippers. He had a mischievous smirk, which for some reason made me giggle.

"We're not laughing at you," Eli said, trying to calm Jimmy down.

"Talk to the hand," Jimmy said, holding up his palm.

"Mr. Hand," Eli said, "why do you have so many age spots?"

"Just get in the water before someone sees us," Jimmy told him.

Trying to be like one of the boys, I immersed my mask in the water and spat on the lens. After adjusting the strap, I pressed the mask snuggly against my face and dropped backward into the sea.

The overwhelming abundance of fish was too much to handle. Something brushed my leg and I screamed and groped for the surface.

Brixton popped back up. "Is there a shark?" He looked around worriedly.

"No," I said sheepishly.

"You're afraid of fish, aren't you?"

I could feel myself blushing profusely.

"Why didn't you tell me?"

"Because people always make fun of me."

Eli surfaced and slid his mask up onto his head. "What's the hold-up?"

"Jackie's afraid of fish," Brixton said. "Don't you dare." He tried but was cut off by Eli's laughter.

"There has to be a good story behind this," Jimmy said. I didn't realize he was in the water.

"I don't know if it's good," I said. "Growing up we had a pond in the backyard that my brother liked to stock with trout. One day he and I were driving back from the fish farm. I was in the passenger seat with a big-ass bucket full of trout between my legs. My only job, which my brother reminds me of to this day, was to stir the top with my hand now and then, to oxygenate the water. I guess I wasn't doing a good job of it because the trout began surfacing to get air on their own. They jumped out of the bucket into my lap and flapped all over me. Fish were sliding across my face, in my hair and on my clothes. It was horrible. I dove into the back seat while the fish flopped around in the front. My brother pulled over screaming, 'You're killing my fucking trout.' He angrily collected them all into the water. There was no way I was getting back in the front. Randy had to drive home with one hand in the bucket. Ever since, whenever I get anywhere around fish I have a panic attack."

"You poor thing," Brixton said, trying not to laugh too hard. "I'm sorry. It's a funny story."

"I know," I said. "And I'll be OK. I don't need to go back."

"It's going to be worth it," Brixton said, handing me a flashlight. "See the cave over there on your left? That's where we're headed. Follow Eli; I'll be right behind you. Everything will be fine."

I did feel safer swimming with the boys as my buffer, plus the aquatic terrain had a calming effect. There were hundreds of fish, but I focused on their beauty instead of my phobia. I was floating in place when a portly blowfish swam up to my face and smiled at me—I swear to God. I had to smile back. The fish turned his fat body around and beckoned me to follow him. I floated effortlessly, oblivious to the outside world.

Reality set in as soon as we entered the cave. The atmosphere grew dark so fast it was discombobulating. My flashlight didn't help much as it made for cumbersome swimming, which was hard enough because I had to keep my body near the surface so I wouldn't slam a knee into the rocks below. There was no turning back—the boys were on a mission. The last thing I needed was to be thought of as a killjoy.

As we continued deeper into the shadowy void, our group passed a departing couple. I wanted to leave with them but powered on. We swam for what had to have been the length of a football field before reaching an inviting cavern. The four of us climbed out from the water and lay on the smooth flat rocks. We were all wearing ear-to-ear Kool-Aid grins.

Eli's contagious laugh echoed and bounced off the stone walls of the cavern. The amplified laughter was irresistible. By the time we got ourselves under control, my cheeks were sore and my sides hurt.

"How about giving us some alone time?" Brixton said and winked deviously at me.

"Ten minutes," Jimmy said bluntly.

The boys eased into the water and soon it was just us.

"You up for making a fantasy of mine come true?" Brixton asked, his erection visible through his wet shorts.

"Absolutely," I said.

"We don't have much time. I'm the pirate and you're my captive. Where's the treasure?" he demanded, grabbing my wrist tightly. His words echoed from the walls.

The haste of his actions caught me off guard but I recovered. Somehow I recalled the name of the pirate Eli had mentioned. "I don't know, Long John Silver. As you can see, there is no treasure here."

He spun me around and pinned my hands up against the wall. In the process, he kicked one of our flashlights behind a rock. The cavern grew darker still. "Tell me or I'll be forced to have my way with you, woman."

I coyly wiggled out of my bikini bottom, daring him. Brixton stepped out of his shorts, releasing my hand, and slid his engorged phallus between my legs. I was already wet, filled with boundless desire for my lover. The head of his cock rubbed back and forth across my vulva. I licked my finger and slipped my hand between my legs, rubbing along his shaft, hoping to give him the same level of pleasure he was giving me.

"Where's the treasure?" he said with a snarl that ended in an appreciative moan.

"I was never privy to the location, sir," I cried.

"You'll regret this," he hissed.

"Promise?" I said, guiding his cock inside me.

"You're nothing but a strumpet," he said, plowing into me. I looked back at him, amused by his choice of words.

I performed a fabulous kegel routine on his member, my muscles clenching down firmly. I knew he would be powerless against this move. The captive had become the captor. I probably should have eased up a bit. My ambition cut his fantasy short. A deep moan escaped his lips before he pulled out and drenched my back with dewy pearls.

"You felt so good," Brixton said. "Now it's your turn."

"I can wait until tonight," I said. "Just being with you in the BVI is an orgasm in itself."

"I'm fine with that if you're cool."

"As a cucumber," I said.

"That you are, Jackie Notter."

"I do have one question. Did you call me a strumpet back there?"

He laughed. "Yes."

Brixton climbed down the rough terrain, extended his hand, and eased me into the opaque water.

"Tonight, when we're alone, it will be all about you," he promised.

"You had me at *tonight*," I responded.

We caught up with our crew halfway out of the tunnel. As we approached, it struck me that he hadn't

191

cleaned up his cum like he had meticulously done before. Was he starting to trust me?

"Thanks, guys," Brixton whispered to the boys.

"Wave," someone yelled from the front of the cave.

"Shit!" Jimmy said. We looked up and saw a gnarly wave bearing down on us. Jimmy wrapped the three of us in his arms. The sea rose rapidly, thrusting us backward. Thankfully, Jimmy didn't slam his back into the rocks. He was mad enough already.

The water subsided as quickly as it had arrived. "Let's get the hell out of here," I insisted.

"Hang on," Jimmy said. "There may be another one."

Swimming out of the cave was terrifying. The mouth loomed in front of us large and bright, but reaching it took forever. With each stroke toward freedom the walls closed in tighter. My heart pounded out of control as a claustrophobic panic overwhelmed my senses. I started crying silently, the seawater hiding my tears. The entrance felt like it was getting further away, like a bad dream. I wanted to swim faster but Eli was blocking my way. Eventually, the channel grew wider, offering room to maneuver around him. I swam like crazy and got the hell out of there.

Once safely out, the soothing rays of the sun calmed my nerves. My fear of fish seemed absurd after surviving that ordeal, although I still kept my head above water so I wouldn't have to look at them.

After checking to see if I was all right, Brixton and Eli swam to our Zodiac. I took my time getting back to the dinghy and found the boys hanging onto the front of the boat, hiding from a group of girls nearby.

"Can you drive us out of here?" Brixton asked me.

"Sure," I said.

They climbed into the boat quickly so as not to be seen. Brixton ducked down while Eli wrapped himself in a towel to cover his easily identifiable tattoos.

I untied the Zodiac and yanked on the starter cord. The engine kicked in on the second try. Right is left when steering a dinghy, which sent me careening toward the girls. I adjusted for my mistake and headed for our bay.

The Baths

Back at Serenity, we hoisted the dinghy out of the water.

"Time to roll," Brixton called to Jimmy.

"Best thing you've said all day," he replied.

"Let's get her untied," Brixton commanded. Eli and I were heading to the front when the engines started with a rumble. Brixton moved the catamaran forward enough for the bridle lines to grow slack, and we removed them from the buoy. Eli threw his line onto the middle of the trampoline mesh. I followed suit.

"Where are we off to this fine afternoon?" Eli asked as we joined Brixton at the helm.

"I thought we'd show Jackie The Baths."

"Brilliant," Eli said. "You'll love this place."

"Can't wait," I said.

Raising the sail this time was easier. I'd only helped once but the task felt like second nature. It was becoming evident to me that I was a sailor at heart. Brixton turned the boat into the wind and filled the sail; it snapped tightly. He shut off the engine and leaned back in the captain's chair.

"Can we listen to Enya again?" I asked.

"Of course," Brixton said.

The haunting first notes of "Sail Away" blasted from the speakers. I was comfortable enough to sing along with the boys. Happiness filled my soul.

When the song was over, Brixton asked me to pick the music. I knew just the album. Jennifer had bought me John Jackson's *One and One*. Every song is perfection. I retrieved the disk from my travel bag and slipped it into the stereo. The slow, breezy strumming of John's guitar filled the cabin.

"Nice," Brixton said when I returned on deck.

"Bloody hell," Eli exclaimed. "That sounds like Cory's demo CD. You have to let me play it after this."

"How did you get his demo before me?" Brixton asked.

"I ran into him in LA. Don't worry, I have a copy for you."

"We can play it now if you want," I said.

"Thanks, love." Eli raced to the galley and soon a simple, yet beachy guitar riff kicked in, followed by Cory's soulful voice. I could see why my choice of music had sparked his memory; there was more than a touch of John Jackson in Cory's opening song.

"This shit is tight," Brixton said.

"John Mayer is helping him with the album."

"How old did you say he was?" I asked.

"Seventeen."

"Damn."

The demo had four of Cory's new tracks. With each song, I could feel Brixton's jealousy building.

Eli caught my eye. A worried look was on his face. "Jackie, do you think you could whip up some breakfast?"

"How about a fried egg sandwich? I make the best."

"Sounds wonderful," Brixton said.

With the helm positioned right above the kitchen, I could hear the boys' conversation as clear as if they were in the room.

"I was supposed to be the first to make the jump to adult singer," Brixton said. "This is bullshit."

"I know. Look on the bright side. You'll be free in June when your contract is up. Do you know who you're signing with?"

"I'm not sure. Mom told me to wait a month to decide. To not rush into anything. She made me promise."

"I'd listen to her on this one," Eli said.

I put John Jackson back on and returned with the fried egg sandwiches.

"This is tasty, Jackie," Eli said after taking a bite. "How is this so good?"

"The secret is a touch of yellow mustard," I said. "You wouldn't expect it to work but it does."

Brixton's eyes grew larger with each bite taken. In less than a minute, he devoured the whole sandwich.

"I wolfed that mother down," he said. "Best damn breakfast sandwich I've ever had."

"Thank you," I said demurely.

Brixton turned to Eli. "Every song I write gets thrown into Committee. After they put their spin on it I hardly recognize my work anymore." He sighed. "I hate it. The contract mom snagged me was all about the money. I want my new one to be about the music."

"You'll get a better contract," Eli said. "Just be patient. Don't let Dusty talk you into re-signing."

The prospect of having Dusty out of Brixton's life pleased me.

"I need control, man."

"Trust me. You'll be the one in control."

"What are you up to?" Brixton asked.

"The world has no idea what's about to hit them," Eli said.

"Do you guys mind if I isolate for a bit? I need to process," Brixton said.

"Of course, mate," Eli said.

I kissed Brixton on the cheek and turned to leave. I wanted to add a few encouraging words but refrained. His work and our life were two separate worlds.

Eli jumped up from the back table. "I can't believe I forgot the flag."

I was expecting the skull and crossbones but he proudly hoisted the Union Jack.

"Do you want to catch some rays?" I asked Eli.

"Sure," he said, grabbing his towel and leading the way to the front.

I laid my towel out on the trampoline and began removing my top.

"Put your top back on," Brixton demanded. "There could be photographers around."

"I don't mind," I said.

"I do. Those are mine and mine alone."

Such a declaration of entitlement could have been taken the wrong way, but I chose to be positive. It was sweet and protective. I put my top back on.

Eli leaned over to me. "Sorry about springing Cory's demo on him like that. I had to share it with him before Sinclair arrives. B took it better than I thought he would."

"As long as he's fine, I'm cool," I said. In all honesty, I was a little upset. Eli could have waited until the trip was over.

"Just be glad I didn't play Cory's cover of Bob Marley's *Three Little Birds*. That would have really set him off." Eli looked over, sincerely. "Don't worry, B will be fine. Hearing Cory's songs will make him work that much harder."

The conversation drifted into a comfortable silence that neither of us felt the need to fill.

I was in a trance, lying face down on the see-through netting, flying across the water. The catamaran was bouncing methodically in the waves, which sent me drifting off to sleep.

"You don't want to burn, sweetheart," Eli said, waking me up.

"Thank you, Eli." I stretched my arms out over my head.

"Man, you were out. We tacked twice. You didn't even stir."

"It was wonderful."

I glanced back at Brixton and waved. He motioned for me to join him.

"Did you have a nice nap?" he asked, kissing me on the cheek.

"The best," I said.

"I have good news. The police caught the people who jumped Dennis. It was a couple teens looking to rough someone up."

"What? How do you know this?"

He showed me the West Seattle Blog's tweet on his iPad. "Looks like his getting jumped didn't have anything to do with him being gay."

I started crying, overcome with guilt. "I am so sorry," I said, "I blamed you."

"It's all right, baby," he said lovingly.

It wasn't all right. I felt like absolute shit. How could I have thought such a terrible thing about Brixton? What was wrong with me? I didn't deserve such a good man.

After a leisurely cruise, we arrived at The Baths, chillin' to the Caribbean vibe.

"Why do they call it The Baths?" I asked Eli while helping to secure the buoy.

"I'm not quite sure, love," he said. "Maybe because the large boulders look like upside-down bathtubs?"

"They do!" I agreed.

"Let me take your picture," Brixton said.

"Really?" I asked.

"Absolutely. Can you grab Jackie's phone?" he asked Eli.

"It's in my purse," I said.

Eli disappeared into the cabin and returned with a gift-wrapped box.

"What is this?" I asked.

"It's your new iPhone," Brixton said. "It's registered to me so no one can track you down."

199

"You're so sweet," I said, opening the box. I felt tears well up and fled to the safety of our bedroom.

"What's the matter?" Brixton asked, joining me on the couch.

"I should never have doubted you. I'm a horrible person. My past makes me paranoid."

"Oh, baby. We all have skeletons." He wiped my tears away with his finger.

"Skeletons? What have *you* ever done?"

"Nothing," he said, avoiding the question.

It felt like there was something he wanted to say. "You can trust me."

His eyes expressed his conflicting thoughts. I could see the pain.

"Maybe it will do me good to get it out," he said. "I've never told anyone, not even Stephanie."

"You don't have to."

"No, I want to. The guilt is like a poison." His eyes filled with sadness. "You know the song that made you cry at my concert? I wrote that about a boy in my class who I used to tease. I was the one that made Billy a target. In the third grade I called him Billy Bunghole and it stuck. One simple name and he was doomed. My bullying didn't last long but I did something worse. I never stopped people from picking on him, and they were relentless. I'm the reason he killed himself."

I drew him close. "You can't blame yourself."

"He mailed me a letter before he shot himself. Said I had wrecked his life."

I held onto Brixton as he wept.

"You have to forgive yourself. Suicide is selfish. It's not your fault."

"But it is."

"It's not," I said forcefully.

"I want to believe that. Look at me blubbering all over the place."

"You needed to get this out. Fuck him for leaving you with this guilt. That's not cool at all."

He wiped his eyes with the sleeve of his T-shirt and looked at me. "So, what was so bad in your past? I've caught glimpses of your sorrow."

"Nothing," I said.

"Come on, Jackie."

"I can't tell you," I whispered.

"That's not fair."

"It's not what I did but what was done to me."

"Oh fuck."

"Yeah," I said.

"Tell me," he pleaded. "Don't be scared. I'm here for you."

I reluctantly told him about my stepfather molesting me. I was going to say that it only happened once, but as soon as I began the truth was impossible to keep inside. I told him everything. Brixton didn't say anything for the longest time, which freaked me out. What the hell was I thinking? Why on earth would he want to be with me after learning that I was damaged goods?

"What I did to you in the cavern. I am so sorry."

"Honey, no. You were just playing. I know the difference."

"I'm glad that fucker is dead. I want you to know that I will never hurt you."

I almost confessed my love for him right there, that I'd never loved anyone more, but I was afraid. "I know you won't."

"There is nothing to be sorry about. You were a child. It's not your fault."

We sat in silence, holding hands.

Brixton patted my knee and headed to the bathroom. He returned with a warm washcloth. In slow, caring strokes, he tenderly washed the tears from my face and then cleansed his own.

"Let's go take that picture," he said, offering me his hand. Heading upstairs, I felt lighter, as if a huge weight lifted. A genuine smile emerged.

"Why don't you stand on the front," Brixton said.

I posed as he snapped one picture after another.

"You are *so* beautiful."

His honeyed words lit up my face brighter than the sun shining upon me.

Jimmy and his boyfriend joined us snorkeling. Tyrone stayed back to keep an eye on the boats.

"I'm not liking this blasted current," Eli said, coming up for air.

"Why don't we walk the path to Devil's Bay and drift back?" Brixton said.

"I don't know," Jimmy said. "Probably too many people." But Eli was already heading for the shore.

The sand in the BVI is fine like sugar, and glows a golden white. I raised my foot and let the granules sift through my toes. The wonderment of the moment caused me to lag behind. I caught up with the gang and followed them along the footpath.

"If we run into any fans could you help take pictures?" Brixton asked me. "Just make it quick so we can keep moving."

"Sure thing," I said.

Almost as if on cue, two girls ran up to Eli and Brixton, screaming and fawning all over them. Jimmy shook his head in an I-told-you-so fashion.

"If we take a picture will you let us go?" Brixton asked. "This is our vacation. We're two normal guys today."

The girls screamed again and handed over their camera. They were freaked out to the point where neither of them could speak.

"Use your words," I said, jokingly. The girls just screamed louder.

I took a few shots, returned the camera, and we were off. The path became steeper as we climbed over a large set of rocks with wooden steps built onto the stone. We had to scoot off to the side as a couple of elderly women passed by on their way down.

"They'll need help with the stairs," Brixton said.

"Oh, bless your hearts for coming back," one of the women said, looking nervously at the steep descent.

Brixton and Eli helped each woman safely to the bottom of the steps.

"Do either of you have granddaughters?" Brixton asked.

"I do," the taller woman said. "One is eleven and the other fourteen."

"Do you have a camera?" Eli asked.

She shuffled around in her bag for a solid minute before finding her Cannon Powershot.

I took the cutest picture of Eli and Brixton kissing the woman on each cheek.

"Put that on Facebook," Brixton said. "Your granddaughters will be jealous."

"All right?" the woman said, confused. *The ego on this one,* I imagined her thinking.

The path through the rocks was a series of low passages, steep boulders and tight squeezes. It led us to the beach of Devil's Bay. I'd never been to a more serene place in my life.

Off in the distance a pelican was diving for fish. As soon as he would catch one, a smaller bird would land on his head and wait for the scraps.

"Can we sit here a bit?" I asked.

"Of course," Brixton said.

We watched the pelican's fishing routine until we heard young voices approaching from the path. After gathering our snorkeling gear, the five of us slipped into the safety of the water.

Brixton and I were floating above a gulch on the backside of a boulder. I was mesmerized by the sheer depth of the trench and stared into the darkness, imagining what type of creatures lurked below. I looked up to get my bearings and was horrified to find a gigantic barracuda staring back at me. Razor-sharp teeth lined his mouth. Brixton grabbed my wrist and squeezed hard. He held onto me tightly as if to say, no sudden movements. We backed away slowly. The barracuda didn't seem interested in us, thank God.

We swam over to the gang and told them about our encounter. Everyone wanted to see the barracuda, even Jimmy, which was surprising. Brixton and I left in a hurry. I'm glad it wasn't a shark—we wouldn't have had such a leisurely swim back to the boat. He even held my hand as we swam together underwater.

The Beach

Our final destination was a few miles north. Brixton didn't bother putting up the sails, instead he motored over to the bay. We tied up to a private buoy next to a long stretch of white sand.

"Whose beach is this?" Eli asked.

Brixton stood proudly. "Mine."

"Serious?" Eli said.

"I'm going to build a cabin on top of the cliff. I've already had the old one removed. It will be our own personal oasis." He said this to Eli, not me. I felt a twinge of jealousy.

"It's perfect," Eli said.

"That it is," Brixton agreed. "So, who's up for flying on my Superman harness?"

"Oh, hell yes," I said.

Brixton led us up front to a storage locker. "I came up with the idea for this invention from my Grandpa. He used to fly me around in his arms like Superman. That's what the song is about. Well, what it used to be until it was watered down by Committee."

"Is it safe to do this on the ship?" Eli asked.

"Of course. I perfected the design on my dad's sailboat. You just need a good dismount."

"Let's make it snappy before the fun police shut us down," Eli said.

Brixton unhooked the line for the mainsail and walked to the end of the hardcover canopy. He clipped the line into the pulley system at the top of the Superman harness as Eli secured himself into the straps.

I could see Eli's bulge out of the corner of my eye, pushed up front and center. I forced myself not to look.

"You can take a peek," Brixton said.

"I'll wait until you're in it," I said.

Brixton smiled and walked back to adjust the line. "Put all your weight on it."

Eli grabbed the railing and flipped horizontally, locking himself into the flying position.

"So, what do I do?" he asked.

"Jump with enough momentum to get around the front of the ship. To land, click the hand release and you'll be back on your feet." He tossed Eli a black fingerless glove with a button in the palm.

Eli put the glove on and pushed the button, propelling himself upright. He ran and leaped off the canopy without asking if we were ready.

"Don't worry, we'll catch you," Brixton yelled.

Eli made a perfect arc and flew around the front to the other side. We barely had to move to retrieve him.

"Oh shit," Eli said. "Tyrone's coming." He was approaching full speed in a Zodiac.

"I get a turn before we're cut off," Brixton said. He quickly strapped into the harness and flew around the ship.

Tyrone boarded our vessel and climbed to the top deck. He leaned over with his hands on his knees, waiting to catch his breath.

"Will that thing hold me?" he asked. We all laughed.

"It has a weight limit of 170 pounds," Brixton said. Tyrone was crushed. "But the one I made for Jimmy will hold you."

"Fuck yes! Oops — sorry, Boss," he said to Eli.

Brixton swapped out the harness with the sturdier one and Tyrone flew around the ship sporting a huge childlike grin. He came in strong, humming the theme from the Superman movies.

It was now my turn. With a quick dash, I jumped off the deck and locked into place. I felt like I was flying as I circled the ship.

We played on the harness for most of the afternoon. I had more fun hanging out with the guys than I have in years.

A feeling of peace set in the moment we landed our Zodiac on Brixton's beach. The positive energy emanating from his property was all-encompassing. At the base of the cliff stood a colossal stone fireplace and sitting area. A staircase had been meticulously carved into the rock cliff, ascending skyward like the opening of a fairy tale.

Jimmy had met us on shore to drop off a couple of delicious homemade pizzas. With our bellies full we started in on the rum. I was well into my second drink when Brixton jumped to his feet.

"Oh shit, it's Magdalene," he said with a hint of apprehension.

I thought he was messing with us but there sat Magdalene in a fast-approaching Zodiac. Her dinghy was fancier than ours. It had an actual cockpit, complete with a steering wheel and captain's chair. Magdalene's posture was perfect. The woman looked majestic with her long blonde hair flowing in the wind.

"She's been after me since I turned eighteen," Brixton whispered.

Magdalene was right there. She was docking onto our beach, getting out of her boat.

"I heard you were in the neighborhood," she said to Brixton.

"You heard right."

"Eli," she said, winking at him.

"Mags."

"Hi, I'm Magdalene," she said, turning to me. Her eyes were mesmerizing.

"This is my girlfriend, Jackie," Brixton said.

I could have died right there—his girlfriend.

"It's really nice to meet you," I said.

"Likewise," Magdalene responded. "I have a treat for you guys. I've come to take you to George Clarey's soiree."

"Hell yes," Eli said.

Brixton wasn't as ecstatic. "I'm going to pass."

"Dude?" Eli said.

We all looked at Brixton. He stuttered and stammered but came out with it. "Clarey doesn't like me."

Eli let out a loud laugh. I tried to hold mine back but couldn't. Soon Magdalene joined in the laughter. Brixton stared us down, unamused.

"Do it for Jackie," Magdalene said. "She'll never forgive you for missing Gio."

Oh. My. God! Giovanni Ruffino. "I'll be fine," I bluffed. "We can stay here."

"Nonsense," Magdalene said. She leaned in close to Brixton and whispered something in his ear. He laughed deeply.

"Go meet him," Brixton said. "I'll be fine."

"Come with us," Magdalene insisted.

"Not going to happen," Brixton said, "but it's totally cool if you meet him, Jackie."

"You sure?" I asked.

"Absolutely. I trust you. Hurry back."

"I'll keep you company, mate," Eli said, joining him on the log.

Magdalene didn't have a problem taking me without the guys. I knew that ditching Brixton was wrong, but there was no way I could pass up an opportunity to meet my idol. I grabbed the matching black mini skirt for my tankini and my flip-flops. Before I could talk myself out of it, I jumped in Magdalene's Zodiac.

On the ride over I sat next to Magdalene. She was so in control. So powerful.

We motored around the corner to the next bay. On the far end was a ridiculously large yacht. The crowd on the upper deck was dancing to a heavy beat.

"Clarey could have at least brought his big boat," I quipped. Magdalene laughed. I made Magdalene laugh!

"George is getting married this fall. He's blowing off a little steam."

"Can't blame him for that," I said and cleared my throat. "Please forgive me for gushing, Magdalene, but your album *Musicality* helped me through my divorce."

"Really? That's a sweet thing to say."

"I'm not kidding. That album has such a strong woman vibe. Power woman."

"Power woman. I like that. Can I use it in a song?"

"You can do whatever you want," I said.

Off the top of her head she belted out, "*Power woman with your heart so young and free.*"

"Nice!" I declared.

We docked at the back of the ship where two uniformed gentlemen helped us aboard. Another crewmember secured our dinghy as a bikini-clad server took our drink order on a tablet.

"I'll have a Manhattan," I said.

Magdalene gave me a surprised look that I should have paid attention to. "Cosmo," she requested.

"I'll meet you up top with your drinks," the woman said.

Another crewmember escorted us around the side of the ship to the upper deck where the party was in full force. I almost screamed when I spotted Gio standing at a railing off by himself. He must have been getting in shape for a movie because he was fit, trim, and closely shaved. Magdalene walked us straight over to him.

"Hey, Gio. I want you to meet Jackie. She's Brixton Webber's girlfriend."

"Is he here?" Gio asked with a gleam in his eye.

"No, he wanted to hang out at his beach," Magdalene responded.

"Doesn't matter. Any girl of Brixton's is a friend of mine," he said.

I reached out and shook his hand. My vocals clenched up—I couldn't get anything out. I was lost in his eyes, a 13-year-old again.

"Have you been to the Caribbean before?"

"First time," I managed to say. "It's like a dream."

"It is at that." His gaze drifted back to the sunset.

I couldn't believe Gio was standing next to me. My mind went blank from the rush of it all. I needed to say something, anything to get the conversation back. I blurted out, "So, what was up with people making fun of that video of you at Coachella?"

Gio sighed heavily.

"You were just grooving to Young Vaughn, lost in the moment. I don't get people. That song rocks."

He perked up. I had Gio's full attention. "You're the only person who hasn't given me shit about that video. People can be such dicks."

"That they can," I said.

Our drinks had arrived. I thought it was odd that my cocktail was served in a martini glass but accepted it with no complaints. I took a sip and coughed. The unexpected whiskey burned my throat. "I ordered the wrong drink," I said, embarrassed. "I meant to order a Long Island Iced Tea."

"I thought a Manhattan was a little ballsy," Magdalene said, laughing. "I'll swap it out." She left to find the waitress.

"I like you," Gio said. "Come with me." He led me to the stern and hopped over the safety railing.

"No way," I said.

"Oh, it's happening."

I couldn't believe I was about to reenact *the* scene from my favorite movie. Before I could begin my lines Gio put his finger to my lips and shushed me.

"Let me have your hand."

I smiled coyly.

"Don't peek."

Gio walked us to the railing from behind and helped me up. I held my arms out wide, and he grasped onto them securely, holding me high. The moment was surreal as can be.

"What the fuck!" A woman screamed from behind us. "You've never done that with me."

Gio helped me down.

"This is Brixton Webber's girlfriend."

"I don't care who she is. Why haven't I been able to fly?"

"Maybe you want it too much," he said. "It was nice meeting you, Jackie."

I was completely flustered and blurted out, "You're welcome."

That made Gio giggle, which landed him in even more trouble.

I walked back to the party where George Clarey grabbed me. "Who are you?"

"I'm Jackie," I said.

"There you are," Magdalene said, dragging me away.

"Holy hell, Magdalene. Did you see that?"

"I think everyone did. I've never seen a crowd so jealous."

"My heart was pounding through it all."

"I bet. Wait, are you quoting a line from the movie?"

I laughed.

She handed me a Long Island Iced Tea in a large tumbler.

"Thank you!" I said and took a sip. "This is much better."

"You're a riot."

"Before we head back to the beach do you think we could dance to one of your songs?" I asked, wincing slightly.

Magdalene sighed. "Only for you. Which song?"

"Imperfect Instant," I said. "It's my favorite dance song in the whole world."

"I'm flattered but don't let Brixton hear that."

"Oh, I'm not a fan of his. I didn't mean it like that," I said. "I'm just not a *fangirl*."

"With a sweet guy like him that might work," Magdalene said and headed to the sound booth. The DJ wrapped up the song he was playing and queued the rolling beat of "Imperfect Instant."

Magdalene commandeered the mic. "All right, everyone clear the floor. You too, Brad," she demanded. "Dance with me, Jackie."

Jennifer and I must have danced to that song a hundred times, but grooving with Magdalene was out of this world. I could feel Jennifer looking down upon us with approval. The beat sped up to a frenetic groove. We twirled around and ended up falling on the floor, laughing. When the song was over I was ready to get back to my man.

"Do you think we could find some weed for Brixton?" I asked, forgetting that Howard had given us a bag.

"[Name Removed] made me promise never to give him any."

"Are you telling me that someone has power over Magdalene? I never thought I'd see the day."

"More of a mutual respect for each other. And for Brixton," she added. "He has so much potential. Brixton is going to take the adult world over like Cumberlake. You just watch."

"That would be wonderful," I said. "He's sick of being a teen idol."

"His contract *is* coming up."

"It is at that. Goodnight, everybody," I yelled, and we ran out of there holding hands and giggling.

"I can't thank you enough," I said as we sped away into the dusky night.

"It was fun," Magdalene said. "I like you. You're real."

There it was again. I was real. How long would it be until I believed that too? "I like your diastema. It reminds me of my best friend."

She winked and smiled wide, showing off the gap.

"I miss your British accent," I said. "I can't believe what shits people were about that. Like you're not going to acquire an accent living in one place long enough."

"There's always haters. You must get a lot of abuse from his fans."

"Actually, they think I'm his Aunt Carol."

"They think he's fucking his Aunt?" she said, shocked.

"No! I'm his secret."

"His pop secret?" she joked.

"I like that. Makes it not sound so bad," I said. "After what happened with Eli's girlfriend he doesn't want to risk my safety."

"That's messed up," Magdalene said. "I'll talk with him."

"Please don't," I begged. "It could scare him. We just started dating."

"I won't say a word," she said, patting my hand motherly.

I was surprised how well I clicked with Magdalene. Women aren't my strong suit, but she's like a dude.

Magdalene drove her Zodiac right onto Brixton's beach, raising the engine at the last moment. The front

213

caught in the sand and we were both knocked out of our seat. Eli and Brixton helped us to our feet.

"Thanks for a great time," Magdalene said. "I should probably get going."

"Stay for a while," I pleaded.

"I can't. That was my boyfriend in the DJ booth. I have to rescue him."

"Ok, but shots first," Brixton said. He reached behind the cooler where he'd hidden a fifth of Fireball. I'd never had it before but it turned out to be delicious. Very dangerous for me.

Magdalene shuddered after taking her shot. "This stuff is ghastly."

She gave me a sisterly hug. "Take care, Jackie."

"You too, Magdalene," I said.

"I like her," she said to Brixton. And with that, Magdalene was off.

"I'll see you at Clarey's," she yelled as she sped away.

Brixton held me from behind as we watched her go. "You weren't gone very long," he said.

"I hope you can forgive me for deserting you. I was in junior high when Gio's big movie came out. I had to meet him."

"No worries. Was he cool to you?" Brixton asked. "Sometimes idols don't live up to expectations."

"He couldn't have been nicer," I said.

"Wonderful. Let's get you a drink."

By the time nightfall was upon us the boys and I were feeling no pain. We enjoyed a roaring fire on the beach, relaxing comfortably against a weathered piece of driftwood. Brixton had one arm around me, and the other on Eli's shoulder. A group of approaching male voices caught my attention, and I tensed up.

"It's all right, baby," Brixton said and rose to intervene. Eli grabbed his walkie-talkie in case they needed backup and took off after him.

"I can't believe you're here," Brixton shouted. "Jackie, come join us."

I was shocked to see Simon Paulson and John Jackson. Simon's iconic face was so familiar and welcoming it was like seeing an old friend. He had a subtle expression of sadness—his droopy eyes and mouth following the same downward draw. I wondered what was bothering him.

John had let his hair grow to the point it was curling loosely. His face has dominant features; a strong nose, a wide masculine chin, and ample lips that completed his athletic look. He was sporting light stubble and a fresh Caribbean tan.

"Simon, John," I said, astonished as I shook their hands.

"John Jackson?" Brixton asked.

"In the flesh," John said. He had a laid-back, marbled tone to his voice.

"I hope you don't mind," I said to Simon. "I have to give you a hug."

"Bring it on," he said.

Being in Simon Paulson's arms was beyond compare. The sadness on his face is a façade. He is filled with so much warmth and compassion it emanates from his body. I didn't want to let him go.

"So, whose wondrous beach is this?" he asked with a twinkle in his eye.

"Mine," Brixton said proudly.

"Right on."

"I don't know about all of you," Eli said, "but I need to get high with John Jackson."

"Sure—I don't have any on me, though."

"Quite all right," Eli said, "we have a bit left."

"We're not supposed to get Brixton high," Simon whispered in John's ear.

"What the hell?" Brixton said. "Have you been talking to [Name Removed]?"

215

Simon was trapped. He looked back and forth. "No," he lied poorly.

Eli wasn't deterred. He loaded the pipe and offered it to Simon, who glanced at it and looked away. But it's hard to say no when it's right in your face. "Fine," he said, accepting the pipe reluctantly.

My head was spinning and I hadn't even taken a hit. In one day, I met Magdalene, Giovanni Ruffino, Simon Paulson, and John Jackson. Was I dreaming?

Simon took a long drag and released a swirling cloud of smoke. A smile spread across his face. He handed the pipe to John and strolled over to Brixton. "A friend sent me a video of you singing my song The Wrestler when you were twelve. I knew you were going to be a star. How would you like to sing it with me?"

Brixton's eyes glistened. "Holy Christ, yes!"

"I'll fetch your six-string," Eli said.

"Thanks," Brixton said.

Simon had us move to the stone sitting area for the acoustics. Eli returned from the boat and handed the guitar to Simon, who gave the strings a quick run-through. He started playing the opening of "The Wrestler" but stopped and passed the instrument to Brixton.

Simon smiled approvingly as Brixton strummed a note-by-note rendition. In the video Brixton sang Simon's part, but he adapted seamlessly to backup. Their voices blended in sublime harmony. It was a performance of the century witnessed by an audience of three.

Brixton leaned over and gave Simon a one-armed hug when they were finished. "You made my year, man."

Simon was beaming. "Glad I could do it."

I slyly dabbed Brixton's tears away before anyone saw them.

"So, what brings you guys to my beach?" Brixton asked.

"I own the place next door," Simon replied. "Your beach is one of my favorite spots on the island."

"You're welcome over anytime, whether I'm here or not."

"Cool. This beach has the best vibe. I always feel happy when I'm here."

"Speaking of happy," I said, "I have a fantasy of sitting on a beach listening to John Jackson. I hope it's not too much to ask but would you mind giving us a song?"

"Not at all," John said. "What would you like to hear?"

"How about 'Days Like These'?" I said.

"That's a good one," Eli agreed.

"Are kids listening to my music?" John said to Eli. "I don't mean kids. I'm just surprised that someone your age knows who I am."

"People tell me I'm an old soul," Eli said.

John pulled out his phone and hit record. *"People tell me I'm an old soul, maybe. I'm an old soul, baby, I'm an old soul. Every day my life is lived in the moment."* he cocked his head. "What rhymes with moment? Damn, that was really flowing."

"Strong mint," Brixton blurted out.

"What the bloody hell?" Eli said, taking the pipe from him.

"Strong mint rhymes with moment," Brixton said. We all laughed. He started singing. *"Every day my life is lived in the moment, like a strong mint, you know it."*

"Shit, it does flow," Eli admitted. "But does it make sense?"

"Some of my best lyrics are nonsense," John said, picking up the guitar by the neck and headed to the bonfire. He took a seat on a weathered piece of driftwood and began playing the song I requested.

Brixton and I cuddled against a log opposite of John. Eli soon joined us. We sank into the world and listened to John play song after song. It was surreal, one of those experiences where reality is better than the dream.

Simon sat alone at the stone sitting area with a content look. After four songs John handed the guitar back to Brixton. "We should head back to the girls," he told Simon. "Dinner has to be ready by now."

Simon reached for the pipe but thought better of it. "We'll have to do it again. This was fun."

"It was an honor meeting you, sir," I said to Simon, shaking his hand.

"Pleasure was all mine."

"John," I said, "you're awesome."

"So are you."

Simon placed a reassuring hand on Brixton's shoulder. "I've seen how the media treats you. It's such bullshit. All I see is good. Don't let them win. If you can stay out of trouble, there's no stopping this train. Staying out of trouble is the key."

"Thank you, sir. I really appreciate it. I'll try."

"Don't try. Do. Do good and good things will come."

With that, they bid us adieu. We stood in the sand, silently watching Simon and John fade into the darkness.

"What a trip," Eli said.

"Can you believe that just happened?" Brixton said. "I'm shaking."

"It was like a dream," I said.

"Speaking of dreams," Eli responded, "I've dreamt of going to one of Clarey's parties. Do you mind if I head on over?"

"Not at all," Brixton said.

"Can I talk you into going? We could have some mad fun tonight."

Brixton and I looked at each other and smiled.

"You go, honey," I said. "Brixton and I are grabbing a blanket and a bottle of rum and spending the night atop the cliff."

"Wow, it's like you read my mind," he said.

"Want to know what I like about you, Jackie?" Eli said.

"What's that?" I asked.

"You don't look at us like we're stars."

"You're just people," I said with a wink.

Eli retrieved a couple of blankets for us from the boat before taking off.

I called out to him as he was leaving. "Clarey's is the big yacht in the next harbor. You can't miss it."

Brixton placed his backpack on the cooler and we each grabbed a handle. My man led the way up the stairs, which couldn't have been more distracting.

"You have the greatest ass," I said.

"Let me see," he said, pausing as I stepped ahead of him. "Second greatest."

The clearing at the top of the cliff had become lush green as the vegetation grew back from the removal of the old cabin. It was an oasis protected from onlookers by tall bushes and palm trees. The view was stunning. Low, wispy clouds were visible through the moonlight. Serenity was lit up below us. Off in the distance were the silhouettes of tropical Islands.

"Why didn't you keep the cabin?" I asked.

"It was too small, plus it was falling apart. My architect is meeting me here Saturday so we can design a cabin around the vibe of the beach."

"I can't wait to see the plans," I said.

We each held a corner of the blanket and spread it out on top of a thick patch of moss. Brixton lowered me onto my back and kissed me tenderly.

"I'm glad you're here," he said.

"It's been wonderful."

His soft lips moved to my neck. The light touch sent a tingle rippling across my skin. I moaned in appreciation. He slowly made his way to my earlobe and ran his lips ever so lightly along my skin, igniting my desire.

Brixton removed my top exposing my breasts. I worked his tank off at the same sensual pace, lingering to massage his pecs, then lifting it over his head. He slipped off my flip-flops and tossed them aside.

I untied the drawstring at the top of Brixton's swim trunks and pulled the front open. His pheromones, mixed with the sea's salt, created a divine scent. He stood up and I ran a finger across his engorged cock, careful not to grab him outright. I didn't want to shift away from the slow tempo. It was a welcome change from our usual balls-to-the-wall sex.

Brixton slid my mini skirt and bikini bottoms off in a rocking motion. We were now completely naked in the moonlight. He gave my inner thigh a feathered kiss and brought his face to my breasts. I watched as his mouth took in each nipple, kneading and flicking them with his tongue until they were erect. A tropical breeze flowed across their wetness, further stimulating both.

He inched his way down my body, kissing different parts along his journey — the neglected areas not usually associated with sex. He was close to my nether regions but brushed by to kiss the inside of my hip. Just when I thought he was about to perform cunnilingus, the teasing continued. He would veer off and focus on another part of my body. The anticipation heightened my senses to a fevered pitch. When he landed, my back arched in ecstasy. He directed his tongue in long, deep strokes, pressing on my clitoris with each pass. Brixton nibbled and rubbed my clit, patiently, making sure to hit all the right spots. He switched to a rolling, pulsing motion that catapulted me into the stratosphere.

"That's it," I moaned, "don't stop."

I relaxed my upper body and sank into the softness of the blanket. The pleasure happening below was playing with my vision, causing the night sky to pulse in and out to his rhythm. I felt a connection with the energy of the universe. My hips were drawn skyward as if beckoned to the heavens. He rose with me, never skipping a beat.

The alcohol was once again making it hard to reach an orgasm. This only intensified Brixton's determination.

A warm, familiar sensation engulfed my vulva. I wrapped my legs around Brixton's head, pressing my clit against his mouth. Soon I was unable to distinguish myself from him. My thoughts began to dissipate as silver stars appeared in my peripheral. I held onto his head, leaning forward, preparing for the release. A feeling of leaving my body followed my surrender. I left the world behind as I exploded into the night air.

"Oh, God," I gasped, struggling to catch my breath.

Brixton laid his head in my lap and stared up at me with satisfaction. I ran my fingers through his hair in long strokes. He closed his eyes and smiled contentedly, knowing he was the master.

My man tried going down on me again but I couldn't wait any longer — the anticipation of making love was too much. I pulled him close and kissed him greedily on the mouth, tasting myself on his lips. He grabbed my neck and kissed me deeper, his cock thrusting against my swollen vulva. Brixton managed to enter me hands-free. We stared into each other's eyes, locked in the moment, neither of us wanting to look away.

Having sex in the open air made the missionary position feel new and exciting. I wrapped my arms around his neck, our heads nuzzling each other as he rocked in and out of me like a wave. Brixton felt right like nothing else mattered in the world. He looked majestic with the night sky showcasing his muscular body. My man was a god among the cosmos.

He began thrusting harder but still in a rolling motion like he was choreographing a song. His shaft was positioned tightly against my labia.

"That's perfect," I said.

Brixton kept pace with a steady rhythm. He is the only man who has been able to hit my G-spot. I trembled uncontrollably with each powerful stroke, lost in the moment, unaware of time and space. He held my gaze as I grew closer to release. I swear he was staring at my soul when I came a second time. He held onto me as I floated back to reality.

I rolled Brixton onto his back and slid him inside me. Slowly and methodically, I contracted my muscles, gripping and squeezing his engorged cock. His breathing increased and he let out a low moan of pleasure. Brixton began to thrust faster but I pinned him down and elevated my pace.

"Come on," he moaned, spurring me on. I kept up my rhythm, edging him closer until he reached climax. His eyes fluttered and his smile curled as he came. I could feel his cock throbbing with each release as he pushed in as deep as possible.

We collapsed, exhausted. Brixton wrapped the blanket around us and we cuddled together in paradise. He was still inside me when we drifted off to sleep.

We woke in each other's arms, with the morning sun shining upon us. I felt like hell from the mishmash of booze I drank the night before, but still, I couldn't have been happier.

Brixton stirred. "Hey, baby," he said. "How you doing?"

"My head is spinning," I groaned.

He looked at me wide-eyed and freed a hermit crab from my hair.

"What the hell?" I said, freaking out.

He went to throw it off the cliff but had a change of heart and tossed the crab into the bushes.

"I don't remember the end of the evening," he said. "Did I fall asleep on you?"

"I think we both crashed around the same time. That was a big day."

"It wouldn't have been half as fun without my girlfriend," he said.

I smiled so wide my face tingled.

"There's the smile I love," he said, staring longingly at me.

"You make me happy," I said.

We made our way to the beach where we found a CD next to the stone fireplace. "Did you leave this here?" I asked.

"No." He looked at the CD. *Simon & Brixton The Wrestler* was written in Sharpie. John must have recorded their performance on his phone. "Is this real?"

"Let's get to the catamaran and listen."

The problem was we didn't have a dinghy. Eli was still out. Brixton stowed the CD safely away in the empty pot bag and swam with it in his mouth.

Eli appeared from around the corner and met us halfway to the boat. Brixton handed him the CD.

By the time we reached the catamaran my hangover was under control. Water is a powerful entity.

After tying up the Zodiac, Eli walked past us. I had to hear this story. We followed him into the galley. He turned to us with a worrisome look. "Cory's on his way. He'll be here in ten minutes."

My heart sank. I had agreed to leave when Cory arrived but I wasn't close to facing that reality. Brixton held me around the waist. *Please let me stay. Please let me stay.*

"I'm sorry, baby," he said. It was like an executioner's notice.

I walked past the boys to our cabin. Brixton was hot on my heels.

"I wish you could stay. What a time, huh?"

223

"It was the best three days of my life."

"Are you going to be OK?"

"Let's focus on the positive," I said, trying to stay strong.

"You're the coolest, Jackie."

I took a quick shower and threw together my suitcase so I could spend my last minutes with the boys. We sat out at the party table.

"I'm glad I had a chance to meet you, Jackie," Eli said. "You're one in a million."

"You have a beautiful soul," I said. "Don't ever lose that."

"Shit," Brixton said as a seaplane landed off our stern.

Carlos killed the engine, walked out onto the pontoon and threw us a line. Once the plane was secured, Cory Sinclair stepped out. He wore a tan Australian hat that complemented his multicolored bohemian shirt and blond hair. He was adorned with a leather necklace and multiple leather wristbands.

"G'day, boys. Hello, I'm Cory. You must be Jackie."

"I am. I've heard a lot about you."

"Hopefully all good."

"Can you excuse us, baby?" Brixton said. He led his friends into the salon and closed the sliding door.

"She's a doll." I heard Cory say through an open window. "But she can't stay. This is our boy's trip."

"Jackie's cool," Eli said. "She's one of the guys."

"I'm in enough trouble with Rachel," Cory said. "She really wanted to come. If she knew another girl was here I'd be sleeping in the dunny."

Brixton laughed. "You're right."

It made me feel better knowing he at least tried. Leaving would be that much easier.

I gave Eli a big hug. Brixton forced us apart and kissed me goodbye.

"Text me so I know you've landed safely," he said. "Call Stephanie. Her number is in your phone. She'll get you a flight or a room if you want. Whatever you feel like doing."

"Thank you for everything. I'll never forget this trip as long as I live."

Carlos took my hand and helped me into the plane. "It's good to see you again, Jackie."

I shook my head in agreement. I didn't dare speak; I was too afraid that I'd start crying. As we were taking off I was already missing Brixton.

We were leveling off when Carlos turned the plane around. "Why don't you buzz the catamaran?"

"That would be awesome!"

"Just stay to the left of Serenity so the wind doesn't push you into her. I'll have your back."

We came in dangerously low. So close I could see everyone's face. I stuck my tongue out mischievously and rocked my head. Brixton was stoked to see me at the wheel. I felt like a badass.

"Can we fly over The Baths and Willy T's?" I asked.

"Absolutely," Carlos said. "You know, you look like a different person. The Caribbean agrees with you."

"That it does."

Carlos flew us over each Island I'd visited. It was sad saying goodbye but flying past them helped. I'm proud to say I didn't cry.

I was leaving St. Thomas customs when a commotion distracted me. Outside, on the seaplane dock, a gorgeous brunette was being accosted by tourists with cameras. I recognized her face but couldn't place her. She seemed to be enjoying the attention. *Holy shit*, it was Brixton's ex, Candice. I caught her eye as we passed each other. Under our breath we muttered simultaneously, "What the hell is she doing here?"

St. Thomas

I left customs in a frazzle, my head teeming with carnal thoughts of Candice and Brixton intimately intertwined. Why else would she be there if not to fuck him? I wished that Stephanie would call. I texted her more than an hour ago.

The chorus from the Rolling Stones "Shattered" blasted from my new phone. It was Stephanie. Brixton chose the perfect ringtone for her.

"Stephanie, I'm going out of my mind!"

"What's wrong? Brixton said you guys had an incredible visit."

"I'm in St. Thomas. Candice was on the seaplane dock. I don't know what to do."

"Honey, take a deep breath. Everything's cool."

"What do you mean? Why is she here?"

"Her parents have a beach house on St. Thomas."

"Really?"

"Of course. They stay on the American side of the Virgin Islands. I doubt Candice even knows Brixton is in the Caribbean."

"Oh, thank God." I sat down on a boulder and looked around. After stowing my luggage in a locker, I wandered aimlessly into the day. I had no idea where I was.

"You don't have to worry about Candice," Stephanie said. "Brixton was the one who ended the relationship."

"What? Backstage you said she broke his heart."

"She did," Stephanie said. "I probably shouldn't tell you this." She explained something to me that is so personal I don't feel comfortable repeating it.

"*Damn*," I said. "I feel like an idiot."

"Don't," Stephanie said. "Sometimes life can be deceptive. So, tell me about your trip. It sounded like crazy fun."

I was so caught up in the Candice drama I forgot to text Brixton. It took me a while to find him in the contacts list. He had put himself in as B. I was fine with the clandestine nature of it all. It meant no longer relying on someone else to patch us through.

I fired off a quick text to my boyfriend, letting him know I landed safely. He called back immediately. His ringtone was a cheesy electronic version of my lyric: *I wanna take you in the bob bop*. It made me laugh.

"Hey, babe," I answered.

"I needed to hear your voice," he whispered. "I can't get enough of you,"

I was beaming, but at the same time didn't want to scare him with too much emotion. Instead, I chose the sexual route. "You have me hooked. I can't wait to get you naked again."

"Me too, but it's more than sex," he said. "I think you may be my everything."

Hearing this left me speechless.

"Jackie?"

"What are you doing?" Eli shouted. "Oh my God, you are so whipped!"

"Get the hell out of my cabin."

"Hi, Jackie," Eli said.

"Hi, Eli," I said, annoyed.

"I have to go," Brixton said abruptly. "We'll talk soon."

"Wait," I said. "I want you to know I liked your sweet words. My silence was a good silence."

228

"Really?"

"Absolutely," I assured him. "Go have fun."

Home

Stephanie arranged a flight out that day, although the rush was for naught. My absences caught up with me and I was fired from Bellstrom's. Welcome fucking home.

Outside of airport security I spotted my name on a limo driver's sign. The man helped retrieve my bag and escorted me to the car. I stretched out in the back for the ride home, wishing I hadn't answered the call from work.

The depressingly gray Seattle weather would have been enough of a buzz-kill even without losing my job, but it was only the beginning. I entered my bedroom and found my laptop open, a bottle of lotion tipped over on the nightstand, and used tissues strewn across the floor like a masturbatory crime scene. I normally would have been furious but was surprisingly chill. The door to my bathroom swung open and Dennis stepped out wearing only a towel.

I startled him so badly he jumped. "You scared the shit out of me. I didn't expect you home so soon."

"What is this?" I motioned toward his disgusting mess.

"Don't blame me. I thought you'd be in Puerto Rico for a few more days."

My anger went from zero to sixty in no time flat. "How the fuck did you know where I was?" I demanded.

"You left your email open to the confirmation of your plane ticket."

"What the hell? How did you get into my laptop?"

He looked at me unfazed. "You told me you were staying at Lidia's. You're a fucking liar."

Oh my God! Had he read my journal? How much did he know?

"What are you doing with your nose splint off?" I asked, desperately changing the subject. "Removing it early can botch the shape of your nose?"

"Really? Shit!" He dug the splint out from the garbage and raced to the bathroom.

I stripped the bed and started the laundry. Dennis was still in the bathroom when I returned. He was having a difficult time with the tape.

"Let me do it," I said, snatching the roll from his hand.

He hopped up on the counter and I reset the splint.

"So, did you get to see Brixton while you were on vacation?" he taunted.

I tweaked the splint, squeezing Dennis' nose on purpose. He screamed like a child. At least he was still under the impression that I was seeing Dusty. The jealous shit would lose his ever-loving mind if he found out I was dating Brixton.

"All good," I said. "Now get out."

I headed for my favorite deck chair and stayed outside until I saw Dennis slumping down the staircase to his apartment.

A week had passed since I was fired. Being unemployed weighed heavily on me. A growing concern about money, or lack thereof, followed me like a toxic cloud. Brixton had given me more than I needed for the tax on my new car but the extra cash wouldn't last long. I still hadn't told my brother I lost my job. We would be having "the talk" soon.

Brixton and I spoke or texted daily. Our conversations helped stabilize my mood. Surprisingly, the separation proved healthy for our relationship. It placed a veil over our visual attraction, allowing us to explore each other's inner selves.

Work

My first unemployment check hadn't even arrived when my former manager called me back for a one-on-one. I was sitting in Jolene's office waiting for her to get off the phone.

"Thank you for your patience, Jackie," she said after hanging up. Her gratitude sounded forced. Jolene has too much of an authoritative voice for a proper tone of concern.

"No problem," I said, trying to get a read on why she had called me in for a meeting. Jolene slid over an open gossip rag and the truth hit me like a sucker punch to the stomach. The left page was a spread about Eli skinny-dipping at Willy T's. I was in two of the five pictures. In the last one I was identified as Aunt Carol.

Really? I almost said in regard to the Aunt Carol bullshit. "I can explain."

"I don't want to hear it," Jolene responded tersely. "The less we know the better. Have you told Brixton you were let go?"

"No," I said flatly.

"Good. People will find out about the two of you. It's inevitable. And when they do, Bellstrom doesn't want the bad press. Treating our customers and employees with the utmost respect is why this company has gone so far. Bottom line is we would like you to come back to work."

That was about as far from what I was expecting as possible. "I appreciate the offer but I don't get to see him often. Sometimes I have to leave with only an hour's notice."

"You didn't let me finish," she said sharply. "We're setting you up with a flexible schedule. You can have as much time off as you need, no questions asked. And to compensate you for having less work, we're giving you a $5 an-hour raise."

My bitterness faded away. "Thank you."

Jolene reached over and placed her hand on top of mine. "Jackie, you shouldn't have to hide your relationship. It's not healthy."

"Safer than dealing with his fans," I said.

"Point taken. You know you don't have to stay on the department floor. We could use your skills in the corporate office. Put that English degree of yours to use. Maybe you can help with the catalog."

"I would like that. I'm extremely interested in philanthropy if you have such a division." A job like that would be a perfect fit with Brixton.

Jolene perked up. "The Bellstrom family are major philanthropists. They might need some help. I like this idea even better. Let me talk with the brothers and get back to you. In the meantime, call when you're ready to return to the floor."

The phone rang and Jolene picked it up. I guess our time was over. She covered the mouthpiece. "I want you to know that no less than twenty people complained about us letting you go. And it wasn't just guys. You're well-liked, Jackie."

"I appreciate you telling me that."

I shook her hand and left to find Lidia. She was in the break room enjoying a fresh cup of Joe.

"I just had a meeting with Jolene. What did you do?"

A look of panic was on Lidia's face.

"Thank you," I said and kissed her on the lips.

"Sorry about breaking your trust," Lidia said, relieved. "Jolene was the one who came to me with the magazine."

"Don't worry about it. Everything worked out. I'm back."

234

Stephanie called a few days later. "Jackie, before I say anything I want you to know that Brixton is doing fine."

"What are you talking about?" I asked frantically.

"Your boyfriend passed out during tonight's show. He was out for at least five minutes."

"Oh my God! Are you sure he's OK?"

"So far. But he wouldn't go to the hospital. That stubborn little shit is back out performing, closing out the show with an acoustic set. The medics are here. I'm forcing him off the stage if he tries to do an encore."

I felt helpless. "Can you do me a favor and bring the phone out in the hall? I need to hear his voice."

"Sure."

Stephanie opened the door and I heard him singing "Fallen Leaves."

"Please tell him to call me?" I said.

"Of course. I just wanted to let you know before you saw anything in the news. He's exhausted, Jackie. Maybe you can talk him into stopping the meet and greets before the concerts. It's too much."

"I'll see what I can do. Thank you so much for calling."

Brixton texted me twenty minutes later.

I'm OK. Off to the hospital.
Heard Steph filled U in. I'll
call as soon as they let me.

Thank you, babe. Positive
thoughts heading your way.

The story was hitting the Internet, along with a video of him passing out. It happened right after he flew like Superman. His body collapsed as if someone had flicked an off switch. I cried when he struck the ground.

Lidia called soon after the news reports came out. "You all right, Jackie? What's going on with your boyfriend?"

"I'm good," I lied, "Brixton is fine. He's just exhausted. They have him doing too many things. I have to go. He's going to call me back."

"Call if you need anything," she said. "Anything."

"I will. Thanks for being there. Love you."

I should have kept her on the line. Brixton didn't get back to me for two agonizing hours. "Hey, baby, what's happening?" he said nonchalantly when he called.

"What's happening? Are you OK? I've been worried sick."

"There's no need to worry. It's just exhaustion."

"Oh, thank God. You scared me."

"I'm not going anywhere. I was almost caught lip-syncing, though. Luckily my sound tech was quick on the mute. I hate doing that but a few of the dance-heavy songs have been kicking my ass."

"Why didn't you tell me that you've been having problems?"

"I didn't want to complain."

"Don't do that again," I said. "You can tell me anything. So, what can you do to slow down?"

"Well, I can postpone my tour for a few weeks, which extends my contract. Or I can stop my meet-and-greets. They're too much. I used to have that hour before the show to myself."

"I think this is a no-brainer," I said. "Get rid of the meet-and-greets."

"It's not that easy. I'm saving up the money from those to house all the homeless in Juneau."

"Oh, baby, you are so sweet. Your fans will understand. Just go public with what you're doing."

"No way. If I did that all the homeless would be on the next boat to Juneau. I wish I could talk about it. The media has been brutal. Like I'm some kind of egomaniac who charges people to bask in my glory."

"Screw the media. Do what's right for you. If you postpone your tour you're just postponing your exhaustion, not to mention your freedom."

"You're right. I have three days before my gig in Barcelona. Maybe I can get my energy back by then."

"Hello, Mr. Webber."

"Hi, Doc. Sorry, baby. I have to go."

"Take care, Brixton."

"I will. Miss you."

"I miss you too." I wanted to say I love you but was waiting for him to say it first.

Brixton held a news conference two days later. He was honest and spoke from the heart, even tearing up when discussing canceling the meet-and-greets. For the first time in ages the media couldn't attack him. So, of course, they buried the story.

He called later that day. "Hey, honey. Did you see my news conference? Shut those fuckers up."

"You were brilliant."

"My fans are the ones who are brilliant. They started a GoFundMe and in less than four hours raised $25 million with one-dollar donations. Can you believe it? At this rate I'll also be able to renovate an old building into a secure shelter for abused women."

My emotions got the best of me. I had a feeling he was creating the shelter to honor me.

"You all right?"

"Yeah. I'm just blown away by your fans. Look how you've influenced them to be charitable. Did I tell you I'm going into philanthropy?"

"What? No? What? I don't understand."

"Not my own money, silly. The Bellstrom brothers are opening a position for me to help with their charities."

"That is incredible. There's nothing better than helping people. I'm proud of you, Jackie."

"Thank you. That means a lot. How are you feeling? Are you getting any rest?"

"I am. Dusty has me tucked away in a villa at the Algarve — Portugal's Riviera. The locals here have been so kind. We'll have to come back for vacation."

"I would love that," I said. "Hey, I have a question. Why don't you call me Badness anymore?"

His response was instantaneous. "Cause all I see is good."

I choked up. "Aren't you the charmer."

"The highlight of my day is talking with you. I can't wait to be back in the states so we can be together."

"I can't wait, either. I miss you so much," I said.

"I miss you too. Sorry, baby, but my doc is here. We'll chat later."

Brixton's Calling

It was taking longer than expected for the Bellstrom brothers to create a philanthropy position for me. In the meantime, I was filling in for people on the retail floor. I was currently working in the young men's department. It was an hour past lunch and I was starting to get cranky.

I was finally given a break and was heading to the Bellstrom Café when I heard my boyfriend's ringtone. My mood immediately improved.

"Hey, B," I answered.

"Guess who's home?"

"No way? Are you done with your tour?"

"Wrapped up completely. I was back last night. Sorry I didn't call. I needed some alone time."

"That's OK," I said.

"Do you think you can get a few days off? I want to spend time with you here."

"That would be so much fun. When do you want me to come down?"

"Tomorrow morning if possible."

"Let me talk to my boss and I'll get right back to you."

I ordered a salad and then emailed Jolene, informing her that I was taking three or four days off. I didn't even have to ask. My new arrangement was so empowering.

"We're on," I said, calling him back. "I can't wait." It was nearly a month since we had seen each other.

"Me too, baby. I've missed you. And so has Boris. Check this out."

I heard a text chime in from my phone.

"Brixton!" I said, shocked at the sight of his rock-hard cock.

"I need you so bad," he said.

"I need you too. I can't wait until tomorrow."

The last two hours of my shift dragged on endlessly. Before I left, I found Lidia to share my good news.

"I'm heading home," I told her. "I'll see you in a few days."

"What? Where are you off to?"

"B invited me to his crib." I attempted to be cool by throwing down gangster signs but failed miserably.

"His house? Wow, that's huge."

"Not as huge as this," I said, showing her Brixton's picture. I couldn't pass on the joke.

"Is that his fucking cock?" She looked around, hoping no one heard.

"It is," I said proudly and pulled my phone away.

Lidia yanked on my arm for another peek. "Now I'm really jealous."

"That's enough," I said, clicking off my screen.

I texted Brixton as soon as I arrived at LAX's baggage claim. He was lightning fast with his response.

Meet me out front when U
get your bags. Black BMW
750i. Tinted windows.

Be there as fast as I can.

I snuck a peek outside. His car sparkled in the sun like polished onyx. A police cruiser pulled up and the officer walked over to the driver's side window. The cop was soon smiling and laughing.

Being in first class, my luggage was the second to drop down the conveyor belt. As I walked up to Brixton's car the trunk popped open. I tossed my bag inside and climbed in the back to sit with him.

"You're driving?" I said, shocked that he was behind the wheel.

"It is my car."

"I didn't mean it like that. It's just you're out on your own. No security."

"They give me a little freedom when I'm home."

Brixton was looking California in a plain white T-shirt and multi-colored board shorts. He motioned for me to get up front.

I jumped in the passenger seat and lustfully made out with him. If it weren't for the honking, we would have had sex right there in the white zone.

"We need to get home," he said as he started the car. "Now."

I removed my hand from inside his shorts. "What did the cop want?" I asked.

"Johnny didn't like my tinting."

"You knew the cop?"

"What? No, Johnny Law."

My ignorance gave us both the giggles. It felt good having *him* correct me. With age comes wisdom, but who wants to be seen as a know-it-all?

"This is a super nice car. Don't take this the wrong way," I said. "I'm just surprised you're not driving a Ferrari or something."

"You can't drive incognito in a Ferrari. Besides, BMW gives me a couple new cars every year. Yours was the first one I've bought. How is she?"

"I love my car so much. It's perfect for the beach. You couldn't have chosen better."

He raced up the freeway onramp but was blocked from merging.

"Fucking idiot," he said and pulled ahead. "What's up with that look? Come on. All that man had to do was keep his pace. He didn't need to slow down to let me in. I hate timid drivers. They're the cause of traffic jams. It's why your traffic is so slow."

"We're not that bad."

"Are you kidding? Seattle drivers are shit."

"I'm sure aggressive drivers cause just as many problems."

"I'm not aggressive. I'm defensive. There's a *huge* difference. That's it, I'm sending you to driving school."

"That's not cool, Brixton."

"You're mad because I want you to be a good driver?"

"No, I'm mad because you think I'm not."

"I didn't mean it that way, Jackie. I've taken all sorts of driving classes. I have track time reserved for myself this Friday. I just want you to be safe."

"Sorry," I said and rubbed his leg.

"Why don't you take your apologies and buy us some vodka," he said jokingly. "We're out."

"Of course, babe."

Brixton lived in an exclusive gated community called Pelican Hill. I wanted him to point out his famous neighbors but wasn't comfortable asking. I fell in love with his house immediately. The photos hadn't done the place justice. It was a modern two-story reminiscent of Frank Lloyd Wright.

"What is that?" I asked as we entered his garage. The sports car parked in the last stall looked more like a spaceship than an automobile.

"That's the new i8."

"By Apple?"

"No, BMW. It's freaking awesome. All-electric but it hauls ass. I've had it up to 150 on the track."

"Nice."

"I was going to buy you one but didn't feel safe giving you that kind of attention."

"My Z is more than enough."

The interior of his home was stunning, with a perfect mixture of stone, metal and wood. I especially liked the floating staircase leading to the second level. His living room, however, was a little off-putting. A couple of stand-up arcade games and an air hockey table fit awkwardly in the room. The scent of frat house wafted prominently.

"The place is still like this from a party I threw," he said, lying poorly.

"It's fun," I responded. I didn't care how the room looked. Just being with him was enough for me.

"Let's go see the pool," he said, leading me toward a glass door.

I threw my bag on the couch and followed Brixton down an open-air pathway lined with tropical foliage, some as tall as the roof. The atrium led to an oblong pool surrounded by an enormous patio. A stone fireplace was seamlessly incorporated into the security wall, along with a wraparound couch and a low-sitting coffee table, which added a cool 50s vibe. At the opposite end of the pool stood a covered wet bar. Every detail of the house was meticulously thought out. I had a feeling the architect built it for himself.

"What can I get you, ma'am?" he asked, stepping behind the bar.

Hearing the word ma'am made me wince. I brushed aside the pet peeve and hopped onto a stool.

"I'll have a vodka soda with a splash of cran."

"What do you call that?"

"A Rose Kennedy."

"Fancy," he said. "First, I want you to try a cocktail that Eli invented. We call it a Grape Eli."

243

He concocted a potent drink of vodka and rhubarb soda. Adding a small amount of grape juice turned the drink a dark purple.

I took a big sip. "Wow! This *is* refreshing."

"I thought you'd like it," he said, making himself one.

Brixton casually stripped naked and dove into the pool. I disrobed and jumped in after him. With his hair slicked back, it gave me a glimpse of how handsome he would look with shorter hair. I cupped his face using both hands and brought his lips to mine. We kissed in the middle of the pool with our feet barely touching.

"Get under the diving board," he ordered abruptly. His sharp tone scared me. I didn't know what was happening until I spotted the drone heading our way.

Brixton slipped his shorts back on and walked nonchalantly to a storage bin. He retrieved what looked like a bazooka and fired into the sky. A net tethered by a rope wrapped around the drone, dropping it to the patio. The annoying whirring sound of the propellers was silenced. He grabbed an aluminum bat from the same bin and proceeded to beat the hell out of the machine.

"Mother fucking spying asshole cocksuckers!" he screamed as he delivered blow after blow.

"I think it's dead," I said, coming out from under the diving board.

"I am so sick of these things," Brixton said, dumping the larger sections in the garbage. He swept up the rest of the pieces and reloaded his web cannon before joining me back in the pool.

"Your home should be off-limits," I said. "It's rude."

"Damn straight."

"My heart's still pounding," I confessed.

"Mine too. I kind of enjoyed that," he admitted. "I have a surprise for you. I need a little liquid courage in me first." He headed to the bar to freshen our drinks.

By our third cocktail we were in his bedroom. I was relieved to see that his bed had no posts. At least his surprise wasn't tying me up. I don't think I would do well being restrained.

"I hope you don't think this is weird," he said, reaching under his bed and producing a finely crafted wooden box. "It's for when we're separated. Not separated. In separate towns. For when I'm on tour." He was stammering. "Here."

I was brimming with curiosity as I lifted the top off the box. Inside was an unexpected sight. A lifelike dildo was nestled in plush red velvet. The shape and color were familiar. It couldn't be. "Is that a mold of your cock?"

"It is," he said with a mischievous grin. "Let's just say that Stephanie is getting an extra-large bonus this year."

"From the look of things, I am too," I said. "This is the best present I've ever received."

"That is such a relief. I was worried about giving it to you." He held me close and kissed me on the lips. "Jackie, I hope you don't mind me asking. Is there any way?"

"What?"

"Can I?" He looked at my ass, his face beet red. "I don't know how to ask. I wanna take you in the bop, bop."

The notion wasn't as taboo as he might have thought. I was married to a gay man after all. "For you, anything."

"You are the best!" he said. "I'll make us another drink."

As soon as he was gone I ran to the bathroom to freshen up. I sat on the bidet in total awe of the room. Ten people could fit in the shower. His bathtub was a rectangular take on the old cast iron clawfoot tubs. It looked like a piece of modern art but strangely went with the decor. I loved everything about the room, right down to the art deco door handles.

245

I found Brixton downstairs. "Thank you for doing this," he said, handing me a drink. "It's the one thing that Cand…"

"You don't need to skirt around your ex. I'm cool with Candice," I said. "Besides, we've talked plenty about Dennis. You even had him beaten up."

His face grew stern. "That's not funny."

"I was just kidding."

Brixton bounded up the stairs to his room. With each step, the spider tattoo on his ass came to life. I ran after him to catch up.

"So, we're going to need *lots* of lube," I said, my voice wavering with second thoughts.

"Well ahead of you," he said, grabbing a large tube from his nightstand. "I'll go slow. I promise."

I lay down on my stomach and he opened my legs slightly. There was nervous anxiety in the pit of my stomach as if I were in line for a roller coaster.

When he was convinced that I was fine with the situation, he began with one well-lubed finger. I panicked as soon as it was inserted. Brixton paused and I relaxed, allowing him to slip it in and out. I don't know if it was because it was *his* finger, but the sensation was unusually arousing. A second finger was added and I tensed up again. He patiently coaxed me into a sublime rhythm.

"Are you ready?" he asked, tempting the rim with the tip of his cock.

"As much as I'll ever be," I said. It was a couple of years since I had done this. I was scared. "Go real slow at first."

"I will."

He raised my hips and steadied himself. After a lot of pushing and prodding he managed to get the head inside.

"Oh my God, that feels so good," he said.

His cock was so large it hurt. I wanted to tell him to get out but held strong. He paused for a minute then pushed in further.

"It's getting better," I lied.

He started thrusting slowly. "This is awesome."

There's a point during anal that the pain subsides and an immense pleasure takes over. It took longer than usual but I was there.

"You can go faster," I said.

Brixton began thrusting harder. His cock has so much girth it wasn't poking me like Denis' angry pencil-dick used to. Nerve endings that lay dormant my whole life began to spark, singing out for the world to hear. I put my head down and moaned with each thrust. That's when I noticed the dildo was still on the bed. I shoved it inside me and a whirlpool of sensations radiated front and back, up and beyond.

"I'm not making it much longer," he said, "it feels too good."

"Hold on just a bit."

"Oh God, I can't."

He tried to pull out but I clenched down tightly. Brixton came inside me with a tremble.

I placed his hand on the dildo. "Keep moving it and stay inside me." He thrust the dildo into me wildly while I rubbed my clit. "Don't stop. Don't stop."

Having an orgasm with him in my ass was nothing short of rapturous. My sphincter contracted tightly around his cock while my swollen vulva swallowed the dildo hungrily. Delirious convulsions erupted throughout my body as I seized uncontrollably until I couldn't move another inch.

Although the experience was incredible, it was a relief to have his cock out of my ass.

I returned from the bathroom to find my man lying flat on his back, his erection still pointing proudly toward his belly. Brixton scooched over so I could join him.

He looked over at me and smiled. "That was so dirty. I didn't hurt you, did I?"

"No, it felt good," I assured him.

A commercial airline flew overhead, centered in the skylight above us. We both watched it glide past the window. A text on his phone chimed. He reached over and read the message. "Oh, hell yes. You'll love this. We need to get dressed."

My travel bag was still downstairs in the living room. I snagged a T-shirt from his closet and the turquoise shorts he wore in the BVI. I barely had them on when the doorbell rang.

"Can you get that?" he asked from the bathroom.

"Sure."

I was still in a daze from the dual pounding I had just endured. As I ascended each step, the corduroy in his shorts rubbed playfully against my clit.

It took a while to find the main entrance. We had come in through the garage. When I opened the door and saw who was standing in the entryway, I fainted. Flat out hit the floor. I woke up to Robbie Cumberlake leaning over me, concerned. He had one arm on my shoulder and the other on my waist. A pulsing jolt of electricity passed from Robbie's body into mine. His energy was inside me. It was all too much. I closed my eyes and tried unsuccessfully to hold back the orgasm.

"Did you just come?" Robbie asked. "Wow!"

"What the fuck?" I said, embarrassed.

He laughed and helped me to my feet. I was freaking out. What was Robbie Cumberlake doing there?

In walked the rapper, Splitz Diggity. "Damn, girl. You give good welcomes."

"Hey, Splitz," I said, managing to compose myself. "What brings you guys here?"

248

"It's a wiggavention," Robbie said in his quick but poetic speaking style.

I heard Brixton coming down the stairs. Luckily his shorts were pulled up. I couldn't imagine a worse moment to walk in with them sagging below his butt.

"There's my boy," Splitz said. "Brickity-B, what's up, my brizzle?"

"Splitz Diggity! It's so cool to meet you," Brixton said.

"Been a long time coming," Splitz said.

"Cumberlake. Wassup?"

"Nothing much my friend. Let's go in the living room and have a chat," Robbie said. He was all business.

"What is all this?" Brixton asked, slightly guarded.

Neither Robbie nor Splitz said anything. They had Brixton sit on the couch and took a seat on each side of him. I snagged the comfy chair across from my boyfriend.

"Do you want me to clear out?" I asked.

Brixton looked at me, confused.

"Naw, you cool," Splitz said. He turned his attention to Brixton. "Of all my boys, I don't have to tell you how nasty the media can be."

"Fo' shiggidy," Brixton said. He was going to wish he had dialed it down, but there was no hope with Splitz in the house.

"Along with being nasty, the media is also racist," Robbie said. "Or at least they consciously stir it up."

"Fuck that. They straight up racist," Splitz said. "It took forever to break through the white wall of success. And when I did they still had me walking around in a damn pimp outfit to make themselves feel better."

"Shut up," Robbie said. "You do that cause you like it."

Splitz laughed. "Believe me, Brixton, the media is bigoted as fuck. If a kid is missin' they damn well better be blond and pretty or they ain't getting jack from the dailies.

249

Tie a gay white boy to a fence and leave him for dead—you have news for years."

"Whoa, whoa," Robbie said, trying to reel him in. "That's not cool, man."

"Really, dog? If Matthew Shepard was Jamal Shepard, you wouldn't of heard shit."

"Fair enough."

"What about the coverage of the Trayvon shooting?" I asked. "Everything I've seen has been in support of him."

"That's the ruse my sexy muse. What they have there is a perfect storm of racism. It's a dangerous game the news is playing. There's going to be more and more senseless deaths."

"What does this have to do with me?" Brixton asked. "I don't have a bigoted bone in my body."

"Bigoted bone. Bigoted bone," Splitz said. "Shit, that's dope."

"It's yours," Brixton said.

Robbie looked at both of them, clearly annoyed. "Brixton, the media only allows one white rapper at a time. One. And right now that's Macklemore."

"What about Eminem?" Brixton asked.

"He's old school. Last generation," Robbie said. "Em is grandfathered in."

"The media likes white entertainers white and black ones black," Splitz said. "To stop each attack, you gotta quit acting black."

"No man, not you," Brixton said.

"Don't worry, B. You'll always be my snigga. But the country's racism is holding you back."

Robbie stared at Brixton compassionately. "When you're appropriating black culture, it gives the media an opportunity to sell hate."

"They use your skin to push their spin," Splitz said. His face grew serious. "It harms my community."

"I get it," Brixton said, defeated.

250

"We didn't mean to hurt you," Robbie said. "You're a good man. I have nothing but respect for you. The reason I'm here is I want to take over your contract."

"No way. Are you kidding me?"

"One hundred percent real if you want it. You have mad skills."

Brixton stood up and paced.

"Don't worry, you'd still get to let your freak flag fly," Robbie said. "We'd just raise it from your soul."

"Please tell me that Ubastyle would be producing my music!"

"I wouldn't have it any other way," Robbie said.

"Dude, he's a hit-maker! You have him locked in?"

"Tighter than a deadbolt," Splitz said.

"And Magdalene would be the one bankin' the album," Robbie added.

"Is that why she's been stalking me?"

"Of course. What did you think?" Robbie laughed.

Brixton turned a slight shade of crimson.

"I can usher you into adulthood in the media's eyes. Give you the credibility you deserve."

"I'm sensing a 'but' here," Brixton said nervously.

"There always is," Robbie said. "You'd have to stay out of trouble. From now on you would need to be squeaky clean so the only thing the news talks about is your awesome new album. Squeaky. Fucking. Clean."

"I can do that."

"And you'd have to sell this house. It's tainted in the press."

"Can't I just redecorate?"

"Afraid not. This goes beyond your living room. At this point, there's no winning your neighbors back."

"I haven't had any complaints since I put up the sound wall around my pool. I took away my view for those A-holes."

"Your parties are too wild for this hood," Splitz said.

Brixton closed his eyes. "Fuck. I love this house."

"It wouldn't be as bad as it sounds," Robbie said. "We'd find you a secluded pad where you can let your hair down."

"Speaking of hair, would I get to cut it?"

"Of course. What kind of fucked-up contract do you have?"

"That kind."

"You can do whatever you want with your hair. Just wait until after your contract ends. We'll hold a press conference to announce this new chapter in your life."

"I'm liking what I'm hearing," Brixton said.

"You'll really like this next part," Robbie said. "I'm offering you final say on every song. No more committees."

"That's all I've ever wanted," Brixton said. "I... I need to take this all in." He turned and walked from the room.

I leaned over and whispered in Robbie's ear. "Didn't you used to have cornrows?"

"Yeah, but I was nineteen. Oh shit, so is Brixton."

"Your heart's in the right place," I said. "Besides, the media *is* totally out to get him. They've painted a giant target on his back."

Brixton returned with a dazed expression as if he didn't know if he was dreaming. "I'm in."

"Hell yes," Robbie said, standing up to seal the deal with a handshake. He slipped a business card in Brixton's palm. "Have your lawyer set up an appointment with mine, and we'll go over the details."

"Did my mom have any part in this?"

"Of course. She wants you to be happy. And to make sure that happens, she'll have *no* part of your career anymore."

"I love that woman," Brixton said.

Splitz reached into his breast pocket and brought forth a mighty blunt. "A toast to the boogie," he said, offering it to Brixton.

"What the fuck, Diggity!" Robbie said. "Don't give the kid pot."

"How do you expect me to grow up if you call me kid?"

"Touché," Robbie said.

"Look, I will toe the line for you in public," Brixton said. "I will keep my name squeaky clean, but damn if I'm missing an opportunity to get high with Splitz Diggity. It's too much to ask." He snatched the blunt and took a long drag.

"To Brixton," Splitz continued, avoiding eye contact with Robbie, "the voice of the future."

"The voice of the future," Robbie agreed.

I had the next hit. It took just one toke before the world was pulsing sideways. Splitz has the good stuff.

Robbie hesitated but eventually joined in on the celebration. "I don't want to see you doing this in the news again," he said, shaking the blunt at Brixton.

"Scout's honor," Brixton said, doing the salute. I loved that he promised in such a childish way.

"I hate to toke n' bolt," Splitz said, "but I have to bounce, my brother."

"What?" Brixton said. "We're just getting started."

"Family first."

"*That* I understand," Brixton said.

"Nice meeting you Brickity-B," Splitz said. He stuck out his hand but Brixton was having none of it.

"Come on?" he said, drawing Splitz in for a hug.

"Remember, don't be black," Splitz said as he was leaving. His laughter could be heard down the driveway.

The three of us relocated to Brixton's kitchen and sat at the marble island. I loved how the sides met seamlessly with the top, looking like one chiseled-out piece of stone. The kitchen itself was designed for a chef, complete with three ovens, a ten-burner gas range, and a Sub-Zero fridge that was so large you could almost fit inside.

"OK, training starts now," Robbie said. "I'm a reporter from *Vogue*. Let's start with a rough one. Tell me, Brixton, what are your views on abortion?"

"I don't want to talk about abortion!" Brixton said angrily. Robbie had struck a nerve.

"Sorry, dude. I didn't mean to upset you. It does prove the point I was making, though." Robbie looked at him earnestly. "How I would respond to such a toxic question is, I'm here to entertain, not to make people mad. I don't answer divisive questions. I respect my fans and their opinions. It's as simple as that. OK, another one, tell me a little about your religion?"

"Religion is a private relationship between you and God. It's not something I feel comfortable talking about in public," Brixton said.

"Damn, that's perfect. Stay clear of anything that could make half your potential fans mad: politics, abortion, religion. You don't want your views turning anyone off from your music or your brand. Most importantly, we don't want to give the press the opportunity to talk shit about you. We'll bleed them dry with positivity."

"Can I discuss saving the planet?"

"As long as you don't let the media trick you into saying something contentious about global warming. What I'd like to focus their attention on is your philanthropy."

"I don't know if I'm down with that," Brixton said.

"It's time for people to talk about how charitable you are," Robbie said. "Eli told me about all the money you give away. And that Cool Kids Day you do for the bullied students at your old high school is as dope as it gets."

"That one I'm definitely not talking about. It's a private day for all of us."

"OK, but the rest of your goodwill needs to shine forth. I'll make sure the media not only listens but tells your story."

"What do I do about Dusty?" Brixton asked. "He's been like a brother to me."

"I'll talk to him after you sign the contract. You don't have to worry about that."

"No, I need to break it to him. He gave me the opportunity. He deserves my honesty."

"See, you're already a grown-up," Robbie said.

"Thanks, man."

Robbie looked at him with stoned happiness. "If you could have one wish what would it be?"

"Good health for my friends and family," Brixton responded without hesitation.

"That's beautiful," Robbie said, taken aback. "Let's go in your studio. Ubastyle wanted me to check something with you. He's heard you have an amazing memory for music."

"That's some straight-up truth there," I said, hoping it came out as cool as it sounded in my head, but they both laughed at me.

Brixton led us down a hallway lined with gold and platinum records to a dark room. A flick of a switch revealed a full recording studio, complete with an isolated sound booth. The equipment was set up on a C-shaped desk with an expensive looking electronic keyboard on the side. The central console housed a mixing board, two speakers, and a couple of the largest monitors I have ever seen.

"I love your monitors," I said.

"You need to have the best if you want to hear exactly what you're mixing," Brixton said.

I was confused. "Are you talking about the speakers?"

"Yeah, the monitors."

That made me even more confused. "The speakers are called monitors? What do you call the monitors?" I said, pointing at the computer displays.

"Flat screens."

"It's a sweet setup," Robbie said. "Here, load up the two tracks on this USB drive. Ubastyle wants to see what you can do with a dance mix he made of 'What's My Age Again?' by Blink 182."

Ubastyle had chosen a song about not acting your age. I think he was messing with Robbie for wanting Brixton to act more mature.

Brixton plugged the drive into a MacBook. Once the song was queued, he headed to the sound booth.

"What do I push to have him hear me?" I asked.

"Just hold down this button," Robbie said, "and speak into the mic."

"Hey, Brix. Do you want me to leave?"

"No, baby. You can watch me work."

"Thanks."

"All right, Brixton," Robbie said. "First I'll play the version with Ubastyle on the mic. You can listen as many times as you want."

Ubastyle's version had a reggae twist that I knew Brixton would love. He closed his eyes and absorbed the song.

"I'm ready," Brixton said after one listen.

"Damn," Robbie said. "Let me switch to the instrumental." He grabbed the Mac, brought up the song and added a new vocal track for Brixton to use. After a few level adjustments on the mixing board he was ready. "How's that sound?"

Brixton sang the first verse. "I think we need to bring down the treble slightly." Adjusting it from his touchscreen made the physical levers on the mixing board in our room move. He gave a thumb's up after testing the vocals once more.

My boyfriend nailed the song. He could not have done a better job.

"Wow!" Robbie said. "One take, and he didn't even look at the lyric sheet."

"How was that?" Brixton asked, coming back in the room.

"You're brilliant," Robbie responded.

"What did you think, honey?"

I tried to talk but couldn't. I broke down in tears and left the room. Brixton chased after me.

"What's the matter, baby?" he asked, catching me in the hall.

"That was so amazing." I wiped my eyes. "There's no way I can't be a fan."

"Honey, I want you to be my biggest fan. This album is for you."

"It won't mess things up between us?"

"Not in the slightest. I was just glad you weren't already a fan. It would be weird if you didn't go through this album with me. Come on. Let's get back to the studio."

"There you are," Robbie said. "Are we all cool?"

"Yeah," I said. "Sorry. I was overwhelmed by his talent."

"Don't apologize. That makes me know I'm right about this. Brixton, why don't you lay some of your adult songs on me."

"Play him the one you sang with Simon Paulson," I suggested.

"I've heard them singing The Wrestler," Robbie said. "Eli sent it to me. It was the song that won me over. I want you to know that your friend really went to bat for you. He was persistent, with a capital P."

"Goddamn, I love that man."

"Why don't you sing 'Party Load'?" Robbie suggested. "Eli says it's hilarious."

"Seriously? I was just screwing around with that one."

"It'll be a good icebreaker."

Brixton hesitated. "OK," he said, "but I have to warn you, this song is all kinds of nasty. You know when you're at a party and your lust builds up more and more as you're talking with each sexy guest? It keeps building and building so when you finally come it's like a dam breaking. That's the Party Load. You still want to hear it?"

"Hell yes," Robbie said.

Brixton sang a cappella in the room with us. The setup was a cocky narrative of him working his way through a party. It was the chorus that cracked us up. Brixton didn't mind at all. He kept on singing:

Party load.
Party load.
I want you to take my party load.

Party load.
Party load.
Follow me upstairs
I'm about to explode.

It's my tsunami
It's my tsunami
It's my tsunami
Party, party, party load

When the beach recedes.
Don't go running please.
Get down on your knees.
Come and take my party load.

Robbie and I started singing the chorus with him. It was a catchy tune.

Party load.
Party load.
I want you to take my party load.

We were singing it over and over, thrusting our hands in the air. Brixton grew increasingly embarrassed. "Do you have time to listen to a few other songs?" he asked, trying to get us to stop.

"Absolutely."

"Cool. I have at least thirty songs. I've had this idea to release two albums at once called Day and Night. The Day album would be happy, bouncy tunes and Night would be sexier songs for getting your freak on. Night would start out with foreplay and end in a screaming orgasm. Although there would be two or three orgasms for her at the beginning," he said and winked at me.

"I like it," Robbie said. But you can't come out of the gate with your dick swinging. You have to win people over. Show them you're all grown up by releasing a transition album to introduce your adult sound to the world. Something honest and humble that will grab hold of your listener's soul and never let go.

"I have the perfect title," Brixton said. "After Ever."

"Wow!" Robbie said. "Like a fucked-up fairy tale."

"Exactly."

A red light on the wall flashed.

"That would be our dinner," Brixton said. "Can you bring it in here, honey? There'll be plenty for three."

"Sure," I said.

I sat with Robbie and my boyfriend for over two hours listening to Brixton's unreleased songs. Some were still rough but others were polished gems, mature beyond his years. The sound was like nothing I've heard. Brixton has his own style. It was a new genre of music—a mixture

259

of funk, reggae and pop. The songs hopped in a breezy, happy way that won me over. I couldn't wait to see what was to become of his new album.

Brixton leaned against his front door, gazing upward, dreamily. The low rumble of Robbie's Ferrari could be heard leaving the driveway.

"I've saved something for a day like this," Brixton said and raced up the stairs. He met me back in the living room, his eyes aglow.

"Wanna take some ecstasy?" he said mischievously, holding up two beige capsules and a glass of water. The pills rolled lazily across his palm.

I should have been the voice of reason but instead blurted out, "Yes, I do," and snatched one from his hand.

"Sweet!" he said and popped the other in his mouth. "This is supposed to be pure MDMA, pharmaceutical grade. Not that speedy bullshit I hear is going around."

Once the pill became a reality in my hand I was scared. "I've never done this," I admitted.

"We're in a happy place mentally. We'll have a happy time. Trust me."

"I trust you," I said, taking the glass of water from him and swallowing the pill.

It took a half-hour for the ecstasy to kick in. At first I felt jittery like I drank too much coffee, but soon the sensation escalated to an uncomfortable level. I was completely overwhelmed and disorientated. Beads of sweat appeared on my forehead yet I was chilled to the bone.

"It's too much," I told him.

"Here, drink some water," he said.

"I have to get out of here," I said, heading for the front door. Brixton chased after me into the street and took my hand. His palms were as clammy as mine but his touch was comforting.

"The high will mellow out," he assured me. "This is just the takeoff. That's always scary. We'll be in the air soon enough."

"I think I already am. I feel like I'm skydiving."

"Keep walking. Here, this will help," he said, handing me an open pack of his favorite grape bubble gum.

"Oh, thank God," I said, shoving a piece in my mouth. I had been grinding my teeth like crazy. A sugar rush coursed through my veins as I chewed heartily.

The park in his neighborhood has a giant swing set. We ran toward it like children. Brixton pushed me until I was high in the air, then hopped on his own swing.

I was on a downward arc when the high culminated into a warm glow, enveloping my body. It was as if I had crossed through to another dimension. My soul was brimming with joyance.

"We have to get home and turn on some tunes," I demanded. "I need to dance."

I wanted to jump but was smart enough to wait until the swing slowed down. When I felt safe, I propelled myself forward and stuck my landing.

"The air tastes so clean," I said, filling my lungs.

"Said no one ever about L.A.," he joked. "Now I know you're high."

Every molecule in my body was alive. I couldn't stop touching myself. Brixton leaned over and kissed me. It was like kissing for the first time. His lips, his tongue. We couldn't stop.

A familiar voice said, "Get a room, Brixton." I looked up as a car sped off in the distance.

"Was that Mac Damon?" I said and laughed.

"Let's get back to the house."

261

We ran hand in hand, carried by the wind. My inhibitions were nonexistent. Being high on ecstasy was like playing the greatest game of the coolest people in the world.

Once in his living room, Brixton pushed furniture away for a makeshift dance party.

The first song he played was "Magic Carpet Ride" by the Mighty Dub Kats. The opening groove was incredible. We danced the shit out of that song. Brixton moved and I followed. Or I led and he enhanced my moves. It was as if our neurons were connected—each step a semblance of perfection. We played song after song in our techno-utopia.

"I'm soaked," Brixton said and stripped off his shirt. "Let's take a shower."

I watched the individual muscles in his back flex and contract as we ran up the stairs to his bathroom. Even from behind he was breathtaking.

Brixton stopped in front of the bathroom mirror. "Look how beautiful you are," he said, showing off my reflection.

I was grinning like a Cheshire cat. "I look silly."

"You look like a model."

"You look like," I almost said 'a God', but wisely threw out, "an Adonis."

Brixton has a walk-in shower at least ten feet deep with an array of showerheads and spigots. Large slabs of white marble with random gray veins lined the floor, walls and ceiling. The soft lighting would brighten any morning. At the entrance was a touchscreen. He played a song that found its way into my heart.

"What is this? I love it."

"One of Moby's concert mixes. His free-form is unstoppable."

I disrobed in a mock striptease before stepping into the shower.

We turned on opposing showerheads, filling us both with instant warmth. He spun me around and held on tightly from behind. I was looking down, spacing out on the water falling away from my head, when I noticed a stream of yellow flowing into the drain.

Well, I guess this is happening, I thought. *Boys.* I was surprised at how calm I was about the whole thing.

"I peed on you," he admitted.

"I know," I said dryly.

"Can you pass the soap?" he asked.

"Gladly." I grabbed for a bar but he stopped me.

"That's my foot soap. My body soap is on the upper shelf," he said, handing me a green bar.

Brixton cleansed my back, massaging my muscles as he washed. His hands migrated south until his index finger was up my ass. My clitoris began to pulse. The two portals were locked in a dance of pleasure, reminiscent of the joy they experienced earlier in the day.

We washed each other from head to toe. There wasn't an area we didn't touch. Well, except for our feet. He wanted us to wash our own. So, technically we washed each other from head to ankle. The removable showerhead came in handy to rinse our bodies.

I decided to try something Dennis had begged me to do for years.

"You have such a cute derrière," I said, squatting down and grabbing a handful.

"It's from dancing."

I bent him forward a little. His beige starfish was a puckering delight surrounded by wisps of hair. I licked around the soft skin and then inserted the tip of my tongue. He gasped uncomfortably and I relented. Rising to my feet, I tried to ease the moment with a kiss.

Brixton gently pushed my face away with mock disgust. "No kissing after rim," he said, in an accent so poorly executed I couldn't tell what he was going for. That made me laugh harder than the phrase, which I found hilarious.

"Hang on a second," he said and left the room.

I ran to the sink to brush my teeth.

He returned with the dildo made of his cock. "I want to watch my other self inside you."

I lay down for him on the bathroom rug. Brixton brought his face right up in my business and started rubbing my pussy with the rubber cock. It felt so *damned* good.

"This is awesome. Look how your lips wrap around it."

My man rubbed and prodded my labia, teasing the clit with his tongue, all the while thrusting the dildo in and out of me. I didn't know if he was twisting it or if my body was so overcome with pleasure that I was gyrating. Whatever the case, I was in heaven.

We positioned ourselves into a 69 and I slid his cock into my mouth until his pubes were tickling my chin. He backed off a few inches, thrusting in and out, then planted my pussy flush on his face. A thunderous bolt shot through my torso. I whipped my head up. "What the fuck?"

I could feel him smiling with satisfaction. I grabbed his cock, stroked it, sucked it, loved it. He was alive in my mouth with every throb and quiver. This was *my* cock.

Brixton's tongue sent pleasure up my body in an electrical tidal wave. Unfortunately, the ecstasy was working against me. I was giving up hope on an orgasm when a pulsating surge enveloped my clit. I rammed my pussy into his mouth and rode his face to the finish. My body heaved as the energy drained from my core.

He took me over the edge again and again. Each orgasm was easier to reach than the last. After the fourth one I collapsed into a pile of mush.

"I want you to fuck me," I said brazenly.

He was more than happy to oblige. Brixton lifted my left leg over his shoulder and shoved his cock deep inside.

My desire was insatiable. "Harder," I demanded, "harder."

Sweat poured off his body as he slammed into me. I licked a salty drop from his neck.

"I can't have a hickey," he said, pushing me off him.

"I'm not twelve," I responded sarcastically.

I grabbed the dildo and began sucking on it. As soon as it warmed in my mouth it became him. I closed my eyes and felt Brixton, but at the same time I could feel the real him inside my pussy. My mind was having a hard time comprehending what was happening.

"Whose cock are you imagining?" he asked.

"What?" I said, opening my eyes. "Yours."

He stopped thrusting. "Then who's doing the fucking?"

"You are. That's weird, isn't it?"

"No, it's awesome."

I closed my eyes and slipped back into the fantasy. I didn't have a shred of self-consciousness.

"Let's christen my studio," Brixton said, panting heavily. "I've never had sex in there."

"Really?" I found that a little hard to believe.

We stopped in the kitchen to fill our water glasses. I hopped up on the wooden chopping block and he fucked me right there on the counter.

In the studio, Brixton sat in the control center's master chair, the epitome of power. I turned around and straddled him from behind. It didn't take long before he warned that he was getting close. I slid off his shaft and dropped to my knees. He wrapped his hands around the back of my head and vigorously pumped my mouth up and down on his steel-hard cock. I simultaneously licked the front of his shaft and sucked firmly on the head.

"I'm going to come," Brixton said softly, breathlessly.

He released his hold but I kept going. The ecstasy had given me an insatiable thirst for his sweet nectar. He moaned deeply as the succulent liquid splashed onto my tongue. I didn't swallow until I saw an enticing droplet emerge from the head of his cock. Staring him in the eyes, I sucked him dry.

"You taste so fucking good," I told him.

He relaxed in the chair. His eyes were weighted softly with an air of satisfaction.

"Will you sing me a song?" I asked sweetly.

"Whatever you want, baby."

He chose an acoustic guitar from the wall of instruments before ushering me into the sound booth. Brixton checked the strings and began serenading me with a love song from his latest album. I've never had anyone sing to me, let alone a lover. The moment was so overwhelming I had to fight to keep myself from swooning.

I wanted to profess my love in the silence that followed, but even as high as I was I couldn't work up the nerve.

He gave me a quick peck on the lips. "Let's go sit in the hot tub."

That did sound nice. As relaxing as ecstasy is, there's an underlying tension that left my body in knots.

Brixton set the temperature for 102° and we dove into the pool, waiting for the tub to heat up. The cool water refreshed our senses.

It didn't take long for the hot tub to be ready. Slipping into the liquid was like a full-body hug. Brixton motioned me over, and I settled into his lap, my back resting comfortably against his chest.

"I can't believe how chill my mom was with my contract," he said. "My family rules."

"I had a great family, too, until I was five. My father was the sweetest man. I was daddy's little girl."

"What happened at five?" he asked hesitantly.

"My father died. Haven't I told you that?"

"No. Oh my God, Jackie. I am so sorry."

"It was Dad's love of sausage links that killed him. He called it nature's most perfect food."

Brixton couldn't contain his laughter. "I'm not laughing at him dying. Sausage links are nature's most perfect food—that's awesome. We can make some for breakfast in honor of him if you want."

"I'd like that," I said, pausing to gather my thoughts. "I want you to know that you saved my life. After my father died, my stepfather destroyed me." I stopped short of telling him I'd contemplated suicide before we first met. Losing my best friend had been too much for me to handle.

He turned my head so I was facing him. "You saved me, too," he said and kissed my forehead.

That was the single greatest thing anyone has ever said to me. I was waiting for my inner critic to throw something shitty out but the drugs pushed her away.

"We each have our insecurities, our fears," he admitted, "but us together—we work. Can you feel it?"

"So much it scares me," I said.

"It scares me too. Life will be better from now on. The good always balances out the bad. You're in for so much goodness. We were brought together for a reason."

"I'm ready for some good."

He hugged me tightly and kissed my neck.

"You've been so open with me," Brixton said. "There's something I need to share with you."

He proceeded to tell me about his breakup with Candice and the horrible situation that caused it.

"You would never do that to me, would you?" he asked.

"Absolutely not. I promise you."

The weight of the conversation dominated the tub. We both grew silent. I wanted to change the subject. Thankfully, he beat me to it.

"Do you remember the shitty way I reacted to Cory's demo? How I was so upset that he was gonna be the first to break free from the teen idol bubble?"

"It wasn't exactly your shining moment. At least you realize it now."

"What I should have felt was happiness for my friend. My jealousy haunted me for weeks. That was a turning point in my life. I'm trying to learn and grow, not make life always about winning."

"Are you still jealous?"

"Not even the slightest bit."

"Then you're well on your way."

He smiled.

I was startled by a flash of movement in my peripheral vision. "What the hell was that?"

My man positioned himself protectively in front of me. "I don't see anything. What was it?"

We stared into the dark corner of the patio. "I thought I saw something move. Probably the ecstasy playing tricks on me."

"It's not a stalker. Jimmy has sensors all over the hill."

"Is your security on-site? I haven't seen them."

"Yeah. They have an apartment above my garage. Maybe what you saw was a ghost," he said.

Even though I was in a hot tub, the hair on my arms stood up.

"Doesn't mean it has to be human," he said reassuringly. "Could have been a dog ghost."

"That's funny. Why *are* ghosts always human?"

"I have no idea," he said with a laugh. "How come there aren't bobcat ghosts? Or horsefly ghosts? Maybe that's what it is when you have that eerie feeling that someone is touching you — a horsefly ghost." He lifted a tuft of my hair. It felt creepy as hell.

"Horsefly ghost!" I yelled and knocked his hand away.

Brixton laughed. "All the same, we should get inside and have my team take a look." He threw me a towel.

We tried to act calmly but ended up running frantically to the door. Once safely inside, he called security on the intercom. "Hey, guys. We're heading to bed. Jackie thought she saw something in the south corner by the pool. Can you check it out?"

"Sure thing, boss," Jimmy said.

He was at our side within minutes, laughing hysterically. "Hold on," he said, practically hyperventilating. "Oh my God, watching the video of the two of you running and screaming to the door was the funniest thing I've ever seen. OK, I'm good." He started laughing again but managed to get himself under control. "I need to do a sweep of your room. The sensors are down for some reason."

Jimmy rushed us up the stairs and instructed Brixton and me to wait by the door while he checked the deck outside our bedroom. Once the rooms were cleared, he had us lock the door behind him so he could search the rest of the property.

"Ready for bed?" Brixton asked as if nothing had happened.

"Sure."

"You wouldn't happen to have any more Xanax, would you?" he asked.

"Honey, you know I don't want you to get into pills."

"It's just to take the edge off the ecstasy. Smoothes out the landing," he replied.

My heart was still beating a mile a minute. Xanax sounded wonderful.

269

"The good doctor filled my prescription for my flight. I don't want you taking three this time. One is fun."

"But two is cool."

I was sobbing in the morning, which woke Brixton up.

"Honey, what's wrong?" he asked, taking me in his arms.

"Everything was perfect last night. Why am I so sad?"

"Ecstasy uses all your happy chemicals. We'll be back to normal in a few days," Brixton assured me. "I know what will make you feel better." He picked up his home phone and placed a call.

"Morning, Jimmy. Thanks for taking care of us last night. Did you ever find anything?" He listened intently. "Are you kidding? Shit! Well, I won't bother you then. Really? I did have a favor to ask. Jackie and I are spending the day in bed. Would you mind having some sausage delivered and cooking it up for us? Thanks, man." He looked over at me. "Do you want anything else?"

"Scrambled eggs," I said. "Have him get maple links. Nothing too fancy."

"Did you get that? Coolness." He hung up the phone and kissed my neck.

"I've always wanted to spend a healthy day in bed," I told him.

"I like to recharge for a day or two after a tour. It started with a doctor's order and became a habit."

"I don't like that they push you to exhaustion," I said.

"That's all me. The crew is always trying to get me to slow down."

"I wish you would."

270

"Not much chance of that happening," he said. "It's my perseverance that's brought me so far."

"It's all good," I said. "So, what did Jimmy say about last night?"

"Holy crap. The drone I captured was what was taking the sensors out. It was done on purpose. Jimmy had ten people watching the property. Thought a stalker was trying to get to me. They never found anyone."

"That's terrifying," I said.

"Yeah, but we can't give in to the fear," he said. "Negativity attracts negativity. All we can do is keep a clear head and we'll be fine."

Brixton was right about what would make me feel better. Eating my father's favorite breakfast raised my spirits. More importantly, it showed that he had listened.

I was clearing our tray from the bed when I noticed his shiny erection.

"Are you horny again?" I asked.

"I'm always horny for you."

"I want to watch you masturbate."

He was put off by my remark. "That's not really a spectator sport."

"What are you talking about? Touch it."

"No."

"Grab hold of your fucking cock and stroke it," I demanded.

"Fine," he said, pretending to be angry.

Brixton closed his eyes and disappeared into fantasyland. I immediately regretted pushing him, but at the same time he was giving me relationship gold, showing what feels best to him. He had a short, rolling rhythm that favored his head. I made strong mental notes.

"Best fight I've ever been in," he said after finishing. "I want you to know I was thinking about you the whole time."

"That's sweet," I told him, "but there's nothing wrong with having fantasies. It's healthy."

271

By the look of his appreciative smile I had knocked that one out of the park. "Are you cool with porn?" he asked hesitantly. "It's lonely on the road."

My brother warned me that women who don't let their husbands watch porn are women with cheating husbands. "I'm cool with porn. I'd watch it with you if you'd like."

"You are the best girlfriend in the world," he said.

"I aim to please."

Brixton spooned up against my backside and fell asleep with his arm resting on my thigh.

After waking from our nap, he was in the mood for a movie. The framed painting above his headboard turned out to be hiding a flat screen. He barely touched the bottom and the TV extended out in front of us.

"No way!" I said when I saw that he was ordering Titanic.

"I have to see what all the hype is about."

He slid close as we cuddled up to watch the movie. My fantasy world was playing on the screen as he held me in his arms, although the real world was becoming greater than any dream I'd ever imagined.

We weren't halfway through the movie when he joked, "I'm the straightest guy you'll meet, and even I find Jack kind of hot."

"That right there is the reason guys flip you so much shit," I said, pressing pause on the remote.

He furrowed his brow.

"Don't get mad. What I'm saying is you're so sexy you cause straight guys to want you. They lust for you and resent you for it."

"It's not my music?" he asked, rolling onto his side to look me straight on.

"Of course it's not your music."

"That does explain a few uncomfortable advances," he said and pressed play.

Brixton wasn't prepared for Jack freezing to death at the end. He was trying to hide it but I heard his sniffles. Once he realized he was busted he yelled, "What the hell? There was room for two on that door. Why did he have to die?"

I'd seen the movie so many times I was cried out. I held him close and laughed with him in my arms.

He rubbed his eyes. "That was still the drugs," he said, embarrassed.

"Of course, babe," I assured him.

Jesus Chrisis

When I woke the next day, Brixton was sitting up in bed with his iPad. He smiled at me and turned off the screen. I reached over and grabbed his dick. It was a rock-hard hello start to the day.

I prolonged the blowjob, bringing him to the edge repeatedly and then tapering off. When I had him begging for release, I went down hard and stroked his cock using his own technique. He shot onto his stomach like a sprinkler.

I wiped him dry with a tissue, lifting his cock to make sure I got every drop. Brixton wrapped his arms around my body.

"I'm making you breakfast," he said.

"Well, this day just gets better and better."

I sat at the kitchen island, watching him meticulously cut ham slices into medium-sized pieces of the choicest parts of the meat.

"The trick to Eggs Benedict isn't just quality ham—it's the hollandaise," he explained. "My father makes the best in the world. The secret is fresh mayonnaise."

"Sounds healthy," I quipped.

"Health isn't a concern with this meal. My family makes Eggs Benedict Christmas morning after we open all the presents. Everyone has a task. I'm always on ham duty."

"It sounds wonderful," I said.

"It is. What does your family do for Christmas?"

I let out a deep sigh. "My brother and I spend the day trying to be around my mom as little as possible."

Brixton stopped cutting and stared at me. "How would you like to be my guest this year?"

"Yeah, right."

"I'm serious. Come spend Christmas with me."

"I can't imagine anything better," I said.

Christmas morning. That was so major. But at the same time, I didn't want to get my hopes up. I wasn't sure his mother would approve of the idea.

"It's a date," he said.

To accompany our breakfast, Brixton made the best Bloody Marys I've ever tasted. He set the table out on his bedroom deck where we could bask in the glory of the Pacific Ocean.

The years of love that went into his family's Benedicts were reflected in the mouthwatering taste. It was as if he'd thrown my dish in the air and a slice of heaven descended upon it.

"They're delicious," I said.

He beamed with pride. I found out later it was the first time he made them on his own. He only needed help with the eggs.

"I've been thinking about your plan to house all the homeless in Juneau," I said. "Our mayor allowed a homeless camp in a church parking lot. It wasn't long before the tents were being mocked as Nicklesville—after the mayor. Your housing has to be so perfectly executed that the media can only say good things. You don't want yours ending up being called Webberville."

"Actually, the people in the camp were the ones who named it Nicklesville," he said, "and that was only because the mayor was clearing out the unsanctioned ones."

"Really?"

"I've done my research. What works, what doesn't. I'm not concerned about looking bad in the press. This is all about the homeless. And besides, we're building neighborhoods, not camps. Having an address will give people the confidence to work themselves out of their situation. Houses first," he said with a half-raised fist. "My program will be successful because we're allowing pets. If

276

you're homeless and have a pet, you can forget about finding housing."

"That is so true," I said. "It broke my heart seeing all the pets left behind after Katrina. The government wouldn't allow them in the FEMA trailers."

"You've been to New Orleans?" he exclaimed.

"No," I admitted sadly, "I saw it on the news."

"Eli and I try to go to the Day of the Dead festival every year. We have these wicked skull masks that allow us to walk around freely. You are so going. We'll find an old Victorian dress and have your face painted."

"That sounds like an absolute blast," I said, delighted that he thought to include me.

After our breakfast, we showered outside and slipped into the pool for a leisurely swim. It was a pleasant afternoon—up until his phone rang.

"What? Why is he here?" Brixton asked. "Are you sure he's looking for me? All right, send him in."

"Who was that?"

"The guard at the front gate. Cannon Rockford is coming to see me. Said it was important. Here, put this on." He tossed me a soft white bathrobe.

We met Cannon in the driveway. It was odd seeing a favorite rocker from my childhood in the flesh.

"So sorry to bother you," Cannon said, "There's something I need to talk to you about."

"No worries, it's great to meet you," Brixton said. "This is my girlfriend, Jackie."

"Nice to meet you," I said, shaking his hand.

"Let's go out to my back patio."

Brixton led us to the wraparound couch by his pool. Something didn't feel right about Cannon being there. I offered to give them a little privacy.

"It's all good," Brixton said, placing his hand in mine.

Cannon hesitated before speaking. "I knew your mother."

"What are you talking about?" Brixton said.

"It was June 1994. Suzette was a model at one of my photo sessions."

"My mom was never a model," Brixton said defensively. "I would know about that."

"She was, Brixton. Suzette was the most beautiful woman I had ever met. We ended up spending time together after the shoot."

"I don't want to hear this," Brixton said and walked away with his hands to his ears.

"Brixton, come back here!" Cannon demanded.

"Why?"

"Because I'm your father."

My jaw literally dropped.

"Bullshit!" Brixton yelled.

"The photoshoot was in Brixton, London," Cannon said in a soft, explanatory manner.

"My name is from Eddie Grant's song *Electric Avenue*," Brixton said, "when he sings it at the end."

"That whole song is about the district of Brixton — where you were conceived. Look at my chin. It looks like yours."

"No! Mom said I inherited my talent from God." His eyes welled up.

I could tell Cannon wanted to comfort him but he remained seated. "This doesn't change where your talent comes from."

"Why would mom lie to me?"

"I don't know. She flew back to the states and never returned my calls. I only figured it out this year when I saw the two of you at the MTV Music Awards."

"My whole life is a lie."

"Your life is not a lie. Your life is brilliant. And guess what else you are?"

"What?"

"A big brother to three boys."

"Really?" He perked up. "I've always wanted a brother."

"Do you want to meet them? They're at the park with Grace."

"I don't want to upset your wife."

"I met your mother a year and a half before I started dating Grace. She's cool. Well, as cool as can be expected."

"All right," Brixton said, "let's go before I change my mind."

I stayed behind. This was something he had to do on his own. When he returned, Brixton didn't say a word. He made a beeline to his studio, where he locked himself inside.

The door was open the last time I checked. I found him in the sound booth playing a simple set of chords on an electric guitar. He began singing a solemn tune:

> *A boy becomes a man*
> *when his world*
> *crashes down upon him.*

> *Life can be a scam*
> *When you're not*
> *told a thing about it*

The song jarringly switched to hard rock:

> *I'm having a Jesus Chrisis*
> *Full fledge fuckery*
> *I'm having a Jesus Chrisis*
> *Put me out of my misery*

Brixton's fingers moved deliriously fast across the strings yet the notes remained haunting and tormented. Watching the raw talent emanating from my boyfriend left me wet and wanton. He must have sensed my presence and looked up. Seeing me standing there brought a pleasant smile to his face.

"Don't stop," I said after switching on the mic at the mixing board, "that rocked."

"Come in here," he said.

I joined him in the sound booth without hesitation. He gave me a warm embrace. "Thank you for coming down."

"There's no place I'd rather be," I said and kissed his forehead.

"Want to see what it's like to record a song?" he asked.

"Sure."

"Put these on," he said, handing me a set of headphones. I panicked when he swung the mic in front of me.

"I can't sing," I said. "I'm afraid."

"My father taught me something about overcoming fear. Well, I guess he's my stepfather."

"He's your father," I said firmly.

"You're right, he is. My *father* had me up on the high dive at our local Y. I must have been around eight. I told him, 'I'm scared, Daddy.' His response was brilliant: 'So be scared, and jump anyway.' That philosophy has brought me further in life than anything I've learned."

"But I really can't sing. You've heard me try."

"It's just me. Come on. 'What's My Age Again?' is pretty much talk-singing anyway."

"All right," I said, giving in.

I put the headphones on and Brixton started the song from the touchscreen. He pointed to the first line on the lyric sheet when it was time to jump in.

I was shocked at how clear my voice sounded through the headphones and yanked them off.

"Put them back on," he insisted.

I caught up with the chorus but felt really subconscious. Thankfully he started singing along with me.

"Told you," I said when the song was finished.

He didn't correct me or say I was good. That made me laugh.

"Your talent will be in helping people. Like Prince William does."

"You should have seen Lady Di."

"Who?"

"His mother?" I was surprised that he didn't know who Diana was. "She was the People's Princess."

"You'll be fantastic at philanthropy. You have the gift of being able to talk to anyone at their level. That's not something you can learn."

"Whatever," I said, my inner demons not allowing me to accept the compliment.

"It's true," he said. "A day doesn't go by where you don't amaze me."

"You're very sweet," I replied.

"How about we go blow off some steam?" he said. "I need to clear my head."

"Sounds wonderful."

In the living room, he flipped the power on the air hockey table and it came to life with a whirl.

"I know we just talked about me working on not always needing to win," he said. "Is it all right if I don't hold back?"

"I would be insulted if you did."

I'd like to say I held my own but he destroyed me in all three games. Winning made him happy and that, at the moment, was all that mattered.

"Do you mind if I call Eli?" he asked. "I want to tell him about Cannon."

"Not at all."

Brixton opened Skype on his iPad and clicked on Eli's icon. The call rang and rang. Eli eventually appeared on the screen, shirtless in bed.

"Hello, Mate," he said, rubbing the sleep from his eyes. "What time is it?"

"Are you back in England?" Brixton asked.

"Yeah," Eli said, still in a daze. "I can't see you."

"Oh, shit. Sorry." Brixton removed the tape that was covering the camera.

Eli perked up. "Hi, Jackie. How's my girl this evening?"

"I'm doing well, thank you," I said. "Brixton has some weird news."

Eli's face beamed.

"Whatever you're about to say," Brixton said, "don't."

That made me wonder what things the boys had been discussing.

"Like Jackie was saying, I have some weird news." Brixton paused for a moment and then spat it out. "I was conceived in England."

Eli scrunched his forehead in confusion. "I wasn't expecting that. When did you find this out?"

"Today. My father stopped by to introduce himself."

"Your father? What are you talking about?"

"Apparently Cannon Rockford is my biological father."

Eli laughed heartedly. "Wait until I see your mother—that cheeky monkey. Where did this happen? In Brixton?"

"Apparently."

"You know who was born in Brixton?" Eli said. "David Bowie. Bloody hell! That whole spider thing you have going on. David's band was The Spiders from Mars."

"Spooky," I said.

"That's cool, but I feel like I don't even know who I am anymore," Brixton said. "This whole thing has royally fucked me up. It's been an odd couple of days, to say the least, and to top it off, Robbie Cumberlake stopped by."

"Really?" Eli said, feigning surprise. "What on earth did he want?"

"Shut up," Brixton said. "Thank you so much for being there for me. I won't forget this."

"You're welcome, Mate. You'll have to fly over for holiday. It's your turn. Bring that gorgeous bird with you. We'll explore your hometown."

"That sounds fantastic," Brixton said.

"Prepare to be underwhelmed."

We all laughed. I loved Eli's wit.

"I appreciate you calling," Eli said. "I should get back to sleep. I'm meeting the Queen Mum tomorrow."

"No way! That is so cool," Brixton said.

"It's been my dream. Take care, my friend. G'night, Jackie."

I waved goodbye.

Brixton set his iPad down and looked at me with apprehension. "Hey, honey. I received a text today. Cumberlake landed me a spot on the Tonight Show. I leave for New York in the morning. Sorry to spring this on you last minute. You can stay at the house while I'm away if you want. That's totally cool."

It wasn't *totally cool*. I was hurt that I hadn't been included. Why did he still feel the need to hide our relationship?

"I should probably get back to work," I said, trying to sound positive.

"I can fly you home on my jet. You'll get to spend time with the gang."

"That'll be fun. If this is our last night, we need to get to the bedroom." I took his hand and led him toward the staircase.

The jet Brixton chartered was luxurious to the nines. If I hadn't already experienced one, there's no way I could have contained my excitement. I stepped aboard nonchalantly as if this was normal life.

I was relieved to see the door closing after Stephanie and Jimmy arrived.

"Dusty's not joining us?" I asked, trying to hold back my delight.

The three of them looked at each other without saying a word.

Brixton spoke. "You won't be seeing much of Dusty anymore."

"What happened?" I asked. "Did you talk to him about your new contract?"

The confusion in Stephanie and Jimmy's eyes spoke volumes. They didn't know. Shit!

"No, I haven't spoken to him about that. I'm talking about how he handled the stalking incident with your ex. That was the last straw."

"I've had a sinking feeling Dusty was out to get me," I said.

"That's the understatement of the year," Stephanie replied.

"He was just looking out for me," Brixton said.

"There's a line," Jimmy scowled. "He crossed it."

"As I said, I took care of it."

"So, what's this about a new contract?" Stephanie asked.

"Jackie only knows because she was there when I found out. I need your word that you'll keep this quiet until after my press conference. You too, Jackie."

"Of course," we assured him.

"Robbie Cumberlake is taking over my contract."

Stephanie and Jimmy were as thrilled as I was to hear this news.

"He's giving me complete control of my music. No more bubblegum pop. I'm finally going to break into the adult scene."

"It's about damn time," Jimmy said.

The captain turned off the fasten seat belt sign and Stephanie motioned for me to follow her to the back of the plane.

"That top is smoking hot so don't take this the wrong way," she said. "With Brixton's new contract, I have a feeling you won't be a secret much longer. I'd like to start putting outfits together for you—come up with a style that is uniquely your own."

"That would be great," I said.

The flight was thoroughly entertaining. I was warming up to Jimmy, and becoming fast friends with Stephanie. I really dig that girl. Brixton was in rare form, cracking us up most of the way as he tried out different bits for his interview. My cheeks hurt from all the laughter.

We landed in Seattle, and the jet taxied to a stop by a hangar where my limo was sitting idlingly. The driver stepped out and stood attentively at the back door, waiting to accommodate me.

"I'll give you a call this week," Stephanie smiled.

"Sounds good," I said, and gave her a big hug, then turned to Jimmy. "It was nice spending time with you again."

"You're the best," he said. I tried to hug him but could barely get my arms around his muscular frame.

"Would you mind giving us some alone time?" Brixton asked Jimmy and Stephanie. The copilot was already out the door. Jimmy exited the plane without giving it a second thought.

"Better make it snappy," Stephanie said, pointing at her watch for emphasis.

We waited until she was out of sight before heading toward the couch at the back of the plane. The intense passion in Brixton's kiss stroked my ego to the core. He removed my skirt with such vigor it flew across the cabin and landed on a seat in the front. I unbuckled his belt hurriedly, sliding his shorts to his knees. His hulking cock stood tall and eager. He didn't bother completely removing his shorts before driving his manhood into me. I moaned deeply as he filled me to capacity.

The door to the cockpit opened and the captain looked at us, shocked. "Oh, my God," he mouthed and retreated. His voice crackled over the intercom, "Time to go, Brixton."

"Damn it," he said, frustrated.

I clinched down firmly, offering a couple last thrusts of memorable tightness before sliding off him, then stroked his cock vigorously while sucking hard, determined to bring him to completion. It didn't take me long.

"I'm close," he moaned.

A stream of saliva shot out of my mouth in anticipation. I stroked harder, focusing on the head, and was rewarded with a warm offering of Brixton's private reserve. I savored his essence before swallowing hungrily.

We dressed, laughing mischievously at our naughtiness.

"I'll call after my interview," he said.

"Cool. I had a blast at your house," I said.

"The pleasure was all mine. It was a nice welcome home."

Hello, Mother

I was working in the shoe department when a stunningly beautiful woman asked for my assistance. Her perfectly coifed blonde hair was familiar but I couldn't place the face. It was in her eyes that I found my answer.

"Hello, I'm Jackie. How are you this fine afternoon?" I said with a smile, my voice steady, even though I was freaking out inside.

"I'm doing quite well," Brixton's mother responded. She looked around and grabbed the closest shoe—a pair of hideous jelly sandals. "What's your opinion of these?"

I stared at the monstrosity in her hand, trying to figure out a positive response. I despised jelly sandals when they were in style in the 90s and was horrified that they were making a comeback. "They certainly make a statement."

"What that I wear ugly shoes?" Mrs. Webber quipped.

Her response made me laugh. It was a nice icebreaker. "I don't know why people wear these," I admitted.

"We can stop beating around the bush," she said. "I think you know who I am."

"I do. Brixton has your eyes. Want to grab a cup of coffee, Mrs. Webber?"

"I would like that," she replied.

I let Lidia know that I was heading out for the day. It was our last shift together before my philanthropy gig, but Lidia seemed to understand.

The day was sunny and bright, so I suggested hopping on the trolley to the lake. We sat aboard in silence, watching the buildings pass. Once we were alone in the park, Mrs. Webber opened up.

"I appreciate you taking the time to talk with me. I've wanted to chat for a while. As you can imagine, I'm not a fan of your relationship with my son. The age difference, it's too much." She looked away. "But even though I don't approve, I've been going along with the ruse that you're his Aunt Carol. Luckily, the media doesn't check their facts too carefully these days."

"To tell you the truth I hate the lies," I confessed. "I love your son."

"Do you mean that?"

I held her gaze. "I've never met anyone who gets *me* more than Brixton. I'm a better person when I'm with him."

"Brix said the same thing. I don't know. Cannon was ten years older than me. I'm a hypocrite. But I'm his mom. I'm supposed to protect him."

We had walked past the park and were standing on the footbridge that crosses the end of the lake. Seaplanes were taxiing in and out of the charter company across the way, reminding me of my flight to the BVI.

"Then let him be," I said. "Brixton and I could spend a few months together or the rest of our lives. No one knows, but right now he's happy. Besides, I'm not as old as my age and he's not as young as his. We meet in the middle. It works."

"I'm trying," Mrs. Webber said.

"That's all we can ask. Your son is a good man. I can't thank you enough for the way you raised him."

"It hasn't been easy."

"I can imagine," I said. "Would you like to go to my house, Mrs. Webber? We can relax on my deck without all these people around."

"That would be nice, and please, call me Suzette."

We took a cab to my car and then drove to the beach with the top down. Lidia keeps a scarf and Jackie O

288

sunglasses in the glove box. Suzette looked glamorous in them. I have no idea why Brixton was shocked that she had been a model, but I guess when it's your mom you look at things in a different light.

Luckily Dennis and Randy were both at work. I wasn't worried about my brother but Dennis would know Brixton's mom in a heartbeat.

We sat out on my deck, taking in the Puget Sound and the Olympic Mountains view. My neighborhood is so chill it would put anyone at ease. Just to be safe, I poured us both a tall glass of Prosecco.

"I love the ferries that pass by here," Suzette said. "It reminds me of Juneau." She took a sip of her drink and relaxed into the lounge chair. "I wish Cannon had stayed the hell away. Brixton hasn't spoken to me in a week. My son has never behaved like this."

"He's still in shock."

"I felt horrible for cheating on Tony. He's been an amazing father. As far as I'm concerned, Brixton *is* his son. I haven't had the heart to tell him the truth. I'm scared."

I repeated what Tony had told Brixton as a kid, "So be scared and jump anyway."

Suzette was taken aback by the comment. I didn't explain where I had heard it.

"You need to come clean with your husband. Honesty is what will mend this situation. And Brixton will be fine. Tony is still his father. He's the man who raised him."

"I don't know if I'm that strong," she said.

"Sure you are. There's never been a time Brixton has needed your strength more. This whole thing has screwed up his faith in life and God. That's a bad place for your son to be."

"You make it hard not to like you," she admitted.

"I like you, too. I can see us being friends."

"I would like that," she said and patted my hand. "I hate to cut this short but I have a meeting in a couple of hours. Would it be possible to give me a ride back to the Four Seasons?"

"Traffic will be a nightmare this time of day. It'll be best to take the Water Taxi."

"That sounds fun," she said and finished her Prosecco.

On board the Water Taxi, it was a swift 10-minute ride across Elliot Bay to downtown Seattle. Eight city blocks separated the dock from the hotel but Suzette insisted on walking.

We were admiring Hammering Man in front of the Seattle Art Museum when a clean-cut man in a business suit walked past us and said, "Nice titties," as casually as if he was talking about the weather.

"What the heck is up with men?" Suzette asked. "They're so disgusting."

"My brother didn't believe me when I told him guys harass women like that. I had to record one of my strolls down the boardwalk to prove my point. Three guys pulled that crap on me. Randy goes on my walks now whenever he can."

"That's comforting," Suzette said. "Brixton mentioned the trouble in your neighborhood."

"Where I live is pretty safe. The problems are more on the restaurant end of the beach. Alki attracts every walk of life. You could have the Gates family playing in the sand next to gang members."

"I adore Bill and Melinda," Suzette said. "They are the epitome of giving."

"My first day in philanthropy with Bellstrom is tomorrow," I responded.

"You're going to love it," she said. "Giving back to the community is the greatest joy in my life, after my son, of course."

We had reached the Four Seasons. The view from the street looked out onto Elliot Bay and across to my neighborhood. "You can almost see my house from here," I said. "It's on the right just past where the road bends."

"You live in a beautiful part of the world. It was a pleasure meeting you, Jackie. I wish we had more time to spend together."

"Same here. I like you, Suzette. Give Brixton a call. I have a feeling he's ready to talk."

"I appreciate that."

She hailed a cab and handed the driver $25. "Please take Ms. Notter to the Water Taxi."

"I don't mind walking," I replied.

"Honey, I wouldn't want you down here alone with that awful man lurking about."

I liked that she cared. "Thank you."

Brixton FaceTimed me later that evening. This was a first. Due to security concerns, Jimmy had forbidden me from using my phone for video chats. I answered and his handsome face lit up the screen.

"What did you say to my mom?" he asked abruptly.

I panicked. "What do you mean?"

"How did you get through to her? She's being so cool about our relationship."

I took a moment to catch my breath. "You scared me."

"Sorry," he said, laughing.

"I just spoke to her from the heart," I said. "That's all."

"Thank you, baby," he responded. "I love you."

A smile spread across my face. That was the first time he'd spoken those wondrous words.

"I love you too, Brixton."

Sail Away

I called my sister's phone again but it went straight to voicemail. "Jacks, I'm getting worried. Call me."

Jackie's car was still in the garage. She had to be somewhere in the area. I left a note on the kitchen counter and set out to search the neighborhood.

Two teens were sitting on a bench at Anchor Park. My sister was nowhere to be found. I strolled around the corner where a crowd had formed above Jackie's favorite spot on the beach. Police cruisers and an ambulance were parked nearby, which sent my heart racing. I sprinted down the steps and tried to pass the officers gathered on the sand.

"Sir, this is a crime scene," a policeman stated firmly. His name tag identified him as Officer Pettigrew. "You have to stand back."

"I'm looking for my sister."

"And who are you?" he replied tersely.

"Randy Notter. Please tell me she's OK."

The officer flipped through his notebook. The man's demeanor grew stern after checking something from a list. "Sir, you need to come to the station with me."

"What are you talking about? Where's Jackie?" I pushed my way past him and spotted Jackie in the sand, lying on her side with her hands up to her face like an angel. Officer Pettigrew and a female officer tackled me to the ground.

"Wake up, Jacks," I cried. "Wake up!" She didn't move. "Please get up."

Office Pettigrew propelled me to my feet. I looked dumbfounded at the crowd on the bulkhead staring down at me. "She's OK, right?" I pleaded with the officer.

"I'm afraid she's gone."

My legs buckled and I hung in the man's arms. It was at least ten years since I had thrown up. My chicken salad flew across the sand.

The two officers waited for me to compose myself before lifting me back to my feet. Their firm grip on my arms remained.

"Let go of me," I cried. "What did I do?"

The officers dragged me to my sister and forced my head so I had to look. It wasn't her that they wanted me to see. What interested them was the name written in the sand next to her hand. It was mine.

"Oh, fuck. Dennis, what have you done?"

"Who's Dennis?" Officer Pettigrew asked.

"My sister's ex-husband. That's his handwriting. He makes capital Rs with that stupid point where the curve should be. I'll take you to him. He lives down the block."

The officers released their hold but warned me about running.

"Where would I go?" I said, broken.

Back at the house, I pounded on Dennis's door. "Come on out, Dennis. What did you fucking do?"

"Go away!"

"What did you do?"

"Why does she get to have him?"

The officers moved me aside. They were announcing their presence when a gunshot rang from his apartment. A heavy thump was followed by an eerie silence.

"What the fuck is going on?" I yelled.

Officer Pettigrew kicked open the door and I caught a glimpse of Dennis on the floor. A pool of blood was spreading around his head. The coward took the easy way out.

The next day I woke up from what I thought had been a bad dream. It was a few minutes before reality set in.

I walked hesitantly into Jackie's room and began looking through her belongings, trying to find something to shed light on this nightmare. I knew she wanted Dennis out but hadn't recognized the urgency.

Jackie's password for her MacBook was on the back cover of a rumpled notebook. I logged in and searched her files for clues. The latest document she had been working on was a story about Brixton Webber. At first I thought it was a fantasy but I soon recognized some of the events. Hearing what my stepfather did to her sent me into a rage. How had I been so blind? I wanted to die so I could see Jackie again and apologize.

That evening the phone rang with an area code I didn't recognize, so I ignored the call. A moment later it rang again. Reluctantly I answered.

"Is this Randy?" a panicked voice asked.

"Who's this?"

"It's Jackie's boyfriend. I read something in the West Seattle Blog. Please tell me it's not true. Jackie won't answer her phone. Oh my God." He began to weep.

"I am so sorry, Brixton. Dennis shot her."

He let out a howl like a dying animal. I heard a loud clunk as his phone fell to the floor.

He composed himself enough to pick back up. "I can't... I can't do this."

I was left with a dial tone echoing in my ear.

Brixton called back a half-hour later. "I should have moved her down here. That was the plan."

"It's not your fault."

"It is my fault. I should have done something."

"I know how you feel. But in the end, Dennis is to blame, no one else."

"I can't believe this is happening. I loved your sister so much."

"I have something that may help. Give me your email address. I'll send you the journal she kept about her time with you."

Brixton called the next morning thanking me profusely for the story. Neither of us were in the mood to talk. He promised he'd call back later.

Jackie's Day

I scheduled Jackie's memorial for a month after her death to pass it off as more of a celebration of life rather than a funeral. But now a month had passed and the memorial was tomorrow. I still wasn't emotionally prepared.

Brixton and I were standing in the doorway of Jackie's bedroom. I had kept things the way she left them the day she was killed.

"Thank you for letting me stay here," he said.

"You're welcome anytime."

He forced a smile and hugged me.

I tensed up. "Sorry, I'm not a hugger."

"I don't care," he said, squeezing me tighter.

I ignored my upbringing and hugged him back.

"You and Jackie have the same smile."

"I miss her," I said.

"Me, too." His voice was quivering on the verge of tears.

The doorbell rang, snapping us back to the present. It was Lidia. She took one look at Brixton and broke down. He received a better hug from her.

"Thanks for coming," he said. "I want to go to the beach where they found Jackie. Will you come with us?"

"Of course, Brixton."

"You better put on a hat," I said, throwing him a baseball cap.

"Thanks," he said and tucked his hair up under it.

A cement bulkhead in front of our house serves as a barrier, separating the road from the beach below. There are large boulders at the base for added protection against the surf. They appear to run the length of the bulkhead except for one spot where the sand reaches the wall. This was Jackie's oasis.

"She liked to sit here with her back against the wall," I said. "We would hang out for hours. Jackie... Jackie died lying in the sand, with the look of an angel on her face."

Brixton fell to his knees and began to sob. Lidia kneeled by his waist and took him in her arms.

"It's all right," she said. The three of us had a good cry.

We composed ourselves and sat silently, watching the ships cross the Sound. If it weren't for Brixton, I wouldn't have returned to Jackie's spot for years.

"I need a drink," Brixton said, standing up.

We held Jackie's memorial in Salty's banquet room. The restaurant was within walking distance of my house and has a 180° view of downtown Seattle. Jackie adored that view.

I'm uncomfortable speaking in public but I forced myself to get up and talk. If it had been my memorial, Jackie would have spoken for me. I felt better for having done it. Brixton stayed in the AV room watching through a tinted window. He didn't want to take attention away from Jackie.

Brixton and Lidia prepared two slide shows. The first set were photographs of Jackie in her childhood, up through her teens. The second showcased the latter part of her life. They put a lot of effort into it, but the photos were still hard to watch.

The packed room warmed my heart as friends, family and coworkers rose to offer their memories. After the stories dried up I took the stage again.

"Thank you all for being here. I would like to invite Jackie's boyfriend to say a few words. This man had an immense impact on her life. Jackie wrote that the best gift he ever gave her was a sense of great self-worth. That says it all. She died happy because of this incredible man."

I motioned for her boyfriend to come up. A gasp filled the room as Brixton walked through the crowd to the podium. It didn't take long before people pulled out their phones for pictures.

"Please, no pictures or videos," I said. "And *no* posting on social media. Be cool, people."

Brixton whispered in my ear, "Thanks, brother," then took the mic. "Hello. I'm Brixton Webber. Jackie was my girlfriend. I loved her." Tears streamed from his eyes but he managed to pull it together. "I loved her with all my heart. It was at my Seattle concert earlier this year that I first saw Jackie. She was in the front row trying to sing along to lyrics she didn't know. I've never encountered a more natural beauty in my life. I had to meet this woman with the amazing smile, and arranged for her to come backstage. That was the start of our brief but wonderful relationship. Jackie was a breath of fresh air in my crazy world. She never once treated me like a star—I could just be myself." He paused and looked off into the distance. "I tried to be cool in the beginning so I wouldn't scare her off, but the truth is I knew she was my soul mate right from the start. I'm devastated. I don't know how to move on."

Stephanie climbed on stage and embraced him. "Why don't you roll the video," she said to the man at the controls.

Brixton had all the celebrities Jackie met send in videos. While those played, Eli snuck up on stage. He spoke when the videos were over.

"Hi, I'm Eli Strut—Brixton's mate." A high-pitched girl's scream of adoration pierced the room. Eli continued unabated, "I didn't know Jackie for long but she left an impression. I've been trying to figure out how to describe her. The best way I can say it is this. When you walk into a grocer's and you grab a trolley and there's not a wobble or a squeak in the wheels. That was what she was like, a one in a million trolley that just glides. Jackie was as close to perfection as I have ever known. When I first met her we shared a moment up front of Brixton's catamaran. After a while our conversation turned to a comfortable silence. We had only met the day before and already we didn't feel the need to fill the void with meaningless chatter. It was in that moment that I learned more about Jackie than any time talking to her. I love you, Jackie."

Short clips of stars from Magdalene to Simon Paulson began to play on the screen. They each said the same four words, "I love you, Jackie." The video ended with a close-up of Gio speaking through watery eyes. The moment was too touching for applause but the crowd couldn't help themselves. It was Gio after all.

Brixton took the mic again. "I love you, Jackie." He rolled my father's piano to the center of the stage and sat down on the bench. "I haven't been able to write a song to memorialize Jackie. I guess it's because I'm still in denial. Instead, I'm going to sing Harry Nilsson's rendition of 'Without You.' This is one of Jackie's favorite tunes."

He put everything he had into the song, belting it out with heartfelt emotion. Somehow, he kept it together until the end. When he finished, only sniffles filled the air.

"I did write a happy song about Jackie a few months back. It's a silly ditty that made me feel good when we were apart—nothing I planned to release. Jackie, this one is for you."

Jackie.
Jackie is everything.
Everything I need in this world.

She's my.
She's my everything.

He stopped singing. "I'm sorry. I can't do this. Jackie *was* my everything." He walked off the stage in tears. My mom tried to comfort him but he brushed past her to Eli. I glared at my mother, still furious at her for allowing Jackie to be abused. She turned awkwardly and walked back to her seat.

I grabbed the mic. "Please stick around. Jackie would have wanted this to be a celebration. There's an open bar on the deck. If you drink too much, Lidia has taxi vouchers."

Although my house was within walking distance, Jimmy drove us for safety reasons. We raced up my stairs to avoid being seen.

"Let's get a drink," Brixton said. He put his arm around his friend and they walked to the kitchen. "I need to know something, Eli. That shopping cart metaphor was really out there. When's the last time you were even in a grocery store?"

"I go all the time with my Mum," Eli said. "After hours, of course. You should come. It's rather a normal thing to do."

"I totally get it," Brixton said. "Back home, I help my grandpa in the backyard. He says it's to keep me grounded, but mostly I just enjoy being around the old man."

"Exactly, mate."

After we settled in, Brixton led me to Jackie's room.

"So, what are you planning on doing with the house?" he asked. "I noticed a realtor's card by the phone."

"Don't worry about that."

"Dude, come on."

"I have to sell it. I can't afford the mortgage by myself."

"No you don't," he said and handed me a USB drive.

"What's this?" I asked.

"It's Jackie's story. I want you to publish it."

"I can't do that!" I said, shocked. "It's so personal."

"Yes, you can. I want the world to know her. I've set you up with a publisher. You'll get an advance as soon as you hand the story over."

"I couldn't read parts of it because it was so intimate," I said. "I don't know, man."

"Her story needs to be told. I've gone through and added some of the missing details. I had to change a few things for security and legal reasons. I probably should remove even more."

"You sure you want to do this?"

"Absolutely. It was a mistake to keep her a secret."

"Will Cumberlake let you?" I hoped the answer was no.

"He was surprisingly chill about the subject. But I did have to promise to go to rehab. It's the only way to release the book and still redeem myself as a role model to my fans."

"I need time to think about this," I said.

"Take all the time you need. Look, you're my brother. You'll always be my brother. I want you to be taken care of. All I ask is that you keep Jackie's room the way she left it."

"I don't know if that's healthy," I said.

"Yeah, maybe not," he said. "But keep it this way for a while. I can still smell her."

"Me too." I looked around. "Feel free to take anything you want."

"Thank you. There are a couple items that I wouldn't mind having. And there's also something I need to dispose of," he said with an embarrassed smirk.

"I don't want to know."

302

Eli poked his head in the room. "Dude, you have to come see this."

We followed Eli to the deck. News had traveled fast. Three media vans were parked across the street and the front yard was packed with fans. What was so touching is none of their signs had Brixton or Eli's name on them; they were all some form of, I love you, Jackie.

Six Weeks Earlier

Brixton's new contract with Robbie Cumberlake was a done deal. His dream of having full control over his music was a reality. Robbie would be making the announcement at their press conference the next afternoon. To celebrate, he wanted some dirty Skype time.

My brother was visiting a friend, which left me with much-needed alone time. Earlier in the day I had gone OCD on the cleaning in case Brixton wanted me to give him a video tour with my laptop.

I was lying on my bed wearing sexy black lingerie, waiting for my man to log in. It was ten minutes past the time we agreed on but it was no big deal. That slipped into a half-hour, then an hour. Finally, my phone rang.

"My connection isn't working," he said, frustrated. "I can't figure out what's wrong. It just spins and spins."

"That's OK, baby," I said, disappointed.

"Why don't you just let me in?"

"What? Oh my God." I ran to the window. Brixton was standing on my side lawn. The shock of his presence sent so much adrenalin racing through my body I felt nauseous.

"You cut your hair!"

Gone were his long locks. Brixton's hair was now medium length and a natural dirty blond with sun-soaked highlights. The style was loose and tousled as if he had been surfing all day. He was rocking black pants and an un-tucked blue dress shirt with rolled-up sleeves. The watch on his wrist probably cost more than my car.

"Get down here," he motioned.

I hurriedly put on a lacy black robe, bolted down the stairs, and flew into his arms. He spun me around and we kissed. My tongue chased his as I explored his mouth with abandonment.

"Are those leather pants?" I asked as I groped his crotch.

"What the fuck is this!" Dennis screamed.

"Get out of here, Dennis," I shouted.

Brixton grabbed him by the collar and shoved him backward. "You stay the hell away from Jackie."

With a knee-jerk reaction, Dennis swung his arm back as if he was throwing a punch. That was a mistake. Within seconds, he was knocked onto his back, Brixton dominating him with his fist raised, ready to strike.

Jimmy appeared from around the front of the house and separated the two.

"Let me go," Brixton yelled. "This is the fucker who was stalking me when we thought it was Jackie. He almost ruined everything."

"I wasn't stalking anyone," Dennis lied. His erection told a different story.

"Fuck you!" I shouted.

Jimmy grabbed Dennis forcefully around the shoulder and escorted him to his apartment. "You're going to have a little company tonight. I hope you like the Game Show Network."

"I love your new haircut," Dennis yelled back to Brixton

"If you tell anyone about us I'll kill you!" I screamed. "No one."

"I don't understand what's going on?" Dennis sobbed.

"Come on, let's get you upstairs," I said to Brixton.

"Sorry I was late. I had to give a cancer patient a ride on my jet."

"Of course you did."

He came to a stop halfway up the staircase. "This chimney is awesome!" he said, running his hands across the stone surface. "It's so retro."

I pulled him inside. "Where did you learn to fight like that? You're kind of a badass."

"It's just self-defense," he replied. "I've meant to get you in front of my trainer. You need to know how to drop a man."

"Anything to give you peace of mind," I said.

"You have a piano!" he said and walked to the upright in my living room.

"It was my father's. He bought it to win my mother's love back with song."

"What did he sing?" he asked.

"'Without You' by Harry Nilsson." I could tell he had never heard of it. I found the CD in Randy's pile and brought the track up for him. We sat listening quietly on the piano bench while holding hands.

"I love how he uses his voice as an instrument," he said when the song was over. "If it's not weird I'll sing it for you."

"I would love that. Dad's sheet music should be around here somewhere."

"I don't need it," Brixton said.

He gave the keys a run through, starting at the highest note and walked his fingers down the octaves. Using only the tuning key and his ear, he began adjusting the notes he found to be off.

"Do you have perfect pitch?" I asked, shocked.

He shrugged his shoulders as if embarrassed by this rare talent.

While he was tuning the piano, I fixed us a couple Grape Eli's. Earlier in the week, I had bought the ingredients so Lidia could see what all the fuss was about. Finding the rhubarb soda was the hardest part, but I found it at Metropolitan Market.

"Much better," he said and patted the seat next to him. I placed his drink on top of the piano.

"Is that what I think it is?" he asked.

"Of course," I said and joined him on the bench.

Brixton took a healthy pull from his glass. "It's delicious."

He began playing a note-by-note rendition of "Without You." The song is not easy to sing, as the chorus puts a great deal of strain on the vocals. He navigated through the verses as if he had sung it his whole life. The room fell quiet as the last note reverberated to silence.

"I need to know the truth," I said. "Have you ever heard this song before?"

"Never. But I love it."

"You realize you're a freak," I said half-joking.

"Yeah."

"You're truly gifted, Brixton."

"I want to see your view," he said, ignoring the compliment, and opening up the drapes.

"It's the best part of the house."

"What mountain range is that?" he asked. "It's beautiful."

"The Olympics. Our sunsets have been amazing lately 'cause of the forest fires."

Brixton slid up behind me and nuzzled his face against mine. "I wish I could stay a few days."

"Me too."

"My family is looking forward to having you up for the holidays. It's all they've been talking about."

"Really? I was worried that your mom would have a problem with it."

"She's still being cool," he said. "Speaking of my mother, I think I have a solution to your Dennis situation. Mom needs a place to stay when she's in Seattle for her charity work. She liked your neighborhood. What if I pay rent for the apartment and fix it up for her?"

"Dennis would finally be out of my life. Come with me," I said, leading him to the bedroom.

Brixton slipped my robe over my shoulders at the foot of my bed and let it drop to the floor. He let out a hungry moan when he saw my lingerie. We lunged for each other's lips, kissing until we could no longer contain ourselves. Brixton removed my bra as I unleashed his cock from his leather pants. He ripped off my panties while pushing me onto the bed. Brixton's strong hands explored my breasts, his lips moving from one nipple to the next. He traveled down to my belly button, kissing it tenderly, then dove between my legs and ravished my pussy like a barbarian.

Each pass across my clit was a symphony of delights. Brixton is adept at sticking with a move once he's found his groove, and this one was genius. He pressed and licked with his pulsating tongue, completely absorbed in his mission of pleasure.

I leaned back and welcomed the burgeoning orgasm. The tension inside was so overwhelming my body disappeared and my entire being transformed into a giant, engorged clitoris.

"I'm getting close." I grabbed for the ghost of his long hair and ended up almost strangling his neck. It didn't stop him in the least. He finished me off in a head-spinning orgasmic flurry.

"Jesus Christ!" I said. "You are so fucking talented."

He didn't ask if I wanted another orgasm. He just dove back in. By the third one, I was primed and ready for his cock.

"I need you inside me," I said.

"There's nowhere I'd rather be."

Brixton carried me to my leather reading chair and placed me in a seated position. He stared into my eyes as he entered forcefully. His girth filled me with pleasurable pain. I tightened my muscles around his cock as he plowed into me relentlessly. He was thrusting so vigorously the back legs of the chair buckled, toppling us to the floor. Brixton landed hard on his wrist.

"You OK?" I asked.

"I don't know," he said, holding himself up by one arm. I rolled him onto his back and climbed on top.

He massaged his sore wrist. "I think it's fine," he said.

I lowered myself onto his cock and then popped back up as far as I could while still keeping his head inside me. I continued with this deep rhythm, sensing he was about to explode.

"I'm going to come," he said.

The power of his orgasm forced his eyes shut, and his body trembled as he came inside me. Brixton lay on his back, catching his breath.

It didn't take long before he was rock hard again. He rolled me onto my side, raised my leg over his shoulder, and entered me. I leaned forward and held onto his backside, aligning myself perfectly against his shaft. Brixton's cock rubbed my clit with each thrust, igniting exterior embers while simultaneously fanning my internal flame. The thunder down below rapidly spread throughout my body, erupting in an explosion of volcanic proportions, leaving me quaking in the tremulous aftershocks. I collapsed onto him breathlessly.

We held each other tightly, luxuriating in the warm afterglow.

"I love you so much," he whispered.

His words were music to my ears. I leaned my head back and gave him a sensuous kiss. "I love you too, Brixton Webber."

Lying in his arms was intoxicating. Our sexual bond was a transport to a secret world where only we existed.

"You hungry?" I asked, after hearing his stomach rumble.

"I kind of am. Let's get a pizza."

I grabbed my laptop and ordered from Pagliacci's website.

310

We ate in bed. Being with him at home was familiar as if we had been doing it for years.

He offered me the last slice but I let him have it.

"How about showing me your beach?" he said.

"I would love to."

His leather boots were not exactly beach worthy. The saltwater would wreak havoc on them.

"What size shoe do you wear?" I asked.

"Eleven."

"Perfect. That's my brother's size."

I jumped off the bed to retrieve Randy's black rubber boots from the hall closet. Before handing them to him, I found a pair of thick socks.

"Do you need a hat?" I asked, holding up a driving cap, assuming he would want to go incognito.

"Probably should," he said, reluctantly putting it on.

"You look very English."

"Thank you, ma'am," he said and tipped his cap.

I cringed. "Honey, you don't want to call a woman who is older than you, ma'am. Ms. is more happening."

"Damn, that's good advice."

"We should make a couple roadies," I said.

"Roadies?" he asked perplexed.

"Drinks for the road. I guess that would be confusing for someone in your profession."

"A little. I would love a roadie."

Out on the street I took a detour to show Brixton the view from my park. We walked along the path above the water and out onto the small pier that makes up Anchor Park.

"The Seattle skyline is incredible," he said, lost in the aesthetics.

"We met right there at Key Area," I said, pointing to the pyramid-shaped building.

"Best day of my life," he said, holding my gaze. "Which stadium were we in for the Spinnaker's game?"

"The one on the right with the lit-up arch."

Brixton was staring off into the distance with a faraway look. "I just love your beach," he said.

"What?" I asked confused. The beach was around the corner, far out of view.

"Your beach," he said pointing toward it.

"What the hell? I've never seen the tide out this far at night. Come on." I led him to the cement staircase at the base of the park and down onto the compacted sand. "It's so weird how low the tide is. We'd normally have to use the path along the road to get to the main beach."

The anonymity that the dark offered was comforting but at the same time unnerving. Alki isn't the safest neighborhood at night. I was growing concerned by the two guys up on the walkway keeping pace with us.

"I think we're being followed," I said.

"What? No, that's just Jimmy."

"Are you sure?"

"Here, I'll call him."

I watched as the hulking figure answered his phone.

"Oh, thank God. Wait, is that Dennis with him?"

"Probably. Jimmy said he was keeping an eye on him."

I grabbed the phone. "Jimmy, I don't want Dennis watching us. Can you block his view?"

"I already am, boss."

"He called me boss," I said after hanging up.

"You kind of are. Jimmy's here to protect both of us."

"I feel plenty safe with you."

I slipped an arm in his and we strolled to Alki Beach. The low tide had exposed a century-old landmark.

"That strip leading out into the water is the last remnant of Luna Park," I said. "This whole area was an amusement park in the early 1900s."

"I can totally picture it."

312

We stepped onto the first concrete slab and followed the path above the surf. The low rolling waves passing by had triggered Brixton's bladder. I held onto his drink as he headed out a few feet further.

"Don't venture too far," I said. "It ends abruptly."

Two ferries were crossing in front of us. He watched them come and go, blissfully content in the moment.

On the way back to shore he nearly stepped off the cement path into the water. That would have been a cold awakening.

"Standing out there all I saw was water. It was as if I was a part of the ocean."

We had made it to the main beach, a few blocks from the shops and restaurants of Alki.

"The sand is amazing," he said. "I didn't expect it to be so Californian."

"Alki is an oasis in this otherwise rainy city," I said. "If it was daytime we could collect sea glass."

"Sea glass?"

"This is a party beach. Pieces of broken bottles get tossed around in the surf until they're worn smooth. Here, I'll show you."

I turned on the flashlight app on my phone and kneeled in the sand. It was a lot harder finding the glass at night but I eventually did—a nice rounded green piece. Brixton marveled at its splendor. He brought his phone out and began searching.

"I found a brown one," he said, admiring his chunk of glass. "I guess assholes can make the world a better place."

"Yeah, unless you're a dog owner. The glass cuts the shit out of their paws."

"Did you see what you did there?" he said. "You turned a positive into a negative. We need to get rid of that voice in your head."

His comment kind of irked me. "How would you like it if I pointed out every time you obsess about winning?"

"If you think it will make me a better person, I'm all for it," he said. "I wasn't being a jerk. Stephanie has a technique she has me use to shut down that same negative voice."

"That is not the person I want to be," I said, repeating her phrase.

"You've been talking to Stephanie."

I shrugged my shoulders innocently.

"I love that you don't want to fight," he said. "A misunderstanding like that would have sent Candice off for hours."

"I've had enough drama to fill a lifetime," I said.

"That's good because I don't do drama."

"We'll make a great team then."

Brixton offered his hand and I slipped my fingers between his. He guided us toward the shallow surf and we walked along, kicking the water out in front of us.

"There's something I've been meaning to ask you," I said. "It's about your concert. I hope you don't mind."

"Not at all."

"How did they make it look like you flew through the ceiling?"

"It was simple. When the pulsing light descended upon me, I dropped through the floor and a hologram took my place. The hard part was learning the skateboard routine that distracted everyone from seeing the screens going up."

"It was perfection," I said, squeezing his hand.

"There's something I've been meaning to ask you too, Jackie. How would you like to help my mom and I with my philanthropy?"

I stopped abruptly and turned to face him. "I would like that more than anything."

He held me tight. "Of course, this means you'll have to move in with me."

www.ingramcontent.com/pod-product-compliance
Lightning Source LLC
Chambersburg PA
CBHW030022180626
46810CB00001B/163